WILLIAM MacLEOD RAINE
A GUN FOR TOM FALLON

WILDSIDE PRESS

Original title: *Reluctant Gunman*

To George A. H. Fraser,
Scholar and Raconteur,

who can quote the verses of a hundred poets
but none with more haunting memories of
our vanished youth than his own:

And the strings of pepper hung
On the house-fronts in the sun,
Blazin' red as some young puncher's new bandana,
And the scented smoke that came
from the piñon wood aflame
Smelt like incense to our Lady of Mañana;
The scarlet lips,
The clickin' chips,
The drinks Ramon poured for us!
But the friendly lights are dark
And the coyote's lonesome bark
Is the only music now in old Dolores.

LYNCH MOB

"Don't act like crazy men," the Sheriff pleaded. "There is law in this country. Fallon is entitled to a fair trial, not a cooked up lynching by a bunch of hotheads. If he is guilty he will be executed. Give him fair play."

"Only one way to decide this," Faunce answered. "A vote. All who are in favor of a miners' trial right now say yes."

There was a loud shout of assent.

"That settles it, Mr. Sheriff," Faunce said, a cold sandpaper rasp in his harsh voice. "We'll take care of Mr. Fallon *muy pronto*."

CHAPTER 1

It had been a long day's ride from Tomahawk to Copper Fork over rocky steeps and mesquite deserts skirting the foothills of the Whetstone Mountains, but at last Tom Fallon had reached the ridge from which he could look down on the sprawling camp.

He scarcely gave it a glance, for Arizona was exhibiting one of its most gorgeous sunsets. In the crotch between two peaks a vast fire had been kindled, a sea of molten gold in which floated islands of garnet and tourmaline, insets of topaz and turquoise and amethyst. Tom was a carefree run-of-the-range cowboy, tall, lean, and tanned to a coffee-brown, but in him was an inarticulate response to beauty. Watching the slowly changing picture, he was filled with emotions he did not try to analyze. The wonder of it filled him with awe. He watched the brilliance slowly fade to purple with only the clouds above still painted crimson by the vanished sun.

In that sparsely settled country he had met few travelers during his journey, but while his long lithe body sat eased in the saddle four riders passed and took the descent leading to the town. One of them flung up a hand in greeting without speaking. By their clothes he judged them cowpunchers. They too, he guessed, had come a long way, probably to join in the fiesta which started this evening with a ball at Heilman's Crystal Palace dance hall. He had seen them a few days earlier at a restaurant in Tomahawk and again swaggering into a saloon, but he did not know them by name.

As Tom rode down the long steep slope he saw that Copper Fork lay at the junction of two gorges which he later learned were called Gregg's Canyon and Wild Cat Gulch. Along the walls of these the houses of the camp were perched precariously above the two long winding business streets following the ravines. He was used to wide-open spaces and he did not think he would like this town hemmed in by ramparts shutting out the sunlight. The search for gold could be a glamorous adventure but mining for copper was a prosaic routine.

The town was less than a year old and it still had the helter-skelter appearance of a mining rush. Frame stores had been flung up next door to *jacales* roofed with bear grass. On the hill ledges adobe shanties stood side by side with neat wooden residences back of rose gardens.

Lights began to star the darkness before Tom came to Cochise Street. He could see by the activity on the street that it was going to be a night of revelry. The rattle of chips sounded from the gaming houses and also the whoops of miners already fortified with drink. A banner stretched across the road announcing a mammoth dance at Heilman's Crystal Palace.

Since the place was filled with visitors Tom decided before eating to make inquiries about sleeping quarters. He tied at the rack in front of the Crystal Palace and pushed through the bat-wing doors into the big hall. A long bar ran down the right side of the room and beyond it was a raised platform on which sat three Mexicans, two of them with fiddles and the third playing a guitar. A few dancers had already arrived and were prancing over the floor in a quadrille.

Heilman stood near the door to welcome his guests. As Tom shook hands with him he was impressed by Heilman's warm greeting. The proprietor was a tall handsome man about thirty years old with laughing eyes and curly chestnut hair. He was doubtful about the cowboy's chance of finding a vacant room but suggested he talk with Sam Rosenstein, the owner of the store next to him. Sam was at the head of the committee to arrange rooms for those attending the fiesta.

Tom thanked him and walked out of the hall. He recognized a couple of men loitering on the opposite side of the street. They were two of those he had seen on the ridge outside the town.

Rosenstein's was the most important store at Copper Fork. The owner and his two clerks were busy waiting on customers and Tom lounged against a counter until one of them would be free. He could sleep out if necessary, as he had done many a time, though the night would be cold and he preferred a bed if he could get one. But not till after he had sat down to a rare steak with some vegetables and two or three cups of coffee.

The storekeeper had lived in the West for forty years and was a good judge of its men. His gaze took in Fallon's clean youth—his well-packed shoulders, upright stance, and eyes direct and honest.

"I suppose you figure on helling around tonight," he said.

"Not this tired buckaroo," Tom answered. "I aim to hit the hay soon as I have had a good feed."

"All right. I'll let you have a blanket and you can sleep in my loft. There's no bed there but I reckon you can make out."

Tom said that would be fine and left to find a corral and food for his mount. Half an hour later he was in a restaurant eating the steak he had promised himself.

The waiter was garrulous. In ten minutes Tom had learned that Copper Fork was the livest town in the territory. It had no bank yet but one was being built. In the meantime when the miners' pay was brought to the camp it was kept in Rosenstein's big safe. Except in Tucson there was not any other store as large as Sam's in the territory. Sam was all wool and a yard wide.

"I am surprised he would trust a stranger to sleep in the store," Tom said.

"The only way to the loft is by an outside stairway," the waiter explained. "You couldn't get down to the store. Anyhow, Sam sleeps in the back room."

The sound of a shot came booming down the gulch. This was probably a cowboy or a miner venting his exuberance. On a night like this several bullets from six-shooters would be flung into the air.

"I've a notion this live town of yours has quite a few tough characters in it," Fallon mentioned.

"Y'betcha. There have been five or six killings since I came, but all of the deceased gents are better dead. Tinhorns and such. Most of our miners are Cousin Jacks. Those Cornish lads don't go in for gunplay. If they have a difficulty among themselves they settle it with their fists."

"I hear your stage was held up twice."

"That's right," the waiter agreed. "By strangers. The road agents couldn't have come from here. There's only one way out of this camp and any horsemen going or coming would have been seen."

"Did they get much?"

7

"Not too big a haul. Both times they missed the date of the mining pay shipment."

Tom finished his supper and moved out into the noisy street. Men overflowed from the sidewalk into the road. A teamster, trying to get his wagon through the crowd to a corral, yelled to those in his way to make a passage for the horses. In front of the Bon Ton a barker shouted his invitation to the miners to come in and try their luck. There was a vitality about this raw lusty camp that appealed to Fallon. It was the sap of young blood racing through its veins.

The food he had eaten refreshed Tom. He was not quite ready for bed yet, not until he had savored some of this riotous night life. Though he was untamed as a young colt, he did not intend to do any gaming or drinking tonight. All he wanted was to linger around the outskirts and watch the camp at play. Not for long. An hour or less would be enough. He needed sleep.

CHAPTER 2

Cowboys from the San Simon and San Pedro valley ranches jostled one another on the street. Miners decked in their best, their wives beside them, disappeared into Heilman's Crystal Palace from which beat the blare of the musicians and the thump of dancing feet. Tom noticed that Rosenstein's store was still open to catch the trade of range riders who might need boots, levis, chaps, or sombreros. He decided that it was time for him to bed. Next day, after he was rested, he would take a more lively interest in the fiesta.

"You're just in time," the storekeeper told Tom. "I'm ready to close."

The only customer in the place was a miner's middle-aged wife. She was just about to leave and as she moved toward the door Tom saw a sudden panic fill her eyes. They were fixed on two men who had followed him into the building. His head pivoted. The men were masked and carried pistols in their hands. One was a huge fellow wearing a canvas-lined overcoat with jean trousers, his companion small and bow-legged in chaps and a slicker.

"This is a stick-up," the big man announced. "Reach for the ceiling and no funny stuff if you don't want to be drilled."

The miner's wife gave a scream, turned, and bolted out of the side door. Her shout came back to them from the street. "They're robbing Sam's store."

The small bandit had slammed a bullet at her as she was disappearing. The hands of Rosenstein, his clerks, and Tom were in the air. These men meant business.

"Go easy," Rosenstein said. "We'll not make you any trouble."

"Get that safe open fast," the outlaw in jeans ordered with an oath. "We want the pay roll." He collected Tom's .45 and tossed a gunny sack to him. "Put the loot in that."

The store was lit by large lanterns hanging from the ceiling, but the safe was in a dark corner to which the light did not penetrate.

"I'd better light a lamp to read the combination," Rosenstein said.

The roar of guns from the canyon street outside hammered a warning. This was a hurry-up job. The robbers had to be on their way out of the gulch before the town rallied from the shock and began to fight back.

"Don't pull that stuff," the big man warned. "Open that safe quick or you'll go out in smoke."

Rosenstein tried no stalling. His fingers fumbled at the combination and on the first try missed getting the safe door open. The little outlaw, plainly worried at the sound of the guns in the street, cursed savagely and slapped the head of the storekeeper with the barrel of his weapon. Sam swayed a moment dizzily before he could steady himself.

Tom said, "Don't you see he is doing his best?"

"Get it open," the big fellow snarled. "We're losing time."

The merchant turned the knob again and the door opened.

"Find the pay roll and jam it into the sack, Bob. Don't fool with anything else but greenbacks and gold."

The leader covered the clerks while his bandy-legged ac-complice found the pay roll neatly packaged on a shelf of the safe. He dragged out the canvas bags and dumped them

9

into the gunny sack Tom held. There was a tray full of silver but he did not wait to take that.

"Let's go," he cried urgently, his voice high and shrill. He tore the sack from Tom's hands and started up the aisle.

The big fellow stopped him. "We'd better take the side door to the alley."

Tom's eyes watched the men closely. He could not be sure but it was his opinion they were two of the four he had seen riding into town.

From the front door an agonized groan sounded. A man had stumbled in clutching at his side. He swayed drunkenly to a counter, fell forward against it, and slid slowly to the floor. A revolver dropped from his fingers, a thin trickle of smoke lifting from the barrel.

"God, it's Arch Barrows," one of the clerks cried. "They've killed him." The man's nerve broke and in terror he started a rush for the side door. He was moving fast as a scared rabbit but bandy-legs' bullet traveled faster. It caught the clerk in the shoulder and he flopped down on a sack of potatoes.

The holdup men disappeared into the alley.

With a handkerchief Rosenstein dabbed the blood from his torn scalp. He walked around the end of the counter. One of the clerks still had his hands up, fear in his wide-open eyes. He had come from Ohio a month before and he had never seen anything like this. The other clerk lay on the floor groaning.

"Hit bad, Nick?" the storekeeper asked.

"I dunno," Nick answered. "I'm bleedin' like a stuck pig. Get Doc Pilcher, Sam."

Outside the guns were still crashing but the strum of the fiddles and the thud of boots no longer sounded from the Crystal Palace. The revelers had learned that the shots drumming up the street carried a deadly menace.

Tom was already out of the store. He had stooped to pick up Arch Barrows' revolver as he went. He stood in the doorway an instant, his eyes sweeping the street to right and left. A dozen townsmen were now engaged in the battle, among them Heilman. The bandits had drawn back to the protection of a store entrance. There must be four or five of them, Tom guessed, and guns were blasting at them farther down Cochise Street as well as from the upper end. A bartender in his apron stood in front of the Bon Ton saloon pumping bullets from a pistol. Crouched behind a wagon, his rifle resting on the spoke of a rear wheel, was a man whom Tom recognized as Tex Scully, shotgun guard of the Tomahawk-Copper Fork stage.

A bullet struck the tire rim of the wheel, glanced off in ricochet, and hit a boy's leg. He went down in the dust wailing in terror. He was trapped in the fire line.

From the entrance to the Crystal Palace a man started toward him but drew back when a slug whistled close to his head. "Damn it, there are killers here," he cried.

Tom moved fast, bullets whining past him as he ran, snatched the boy up, and carried him through an open doorway on the other side of the street. He collided with a girl running out of the house.

"He's been hurt," she cried.

"Let's get him to a bed," he said.

She led the way swiftly. Tom put the boy down gently and pulled the trousers off over the boots.

"Do you think—?" The girl's voice faltered.

"It's not much more than a scratch," Tom told her. "He'll be around bragging about it inside of a week."

She drew a long breath of relief. "He has to be in everything," she explained. "He thought the firing was part of the fiesta."

"And you were hurrying out to bring him back," Tom said.

The girl was young, unsure of herself. A deeper color ran into her cheeks as she stammered thanks. Her face was not beautiful, but there was beauty in her—a shy and charming smile, a timbre in the voice like a silver bell, a look in her eyes that promised eager and quivering life not yet fully awakened. Her name, she told him, was Mary Landon and the boy was her brother Billy.

Tom did not stop to become acquainted. The chatter of the guns still boomed angrily in the canyon. As he came out to the sidewalk a heavy-set man ran past him.

"What's all this shooting about?" he snapped at Tom without waiting for an answer.

The man was Wally Pollock, the town marshal. He had been eating his supper at a small hash house when the first shots sounded. To these he had paid little attention. Probably

11

some vaquero with too much tarantula juice in his system was sending harmless fireworks skyward from his pistol. But when they continued he thought it time to take a hand. With an injunction to keep his grub warm he had left the restaurant.

Tom followed him down the street. Beyond the Crystal Palace the visibility was bad. The lanterns outside two of the saloons had been shattered and the darkness in the gulch was heavy.

Somebody shouted to the marshal that bandits were raiding the town. He passed a wounded man lying on the sidewalk. Forty yards below Rosenstein's he made out four shadowy figures grouped together. Flashes from their weapons showed them to him.

Pollock called to them sharply. "Put up your guns. I'm the marshal. You're under arrest."

"Like hell we are," a long man jeered. His trigger finger moved and Pollock crumpled, a bullet in his stomach. He doubled up, spread fingers clawing at the wound, half turned as if to walk to the sidewalk, but slumped to the ground before reaching it.

Tom found cover back of a two-wheeled cart and joined in the battle. He emptied the weapon, firing at the bandits retreating to their horses. The raiders had enough and were intent only on getting away with their booty.

They reached their mounts tied to a hitch rack in front of a saloon, but as the bandy-legged man carrying the gunny sack caught at the horn of his saddle to mount a bullet tore into his body. He dropped to the sidewalk beside his horse. The other outlaws had pulled the slipknots of their bridles and swung into their seats. Two had already jumped their ponies to a gallop, but the big fellow leaned down from the hull as he started and picked up the sack. He followed his companions along the gulch into the darkness.

Heilman ran swiftly to the bandit lying in the street. The man was hit vitally and would not live long. His eyes were glazed and when he breathed there was a rattle in his throat. Heilman bent over him, one knee in the dust, and raised his head. The shotgun messenger Scully was standing back of Heilman whose bulk hid the wounded man.

"Ask him who his pals are," Tex Scully said.

Heilman put the question, leaning close to catch the an-

12

swer. There was a gasp, a gurgle, and the gambler lowered the head gently.

"He's gone, Tex. Just as well for him. He was gallows bait sure." Heilman rose and spoke with quick decision. "Get a posse after them."

"We'd better look after the wounded and get Doc Pilcher to take care of them first."

There was a great deal of confusion. Women had fainted and others were hysterical. Men crowded the street and got in one another's way. Heilman took command and brought order out of the turmoil. He saw that the wounded were given attention, then snapped out orders for the organization of the first posse. Another one could follow later.

"Count me in," Scully volunteered. "Wally was my friend."

"Maybe he'll live, Tex." Heilman's eye fell on Tom. "I'll take you, young fellow. And Palmer. Four are enough."

Within a few minutes the pursuers rode down the gulch.

CHAPTER 3

The posse followed the crooked canyon between the red-brown walls to the rolling hills outside. Heilman led the way, a fine figure of a man who sat his black horse with loose-limbed grace. He had the qualities, Fallon thought, of a natural leader, a man sure of himself, forceful, yet with a touch of friendly warmth that drew others to him.

At the summit of a rise he reined his horse to a halt and voiced an opinion. "They'll head for the border sure, then cut through Squaw Gulch into the rough country south of it."

Tex Scully was not so certain of that. The shotgun messenger was a lean hard man from Lampasas who had gone up the Chisholm Trail with the longhorn herds several times. "Looks to me like they might be making for the mountains to hole up in the badlands around the headwaters of the White or the San Francisco," he said.

"Not those birds," Heilman replied. "Each of them will

13

have a pocket full of money to blow. They are not going to cut themselves off from the señoritas and the gambling joints, and in Sonora they will be safe as a kid in a Sunday school."

"Maybe so." Tex lifted his shoulders in a shrug. Heilman might be right, though he thought it a fifty-fifty bet either way.

Tom felt the gambler was too sure. His nature was to be positive.

They turned south, and after an hour's hard riding reached the upper end of Squaw Gulch. Near the lower entrance Scully swung from the saddle. "Let's have a look-see," he suggested. In this sandy wash tracks would show.

Heilman joined him. It was a dark moonless night. They struck a dozen matches, searching the floor of the canyon's exit. In the loose sand Heilman found hoof marks. "Here they are, Tex," he called.

The Texan was doubtful. "I reckon they are tracks, maybe, but if so I would say they are old ones."

Heilman had a different opinion. "In soft sand like this a track fills up fast. In an hour the ones our horses made will look like that. They must be right ahead of us."

There was a grim eagerness in Heilman's face and bearing. He was no longer the genial host welcoming guests to a ball but a dangerous manhunter on a hot trail. Twice he broke out to curse the desperados who had so recklessly snuffed out innocent lives. Fallon was moved by some of the same urge for vengeance. The road agents had been so needlessly murderous. They had not of course expected to have to kill anybody but when the occasion came they had not hesitated an instant.

As he rode through the night Fallon felt something nagging at his mind, a detail that just eluded his memory. He had no doubt that the bandits had been the four men who had passed him close to the town, but there was something else that he ought to remember. He found himself trying to drag it back to his consciousness. Whatever had escaped him might be of no importance but he was annoyed that he could not recall it.

They were riding through a rough country of arroyos and washes, a desert land sown with mesquite and cactus. In the darkness the prickly pear and cholla tore at their legs and the

14

mesquite whipped their faces. After a few miles of this Scully pulled up his mount in exasperation.

"We're not getting anywhere," he said. "If they came this way we have lost them. Me, I'm going back. I don't believe they are making for the border but for the mountains. We can't do a thing till it gets light enough to see. My opinion is they passed the Gregory ranch on their way north and that's where I aim to be when day breaks. Maybe Clint saw them. It wouldn't have been too dark then. If he didn't we may be able to cut sign at the pass."

Heilman was obstinately sure he was right but the others sided with Scully. In any case there would be no chance to catch the robbers before they reached the border. They might as well go back and strike the Gregory ranch. They could get breakfast there and then decide what to do.

"All right," Heilman agreed grudgingly. "Thought I was leading this posse but it seems I'm not."

Day was just breaking when they rode wearily up to Clint Gregory's steading.

Gregory had news for them. He had been awakened in the night by the barking of his dogs. He thought of getting up to find out what was disturbing them, but had decided not to take the trouble since probably a coyote was exciting them. Ten minutes before the arrival of the posse he had discovered that three horses were missing from his pasture.

"Rustlers are thick as fleas these days," he complained. "You'd figure they wouldn't have the nerve to come right into a man's yard to steal."

"Not rustlers this time," Heilman corrected. "Bandits and killers." He told the ranchman of the attack on Rosenstein's store.

"What did they do with their own horses when they took yours?" the shotgun messenger wanted to know.

Tom Fallon suggested an answer. "Took them into the hills to turn them loose there. They couldn't leave them here where we could read the brands and see who owned them."

"That's right," Heilman agreed. "They had traveled a long way yesterday and by the time they reached the ranch their mounts were worn out. So they roped fresh ones."

"If we had come straight here we might have got the birds," Scully said sourly. "But you were so damn sure."

"A man can be wrong sometimes," Heilman admitted mildly. "It looked to me like they would break for Mexico. They would have got away certain if they had. Now we'll round them up."

The posse ate breakfast at the ranch. While they ate Scully and Heilman discussed what route to take. They differed again. Scully thought they had better cross Cochise Pass into the valleys beyond. Heilman was for scouting the foothills and checking the gulches that ran into the mountains for recent footprints. This time Scully had his way.

Gregory took Fallon's place in the posse. Tom had been in the saddle for twenty-four hours with only a short rest. He stayed at the ranch and snatched a few hours' sleep before he returned to Copper Fork.

He learned there that Marshal Pollock had died during the night. Counting the outlaw, that made the cost of the raid three dead men and four wounded. Fortunately the wounded were all doing well. Two cowboys from the San Simon had identified the bandit who had been killed as Bob Wheldon, a member of the Dutch Frater group of marauders. The gang was a large, rather loosely knit organization, ostensibly ranchers and cowboys but generally suspected of being night riders outside the law. From what Tom could pick up some of them were thorough villains and others merely wild range riders who used their running irons too freely on unbranded calves.

Tom dropped in at the Landon place to find out how Billy's leg was getting along. That was his excuse, but he knew he was a fraud. He wanted to see Billy's sister again. During his long hours in the saddle his thoughts had gone back to her several times. He would like to verify his impressions that she was a girl it would be a pleasure to know.

The door was open and he walked into a long hall with several doors on each side. A stairway led up to a second floor where there must be more rooms. It was evidently a lodging house. On a table was a sign above a small bell, which bore the legend, "Ring For The Landlady."

Tom rang and Mary appeared at the head of the stairs carrying some sheets.

"We have no vacancies just now," she called down.

"I came to see Billy," he answered.

As she came down the stairs she recognized him. "Oh, I am

16

so glad," she said, excitement in her sweet voice. "Billy keeps wanting to see you."

A quick warmth lit her eyes. He thought her shy gladness charming. She led the way to the boy's bedroom.

"How are you doing, Billy?" he inquired.

"I'm fine," the boy replied. "My leg hurts just a teeny bit. Doctor Pilcher says I can go to school next week." He evidently wanted to say more but was too bashful. "Mr., I—I—" he stammered, and stuck there.

His sister said it for him. Tom shrugged off her thanks.

"I happened to be the guy who was nearest Billy," he said. "My name is Tom Fallon. I moseyed over from New Mexico a couple of weeks ago."

She mentioned their name. After a few minutes Tom learned that the Landons were orphans and that she was making their living by running a rooming house. Her dress was neat and tidy but patched in two places.

Mary was a slim girl, rather tall, with bronze hair and blue eyes very clear. She was not pretty, Tom thought, but he liked the planes of her well-modeled face and the neat graceful economy with which her lithe body moved. Her tight-fitting gown outlined the small firm breasts, as was the fashion of the period.

He explained that he had ridden with the posse and had just returned. The rest of the party were still out looking for the bandits.

"Is it known who they are?" Mary asked.

"The one who was killed is Bob Wheldon, one of the Dutch Frater gang. His horse was left hitched in front of the Wagon Wheel saloon. The brand on it is a Circle Y owned by a rancher in the San Simon valley, but the horse was probably stolen."

Later in the day the rest of the posse returned, worn out from their long futile ride. They brought one piece of news which stressed the callous character of the robbers. After picking up fresh mounts at the Gregory ranch they had driven their jaded horses over a precipice where the dead bodies had been found. Evidently they had hoped that these would not be discovered. The outlaws had disappeared into the tangle of steep ranges and gulches where the rivers of the territory had their sources, a region where there were scores of hiding places and game was abundant. In this district of twisting chasms and secret mountain pockets came and went a nomadic population of bad men wanted by the law. Here they found sanctuary disturbed only by occasional not too successful forays led by the sheriffs of adjoining counties.

Sheriff Walter Dunham had ridden from Tomahawk, the county seat, to pick up what evidence he could about the robbery. He made his temporary headquarters at the Crystal Palace.

Sam Rosenstein met Tom Fallon on the street. He had not seen the young man since their first meeting.

"You rode with the posse, didn't you," he asked.

"As far as the Gregory ranch," Tom said.

"I've been told you saw the bandit gang before you reached town. Is that true? I mean when you were coming here the first time."

"I'm not dead sure they were the robbers. My guess is that they were."

"Better come and talk with Sheriff Dunham," the merchant suggested. "He'll want a description of them."

The sheriff sat on the raised platform used by the musicians. Ten or a dozen men were grouped around him. Rosenstein introduced Tom to the officer. Fallon told what he knew.

"These men you met at the edge of town—did you have any talk with them?" Dunham inquired.

"No. One of them sort of flung a hand up as they passed."

"You did not ride down with them then?"

Tom shook his head.

The sheriff's voice had an edge of sharpness. "Why not? You were headed for town, weren't you?"

"That's right. Fact is, I was resting my horse. I had stopped to look at the sunset."

A hard-eyed heavy-set man sitting astride a chair with his arms folded over the back laughed incredulously. His slaty eyes had not lifted from Tom since he had come into the hall. "He stopped to see the sunset. Never had seen one before." There was a jeer in the speaker's voice.

"I've looked at a good many myself, Mr. Faunce," the merchant interposed.

"You ain't a cowboy hurrying to get to town for a drink after a long dusty day in the saddle," Faunce retorted.

"Right now I'm on the wagon," Tom mentioned.

"Says he," a fat man put in. "Hell, I saw him come right into the Crystal Palace to get a drink."

Heilman made a correction. "You're wrong about that, Budge. He came in to ask where he could get a place to sleep and I sent him to see Sam."

The sheriff brushed aside the interruption. "You knew the four men?" he asked Tom.

"I didn't know them at all. Day before yesterday they came into a restaurant where I was eating. At Tomahawk. Later I saw them walk into a saloon. So when I saw them on the road outside of town I recognized them. Looks like they were the robbers certain. When they came into the store—the two that did the holdup—I was sure they belonged to the party. An hour ago I looked into the face of the dead outlaw Wheldon and I would swear he was one of them."

"This fellow is trying to squirm out," Faunce scoffed. "They eat together and they go to the same saloon. He reaches town when they do. He went into Sam's store to scout the place before the robbery. He was right on hand holding the sack while the bandits were getting the loot. Sam identifies him. What does all that add up to except that he was their lookout man?" The ranchman's voice was savagely implacable.

A lean man with a drooping mustache above a weak chin pushed forward. "I got some information," he said importantly.

The man was the waiter who had served Tom the night of his arrival.

"Who are you?" Dunham asked.

"Name is George Silliman. I work at the Denver Chop House. This bird came in the night of the robbery and I waited on him. He was mighty curious about the pay roll in Sam's store. Talked about the stage holdups and acted funny about them. Said he was aimin' to sleep in the loft above Sam's store and how could he get down from there into the store."

Tom's gaze swept around to meet a circle of hostile faces, among them only those of Rosenstein and Heilman apparently not convinced of his guilt. This might grow into something serious.

He said, coolly, "Don't pull on the rope yet, gentlemen. Silliman isn't reporting our talk correctly. Let me ask him a question or two."

"Shoot," the sheriff said.

"Let's run over our talk, Silliman. You were bragging about what a live town this is and how though you didn't have a bank one was being built. Correct?"

"Mebbe so. And you said—"

"Hold your horses a minute. I'm asking the questions. Didn't you say in the next breath that the pay was being kept in Rosenstein's safe?"

"I dunno who spoke of it first. Anyhow you got it out of me that Mr. Rosenstein slept in the store. No use you sayin' you didn't."

"This man Fallon rode on the posse after the robbers," Heilman reminded them.

"Sure. A grandstand play to cover up," Budge flung back.

"I saw him with a gun out on the street during the fight." A miner spoke up.

"Yeah, and who was he shootin' at?" Faunce demanded. "Might of been he killed Wally Pollock."

"Not possible," the miner contradicted. "You didn't reach town till this morning, but I was right on the spot and saw the whole play. I dunno whether this fellow here was for us or against us; yet I know for sure he didn't get the marshal. Wally walked close to the two fellows at the door of the store and was shot from the front. They both blazed at him. This guy Fallon, if that is his name, came running down the street after Wally lay on the ground."

"All right. He didn't kill Pollock. Doesn't prove he wasn't one of these gunmen. Sumner was found wounded lying against an adobe wall—shot in the back. Must have been somebody coming up behind him as Trelawney says this fellow Fallon was doing with his gun smoking. Silliman's story puts a finger on the guy. Why was he so anxious to know where the miners' pay was kept and how to get into the store?"

"This holdup was pulled off before the store closed," Tom reminded Faunce. "If I was one of the robbers why would I need to know how to get into the store? All they had to do was walk in the front door."

"Sure. You-all talked it over and realized you couldn't

break in later without too much noise, and Sam would be wakened and ready for you. So you played it straight, figurin' on a quick getaway." Faunce slammed a heavy fist on the back of the chair. "You're guilty as the devil."

Tom felt the pressure of angry suspicious eyes crowding him but no sign of it showed in his easy bearing or his undisturbed face.

"Gentlemen, you are making a lot out of nothing," he said with quiet confidence. "I have been only two weeks in the territory. Came down from New Mexico. If you want to know what sort of reputation I have write to Mr. Cy Norcross of the Triple X ranch near Tularosa."

"You and yore pals didn't do any writing anywheres to find out what reps Arch Barrows and Wally Pollock had before you murdered them," Budge cried. "I say hang him first and write afterward."

From some of those present came a murmur of assent.

"None of that kind of talk, Budge," the sheriff told him sternly. "This boy is going to get a chance to prove his innocence. Not a thing has been shown against him. He came as a voluntary witness to tell us what he knew about these characters from Tomahawk. All this heat against him makes no sense. If he is guilty we will find it out before we are through."

"That's what *you* say," Faunce retorted arrogantly. "But what you say doesn't go. If we figure this scalawag is guilty— and it looks to me like he is—we'll have a miners' court, try him, and string him up."

The crowd had increased to nearly half a hundred and more were continually dropping into the hall. A chorus of approval to the harsh words of Faunce beat on the ears of Tom Fallon like the voice of doom.

"I beg you not to be in too much haste," Rosenstein urged. "The evidence isn't all in yet. Let us wait until it is. This boy may be as innocent as I am. He doesn't look to me like a bandit. The robbers held a gun on him as they did on the rest of us."

"How does a bandit look different from anybody else?" Faunce sneered. "To meet Billy the Kid you would have thought him a two-bit cowboy not dry behind the ears, too young to vote—but not too young to have killed twenty men. Holding a gun on him was just a play to cover up."

"If I was one of those holdups would I stick around here like a fool instead of riding off with my pals?" Tom asked. "Doesn't seem reasonable to me."

"Took us for a bunch of chumps and thought you could pull a slick play on us," the fat man said. "We'll try you and then hang you—after you have told us who yore pals are."

"Why bother with a trial since you know beforehand what verdict you'll get?" Fallon said. "You have made up yore minds to hang me whether I am guilty or not."

There was a hard core of toughness in the young man. The steel-blue eyes in the lean tanned face showed no fear. There was strength in the well-packed muscles of the broad shoulders and in the poised ease of the long figure.

"Friends, don't act like crazy men," the sheriff said. "There is law in this country. Fallon is my prisoner. He is entitled to a fair trial in a legal court, not a cooked-up one by a bunch of hotheads infuriated at the needless murders the bandits committed. If he is guilty he will be executed. Give him fair play."

"Only one way to decide this," Faunce answered. "That is to take a vote. All who are in favor of a miners' trial right now say yes."

There was a loud shout of assent.

"That settles it, Mr. Sheriff," Faunce said, a cold sandpaper rasp in his harsh voice. "We'll take care of Mr. Fallon *muy pronto*."

CHAPTER 4

Dunham was a solid reliable man with a good record. He had fought in the Civil War and later against the Apaches. There was nothing brilliant or flashy about him but he had character and was to be trusted.

"You are wrong about that, Faunce," he replied, his tone reasonable and friendly. "Nothing is settled unless it is settled right. This boy's life is in our hands. We're decent folk, all of us. If we make a mistake now it will shadow all our years till we die. After we have caught the men who rode down this gulch last night, we'll know whether Fallon is one of them."

"That's right," Rosenstein agreed. "We can wait till then."

Faunce rode over the protests of the sheriff and the merchant with strident anger. "How many men have been shot down in this county in the past five years? Forty or fifty at least. Now tell me how many killers have been hanged legally. Not one. They light out. Or they've got friends in office. Or a smart lawyer talks them out of the hole they are in. We plain people are going to take a hand this time. Don't think anything different, Mr. Sheriff. Our say-so goes."

Rosenstein thought this hot outburst of rage against killing came strangely from the mouth of Curt Faunce, a cattleman who had lived violently with no regard for the rights of others. He had shot down at least one man, in self-defense he claimed, and he had been in close association with the lawless element in the San Simon and Sulpher Springs valleys.

Looking at young Fallon, facing this ordeal with such admirable courage, the storekeeper felt that innocent or guilty he was less a villain than many men who walked openly the streets of Tombstone or Tomahawk, their crimes unpunished. If he had let himself be persuaded to join the raiders he certainly had not guessed that two of his companions would run amok in an orgy of murder; and it was strongly in the merchant's mind that the young fellow was a victim of circumstances chance had piled up against him. But Rosenstein knew that nothing he could say would change the current of events. The wilder element in the camp had taken over. Sheriff Dunham could do nothing to prevent this. But at least they could use their influence to see that the prisoner got a fair trial.

Tom Fallon was detained under guard in the shaft house of the Copper King mine while the time, place, and details of the trial were being decided. To Tom it was an ominous sign that the men guarding him no longer showed any anger. There was a touch almost of kindliness in the consideration they showed him. He knew the reason. They expected that he would be dead within a few hours and they did not want to have to reproach themselves later on account of callous harshness. His hands were free and they encouraged him to roll and light a cigarette. The leader of the group saw that food was carried to him from a restaurant. One of them

23

poured him a second cup of coffee from the pot that had been brought to the frame building.

"It's kinda cold," the man said. "Hot coffee will do you good." He was a bald-headed miner named Walsh with a friendly face.

"That's right," another agreed. "Tough on you that you got caught and yore pardners have made a getaway into the hills."

"No partners of mine," Tom replied. "I never spoke to one of them in my life."

"Too bad a young fellow like you got in with a bunch of killers and bandits, but when he does he has to pay for it."

"Even when he doesn't he has to pay for it if he gets in the hands of crazy idiots," Tom answered bitterly.

"Now—now," Walsh reproved mildly. "Don't hold hard feelings at us because you got in a jam. I hate like sin to think of what is coming to you. Try to keep up yore nerve."

The cowpuncher looked at him out of cold hard eyes. "Don't worry about my nerve. I'll take care of that. Just keep yore mind on the pleasure you and the rest of the wolves are going to get out of murdering me."

Within the hour a messenger came to the shaft house with the news that the trial was to be held at once. It would take place in the Mexican quarter of the camp, a high bench known as Chihuahua Town that cut into one of the walls of the gulch. There would be room there for everybody to attend without crowding.

Tom's hands were pinioned before they started. They moved in single file along the narrow trail that led up the wall to the shelf. Darkness had already fallen but the prisoner could see and hear men tramping up the path in front of and behind them. A stiff wind was sweeping down the canyon and it chilled the young man and set him shivering. This was a dreadful journey to be taking, perhaps his last on earth. He set himself to carry through without breaking down but he felt it would have been easier to bear with the warm sun shining on him.

The settlement on the bench was a poor makeshift one. Adobe cabins shouldered tin-can huts and shanties built with mud-plastered poles. In the open plaza great log fires had been set which pushed the darkness back to the quartz wall

24

of the gorge and flung out moving shadows which gave a weird and eerie effect to the night.

A temporary scaffolding had been rigged up as a courtroom, partly in order to give those in the rear a chance to see what was taking place. On it were a dozen homemade chairs borrowed from Mexicans who lived close to the plaza. A few of them were occupied when Fallon was brought up to the platform. Curt Faunce had evidently elected himself master of ceremonies.

He said harshly: "Before we hang you we're going to give you a fair trial, which is a hell of a lot more than you deserve. These six gents in the chairs will be the jury, but any decision they make will have to be backed up by a vote of all present. After the verdict is in we'll hang you on that tree in front of Juan Perón's house. Any remarks?" The man's mouth was a cruel gash. His eyes were glittering with the hunter's excitement of the kill. He was enjoying this.

The man's animosity puzzled Tom. There was in the fellow a perverted lust that took delight in the pain of others. But that did not quite explain his ferocity. It seemed to have an urgent personal impulse. That thought was tucked in the back of Fallon's mind and would return frequently. But just now other considerations were more pressing.

Tom beat down the fear rising to his throat. His voice was steady and held an edge of scorn. "A fair trial? Murder is the word. You've already picked the tree where I am to hang."

Sheriff Dunham pushed through the crowd to the platform. "The boy is right," he challenged. "This trial is a mockery. If Fallon is condemned it will be by hysteria and not on the evidence."

A voice in the background shouted, "You're dead right, Sheriff."

The fury of the mob yelled him down. It hit Tom like a hot wave of fire.

"We've come here to hang a man," Budge cried. "Let's get at it."

"You're in too big a hurry, Budge," Heilman protested. "Some of us aren't sure about this young fellow's guilt. He is going to have a chance for his white alley. You can't railroad him."

There was a scatter of agreement in the crowd, the opin-

25

ion of a small minority. Faunce smiled cynically. "Sure. No hurry about this. We have all night." He turned to the prisoner. "You can have somebody represent you as yore lawyer."

Rosenstein volunteered.

"Suits me," Tom said. "But I'll cut in when I feel like it."

Faunce took charge of the prosecution. He had nothing but circumstantial evidence but he marshaled it with sour and crafty savagery. He lost his temper when Rosenstein cross-examined the waiter Silliman and tangled him in contradictions. The man admitted there had been some shooting on the street before the prisoner left the restaurant but not in any great volume. The accused man had stayed to finish his supper after that. His explanation of what he had said and what the cowboy had said became involved in uncertainty. But when Rosenstein had finished with him his story was still damaging to Fallon. Silliman might be a little mixed but he was not lying.

Tom made an excellent impression as a witness. The blue direct eyes, the lithe straight figure, his manner bold but not defiant, had a favorable effect on many of those present. It stirred in them as unease. To hang this boy might be a mistake. Perhaps they had better wait and make sure. But the reaction of the miners showed that most of those present would vote against him.

There was a stir in the back of the crowd. The high voice of a woman reached the platform. "Let me through. Please. I have something to say." In the tone of her cry rang a frightened urgency.

A way to the platform was cleared for her. In the stress of her emotion Mary Landon had lost her shyness. "You can't do this," she reproached. "He is innocent. He was with me after he rescued Billy from where he had been shot."

Heilman gave her a hand up to the platform. "We'll hear yore story, miss," he said.

She told how he had brought her brother in from the firing zone where he lay in danger. This was a complete surprise to the listeners. The fact had been passed around that somebody had run into the street and picked up the wounded boy but in the confusion nobody had known who had done it.

26

"You claim he stayed with you till all the fighting was over?" demanded Faunce harshly.

She hesitated. Her eyes shifted to meet those of Tom Fallon.

"Tell the truth," he told her.

"He left just before the guns stopped," she said in a low-pitched husky voice.

"You bet. Her story doesn't prove a thing." Faunce was letting his anger rip loose again. "His gun was smoking at the finish."

Rosenstein would not let that pass without a dispute. "It proves he was a game young fellow who went out to save Billy Landon when nobody else took the chance."

Walsh joined those at the platform. "Hey, seems I'm a witness and didn't know it," he announced.

The miner testified that he had seen the young man who came out of the lodging house with a gun in his hand and had followed him down the street. Walsh had a sawed-off shotgun and was only a few yards behind him. He was certain sure that the man had been firing at the bandits.

"Why didn't you come forward before?" Faunce wanted to know suspiciously.

"I didn't know the young chap was Fallon," Walsh explained.

"You guarded him for an hour and didn't recognize him."

"That's right."

"All you know is that somebody came out of a house and got in the fight."

"Out of the Landon rooming house," Walsh corrected.

"But another fellow could have come out too," Faunce scoffed. "You can't swear that Fallon was the only one."

"Well, I'm pretty sure that—"

"In this trial we don't want 'pretty sures' but facts," Faunce said dogmatically. "Yore evidence don't amount to a hill of beans."

But the shouts of the crowd showed that he had lost his following. Nine out of ten of them were honest citizens who had let indignation at the raiders warp their judgment. They came out strongly now for an acquittal.

A few minutes later Tom walked down the path beside Mary a free man. All her shyness had returned. She was very happy at his release but she was ridden by the fear that she had been unwomanly, that her public anxiety for him might be misconstrued. Maybe he thought she was a bold woman interfering before that mob of men. But she knew that she had been forced to do it. As soon as word had reached her that he was in danger the urge to help him had been irresistible. He guessed at her embarrassment.

"Long as I live I'll never forget how you stood up to Faunce and fought for my life," he said gently. "You're a brave girl, Mary."

His hand reached out in the darkness and took hers. The words, the pressure of his strong fingers, sent warmth and comfort pouring through her. Except for her small brother she was alone in the world with no close friends. Tom would of course leave Copper Fork at once. She would probably never see him again, but the memory of him would not go out of her life.

CHAPTER 5

As soon as Tom had left Mary Landon he walked to Sam Rosenstein's store to thank him for his help in clearing him. On the way he met a dozen men, most of them miners, who stopped to congratulate him. Some of them, Fallon felt sure, had an hour before been eager to help hang him. He felt no resentment toward them. They had been victims of hysteria incited by Faunce and his followers.

Though the store was closed to customers, he found the side door open. With the merchant were Sheriff Dunham and Harry Heilman. All of them expressed pleasure at the result of the trial.

"There was no reason for such a trial," the sheriff said. "The evidence against you was too flimsy. I'm surprised at Curt Faunce."

"Curt means all right," Heilman explained. "He's a good fellow at bottom, and he is right about there having been a lot of killings and nobody hanged for them. I reckon he thought it was time to make an example."

28

Tom made no comment. He could not put a finger on the ranchman's motive, but he knew there was one more weighty than a love of justice. The fellow was either diverting attention from the real bandits or had a personal axe to grind.

"I suppose you will be pulling out of here tomorrow," Rosenstein said. "I can't blame you for going, after the way you have been treated."

Tom's level eyes met his. "No, I think I'll stick around for a while."

"Why?" asked the sheriff. "I'd say that wouldn't be safe. Faunce and his hotheads aren't satisfied with the verdict. They are a wild bunch."

"I am not satisfied with it myself," Tom replied. "I don't want to go through life with a 'Not proven' acquittal. Until the guilty men are captured and convicted I'll be around. Maybe I can help run them down."

Heilman backed the sheriff's opinion. "Don't be foolish, Fallon. There is nothing to hold you here. Get out and forget what has occurred."

He shook hands with Tom and returned to his dance hall.

Dunham surprised Tom by offering him a job. "One of my deputies has just quit. If you want his place you can have it."

"You've got you a deputy, Mr. Dunham," Tom said promptly. He added, grinning, "I reckon you think it will be safer for me over in Tomahawk than here."

"Being a deputy sheriff in this county isn't safe wherever your headquarters are," Dunham warned him. "I've had two killed in three years. If I put you on the job of running down the gang that pulled off this raid—and I can see that is what you expect—you will be about as safe as a man sitting on an open keg of gunpowder and smoking a cigar."

"Well, I can't complain you didn't wise me up about the job," Tom answered cheerfully. "When do I start?"

"Right now. Clam up about being my deputy for a few days. Stay here and see what you can find out. It probably won't be much. Be careful not to let anybody think you are being nosy. Saturday or Sunday ride over to Tomahawk and report to me."

"You think there is somebody here in cahoots with the robbers?" Rosenstein asked.

"Looks like it certain. How did these fellows know when

to make their raid and that your store was the place to strike? Faunce had the right idea but he picked the wrong man."

"On purpose?" inquired Tom dryly. "Because he wanted to protect the right man? Or because he was hell bent on getting rid of me personally?"

"Son, don't say that again to anybody," the sheriff reproved gravely. "Faunce is a dangerous man. You have had evidence of that already."

"He is evil," Tom said bluntly. "It is written all over him. I don't say he was in this holdup, but he wanted me hanged, innocent or guilty."

"I can't leave you here if you are going to talk that way," Dunham told him. "You would be a sitting duck for anybody who wanted to pick you off."

"After I leave this room my mouth is padlocked," the new deputy promised.

"See that it is. Don't trust anybody. Sam won't do any talking."

"Good. Can you give me some information about the Dutch Frater gang? I've heard some guessing that they pulled off this raid."

"That may be a good guess. The claim is that they are a bad bunch of cattle rustlers and tough characters in the San Simon country. They hang around a little town in the valley called Wide Gap. Until two or three years ago they did their cattle lifting in Mexico and drove the herds across the Rio Grande, but Colonel Kosterlitzky and his *rurales* made it so hot for them that lately they have had to do their skulduggery on this side of the line. This has never been absolutely proved."

"Bob Wheldon, the man who got killed, was one of them?"

"He was in the San Simon valley for a while and was friendly with Frater. For what it's worth a Cousin Jack told me he thought he saw Dutch himself on the street half an hour before the holdup. But in the darkness he couldn't be sure."

"Can you describe Frater for me?"

"I never saw him, but I have been told he is a big, heavy man, well over six feet tall, about thirty years old. There is a scar from a knife cut on his chin."

Tom nodded. "I've met the gent. He was with the bunch I saw at Tomahawk and with those who passed me on the way to town Monday."

"If you are sure of that we know one to start rounding up. But I don't want any arrests made until we have evidence enough for a conviction." The sheriff added: "He'll have a nice alibi fixed showing that he was playing cards with four or five other crooks fifty miles from here at the time of the raid."

After breakfast next morning at Hop Lee's Chinese restaurant Tom Fallon sauntered up Cochise Street. He was on his way to the lodging house where Nick Kraus was lying with a wounded shoulder. It was possible the store clerk might have some guess as to the two bandits who held up the store.

A man came out of the Wagon Wheel saloon as Tom was passing.

"So you are still here," he said gruffly. "You'd better light out."

It was an order, harsh and imperative. Fallon's eyes met those of Curt Faunce and held to them steadily. He saw a big rangy man, strongly individual, arrogant and turbulent, one with a bony wolfish face thin of lip and salient of jaw.

"You've got it in for me, Mr. Faunce," Tom said mildly. "Why?"

"Don't argue with me. Get out."

"Just like that." Tom smiled thinly. "No reason given."

"You squeaked out of being hanged last night by the skin of yore teeth. You are guilty as sin. I won't have you around this district. If you know what's good for you, light a shuck. Today."

The man's urgency did not make sense—unless there was some secret reason back of it. If the bandits were caught Tom would be a witness against them. But all he could swear to was that he had seen Frater and his two companions with Wheldon both at Tomahawk and here. He could establish a connecting link between them and the dead man and as evidence that would not have much weight. It seemed to him that the animosity of Faunce was personal. Could it carry back to earlier days in Nebraska—to the shooting of his father, Sheriff Tom Fallon, dropped with two bullets in the back one dark night by a murderer unknown? The suspected man, Carl Fenwick, had fled and never been heard of since.

That the initial in the names of both were C. F. might merely be a coincidence. Or it might be that he had after long years come face to face with the assassin of his father.

Tom had been a small boy at the time of his father's death, and he had never seen Fenwick. But Tom bore a strong resemblance to his father and had the same name. If Faunce was Fenwick, at the first sight of young Tom Fallon it must have flashed across his mind that the sheriff's son had come to avenge his death. It would not occur to him that chance had brought them together.

Their eyes clashed for long seconds while Tom's thoughts raced. That there was fear as well as anger in this man young Fallon knew; a fear not for his personal safety but for the power he had built up. Though no spot in the country was more lawless than this southeast corner of Arizona, even among the outlaws a code bound them. Some of the worst of them ignored it, but it had weight with the majority. You could not shoot your enemy in the back at night without warning. If the followers of Faunce believed this was true of him, it would be a blow to his leadership.

"Murder will out," Tom said, his searching gaze fixed on the ranchman. "Years pass. You think your crime is covered —and it jumps out at you."

Tom knew instantly that he had guessed the truth. The sudden lust to kill had leaped into the ranchman's eyes. It was there, urgent and savage. The thin lips tightened and the jaw muscles stood out like ropes. In that flash of time, while Tom's life hung in the balance, he heard the clumping beat of high-heeled boots on the sidewalk.

"Been lookin' for you, Curt," a voice called casually. "Do we start home before or after dinner?"

The demoniac expression on the face of Faunce was blotted out. His hand moved from the butt of the .45 it had been gripping. Slowly the tenseness of the thick body relaxed. He was postponing the hour of decision until a more suitable moment.

He said harshly to Fallon, "Keep away from me, you fool."

The newcomer was a cowboy called Alabam. Most of his acquaintances did not even know his real name. "This kid been annoyin' you, Curt?" he drawled.

32

If Tom had been an older man he would have let this go in silence but youth cannot bear to be ridden down.

"All I said was that—" he began.

His sentence never was finished. The hairy knotted fist of Faunce slammed into his face. Tom went down as if a hammer had hit his jaw. The big man glared at him, half minded to finish the job.

Alabam guessed what was in his mind. The cowboy's left hand slipped under the cattleman's right elbow and clamped itself around the wrist.

"That'll be enough for right now, Curt," he said, half coaxing and half in warning. "You've knocked him unconscious. That ought to learn him not to get brash."

Faunce wrenched his arm free, glared at his fallen foe, kicked him twice in the ribs, and strode down the sidewalk.

When Tom came groggily back to a world crazily tip-tilted it took him a few seconds to realize that his head rested against the shoulder of a girl kneeling beside him. He shut his eyes and then opened them again to make sure this was not a dream.

He murmured presently with a grin an explanation of his plight. "Kindness of Mr. Faunce."

She cried softly, "Oh Tom, are you—did he—?" The question died in the air.

The road had stopped dancing up and down. "Lady, I am —and he did. If I understand your inquiry. I've been kicked by a Missouri mule—jounced around by an earthquake—run over by a train."

"The brute kicked you when you were down. I saw him."

Tom felt his ribs gingerly. "Mr. Faunce is sure sudden and violent. I get the idea he doesn't like me."

Mary understood that he was making light of his injuries because he did not want to be a sissy. If a fellow asked for a licking he must not complain when he got it.

"Why can't he let you alone?" she cried indignantly. "What have you ever done to hurt him?"

"It's not what I have done but what I may do," he told her.

"I don't see how you can harm him. What is he afraid of?"

He hesitated, then decided he might as well tell her since he meant to bring the truth into the open. "He killed my fa-

33

ther seventeen years ago back in Nebraska, shot him at night from behind. I just as good as accused him of it. I'm lucky he didn't shoot me down. If that cowboy Alabam hadn't been there he would of finished me."

The color washed out of her face. "You must leave Copper Fork at once, fast as you can go."

"Not yet. I have some business here. But I will pack a gun." He rose unsteadily, every movement painful. "First off, I'll see Doc Pilcher. Some of my ribs may be cracked."

"I'll go with you," she said. "Then I'll bring your horse to his office."

"Much obliged, but I can travel alone. And I don't want my horse. If you want to be helpful go to Sam Rosenstein and get my .45 for me. He'll find it in my blanket roll upstairs above the store."

"Oh, Tom, a gun can't save you. Don't you see that? You'll have to leave here."

"Let me decide that," he told her quietly. "When you bring the six-gun be sure it is wrapped up in paper so nobody will know what you are carrying."

She watched him walk down the street and knew that every step was a torture. Nothing she could say or do would move him. That was the way men were, bullheaded and stubborn, going their own road even when it took them to destruction. At critical moments they brushed women aside.

Sam Rosenstein was in his store waiting on a customer, but at her distressed plea he turned the miner over to the clerk and followed her to the rear of the room.

"It's Tom Fallon," she exclaimed. "That Faunce has just beaten him up terribly. He wants his gun. It's upstairs in his roll."

"His gun? You don't think he means to try to kill Faunce?"

"I don't know. But he won't leave town." She added unhappily: "He'll be killed if he stays. He accused Faunce of murdering his father in Nebraska long ago."

So that was the explanation of Faunce's determination to have Fallon hanged. Rosenstein felt that he must move fast to get the boy out of town. His experience last night seemed to have taught him nothing.

"Where is Tom now?" he asked Mary.

"He is at Doctor Pilcher's office getting fixed up."

"I'll go with you," Sam said. "After I have got his weapon. Wait here."

"Tom said to wrap his gun up so nobody would notice it."

"All right," the merchant snapped impatiently. "He doesn't know enough to come in out of the rain. And I'll say he certainly asks a lot of his friends. He's hell bent on having his own way and when he gets in a jam we're expected to get him out of it."

"Maybe he'll listen to you," Mary replied.

"Fat chance," Sam retorted.

At Pilcher's office they found the doctor taping Tom's ribs. "They don't seem to be broken," the doctor said. "But they will be mighty sore for a couple of weeks."

"I'm a lucky guy," Tom commented.

"Sure." Rosenstein's voice held heavy sarcasm. "You may live two or three days yet if you stick around here."

"I'm aiming to leave about Sunday."

"You want to strut around like a hero, I suppose. Give me the name of your nearest relative so that I can forward the news."

"I don't figure there will be any news to send," Tom answered mildly.

"Let me get this straight," the storekeeper said. "Did you or didn't you accuse Curt Faunce of killing your father?"

"I let him get the idea. Until I saw how he acted I wasn't quite sure. I know now." Tom's eyes grew hard and steely. "My father was sheriff and just ready to close in on him for rustling. This fellow shot him in the back one dark night. Then he lit out for parts unknown. Maybe you think I should sit around and say, 'Well, ain't that too bad, but there's nothing I can do about it.' If so, take another guess."

Sam touched the parcel in his hand. "You mean to take this forty-five and kill him?"

"No. I mean to see him hanged by the law."

"If he lets you live."

"I'll be packin' a six-gun, the one you have there."

"He shot your father in the back. Don't forget that."

"On a dark night. I'll be holed up then."

"Use your brains, boy. He may hire a gunman to rub you out."

"I'll be watching."

Finally Rosenstein shrugged his shoulders and gave up.

Perhaps this light-stepping, loose-limbed youth whose move-ments had the easy grace of a panther might weather the worst that Faunce could do. But the odds were against him. More than once it had flashed across Sam's mind that this man Faunce was at the bottom of the lawlessness in his dis-trict. If Fallon was a danger to him it would not be difficult to arrange a killing.

Mary walked home heavyhearted. She had known Tom Fallon less than two days but already he meant more to her than any other man she had met. From the hour when he had carried her brother into the house he had never been out of danger. She knew she would keep on worrying about him. There was no escape from that.

CHAPTER 6

Tom moved down Cochise Street with an odd sense of unre-ality. He was a man set apart from others, one condemned to death at some near hour and day unknown to him. It prob-ably would not be quite yet. Curt Faunce would need a little time to make his plan and set his trap. But by this hour to-morrow a bullet might come tearing into his body from any door or window he passed. The clutch of fear began to tie up his stomach.

This would not do. He not only must show no dread; he must not let it affect his actions beyond a point. Of course he had been a fool. Sheriff Dunham had warned him to be wary and inconspicuous. Instead of that, at the first chance he had let himself be surprised into flinging a challenge at Faunce.

After consideration Tom felt that his enemy would cover his tracks carefully before striking. The news that Tom had accused Faunce of murdering his father would spread through the camp like a prairie fire. It would be unwise to leave any evidence that he had killed the son too in order to protect himself.

Tom wanted to have a talk with Tex Scully, the shotgun messenger who rode the Tomahawk stage, but since he did not want to advertise the meeting he climbed the trail leading to the house where Tex and his bride lived. At his knock Mrs. Scully came to the door. Her husband had not come in yet from the end of his run, she explained, but he would be home inside of half an hour. She invited Tom to wait. Perhaps she was a little more cordial because she had heard so much about this young man who had made such a flutter in the camp during his short stay.

Nora Scully was a pretty girl, not yet twenty, with dark lovely long-lashed eyes. Though she might have had her choice of a dozen men, her fancy had lit on Tex, much to his surprise. She was very much in love with him and let it show in her talk. "I wanted a man—I mean a real one," she told Tom with a smile. "And Tex is more man than anybody else I know."

"You made a good choice," Tom agreed.

Her sleeves were rolled up to the elbows of her strong firm arms. She was kneading bread but stopped to give Tom a piece of news. "Tex doesn't know it yet, but I'm going to shift him from that job he has. I'm not going to have him sitting up on the box of the stage for holdups to shoot at."

Tom said she was right to get him out of a job so dangerous.

Her appraising eyes took in this slim lad, shy and apparently gentle, soft-voiced, yet with a suggestion of will and strength in both his bearing and his tanned face. "You're a fine one to talk that way. You are as bad as Tex—or worse. I've heard all about you. You've been here about three days and in trouble all the time."

"Yes, ma'am," Tom said meekly. "Looks like I've run into a streak of bad luck."

The door opened and Tex Scully walked into the room. Nora ran into his arms, her flour-covered hands raised aloft. Tom noticed that the man's eyes adored her. He held her fast for a long moment.

"We have a guest," Nora told her husband. "He wants to see you."

"Why, hello!" Scully said to Tom. "Didn't notice you."

Tom explained that he had come to get information about the stage holdups. His idea was that the gang which had robbed the stages was responsible for the raid on Rosenstein's store.

Scully was of the same opinion. The road agents had however been masked and he would not be able to identify them. He added sharply that he beileved they would have captured the raiders the night of the robbery if the posse had headed straight for the Gregory ranch. Heilman's obstinacy had taken the pursuers in the wrong direction.

"Yes, I've wondered about that some. He was so sure." At that moment the elusive detail which since the robbery had several times nagged at Tom's memory popped into his mind. There had been a fifth man with Dutch Frater and his companions at Tomahawk. The extra man had been Harry Heilman.

The shotgun messenger followed Tom to the door as he was leaving. "Come outside a minute," Fallon said in a low voice.

Scully shut the door behind him.

"Sheriff Dunham thinks the bandits had an undercover man here to line up the holdup for them," Tom said. "Could that man have been Heilman? Ever since the robbery I've known that there was something I should remember. I know what it is now. Heilman was with Wheldon and his pals when I saw them at Tomahawk."

Scully slammed a fist into the palm of his other hand. "By jinks, you've hit the nail on the head. That's why Heilman led our posse astray. He knew the horses of the robbers were fagged and we might catch up with them."

"Remember how busy he was bossing us all after the bandits lit out, how he said two or three times the killers ought to be hanged soon as they were caught."

Tex Scully stared at Tom, the light of an astounding discovery in his eyes. "I have sure been dumb. Heilman pushed me aside to be the first to reach Wheldon after the firing stopped. He bent over the man playing like he was asking the man to name his pals, stooping over him so close I couldn't see the wounded outlaw. Next day when I looked at Wheldon's body where it was lying in the Wagon Wheel I noticed purple bruises on the throat. I know now how they came there. With me not three feet away from Heilman he strangled the dying man so as to keep him from talking."

"If he did that he was taking an awful risk," Tom said.

"He counted on the darkness and the confusion. It didn't take five seconds to squeeze the life out of a man almost dead. The one thing he dared not let happen was to let Wheldon name his accomplices."

"Of course we are guessing," Tom suggested. "It looks bad for Heilman, but we haven't evidence enough to make an arrest. After what happened to me I don't want to make a mistake and accuse an innocent man. You and I had better clam up until we have built a case that will stand up. I can ride over to Tomahawk Saturday and tell Sheriff Dunham what we suspect."

Scully thought that would be a good idea. He promised to keep quiet about what they thought but he was convinced that Heilman was guilty. Tom was not so certain. He recalled the warm friendliness of the dance hall owner. The man had shown none of Faunce's urgency to have him hanged. Evidence against him so far was slight and might be wholly misleading.

Before leaving for Tomahawk Tom dropped in at the Crystal Palace to find out what impression he would get of the man now. Heilman was practicing some billiard shots but at sight of Tom he dropped the cue at once and came forward to meet him. There was no question as to his charm. His smile was kindly. He had the gift of making people feel he liked them.

"I've been wanting to see you, boy," he said, and dropped a hand on Fallon's shoulder lightly. "What's this I hear about you and Faunce having trouble?"

Tom told him briefly what had occurred.

Heilman shook his head regretfully. "That's too bad, Tom. I'm sorry you made such a charge against him. For two reasons. Curt is a hard man, but I'm sure he wouldn't shoot a man in the back. The killing of yore father took place a long time ago. You say you had never seen his murderer. When you tried to pin it on Curt you made a mistake. Two mistakes, in fact. The second is that he is a proud man who will feel his good name has been attacked. He is a Southerner, very touchy about his honor. I am afraid he will not be content until he has rubbed you out." After a moment Heilman concluded gravely, "My boy, Arizona is no longer a safe place for you."

"I am leaving Copper Fork for Tomahawk," Tom said.

"That is good for a start, but don't stop there," Heilman advised. "Keep going."

Tom promised to think about it. He still was in doubt about Heilman. If Scully's suspicion was well grounded—that the gambler had murdered his dying accomplice to save himself—the man must be a thorough villain. But it was hard to believe this of one so gay and buoyant and friendly. Faunce had the mark of evil stamped on his face. Heilman on the contrary showed the cheerful countenance of one who liked his fellow men. He had opposed Faunce when the latter had been set on having Tom hanged. The narrow street had been dark on the night of the raid and there had been a great deal of confusion. Since the body of the gambler had been between Scully and the dying man he could not have actually seen Bob Wheldon strangled. Yet when Tom had looked at the corpse of the dead man next day to identify it he had noticed what looked like the bruises of finger marks on the throat. There was another explanation of how they might have got there. Some miner or cowboy infuriated at the callous raid could perhaps in a rage have choked the neck of the dead outlaw.

While Tom was walking down the street the long shrill whistle of the Copper King mine sounded. For more than a minute the alarm continued.

"Been expecting that," a mule skinner called to a merchant coming from his store to help unload a wagon.

"Why?" Tom asked.

"Old Mose Hanson just in from the hills reports he saw Apache smoke signals yesterday and fire signals at night. Means some young bucks are off the reservation lookin' for trouble. Till they are corralled it won't be safe to do any travelin' without a guard. The mine whistle sends out a warning."

"Holy Moses! I thought the Apache war days were over."

"So they are, mostly. But once in a spell a few young devils get restless and cut loose. Early this year a bunch of them got two prospectors up in the Whetstones and two months ago a mail carrier was killed not ten miles from Tucson."

"Any particular reason for the outbreaks?"

"I reckon it's just in their blood. After they are rounded up they will go back to the reservation and promise to be good. The government will slap them on the wrists and ask the raiders not to do it again. If I was runnin' it I'd remember that the only good Injun is a dead one."

40

Tom knew that this was the opinion of nearly all of the early settlers on the frontier. All the way from the Mexican to the Canadian border the outbreaks of the tribes had taken a terrible toll of life, including women and children as well as men. But an old squaw man had once told Tom the other side of the story. It was a tale of treaties made with the red men and broken repeatedly by the whites, of a steady pressure on the Indian hunting grounds, of contemptuous disregard for all the native rights in the land. The Apaches, like the Kiowas, Comanches, and Sioux, knew they were engaged in a losing fight and made it on their part a cruel and terrible one.

"You don't think the Pachies would dare attack Copper Fork, do you?" Tom asked.

"We're too big for that," the mule skinner answered. "But only six months ago a bunch of renegades swept over the mountains and looked down on our camp whoopin' and yellin'. After a while they lit out, but they sure scared us plenty." The man stared hard at Tom. "Ain't you the guy the boys fixed up a necktie party for a couple of days ago?"

"I'm the guy who was proved innocent," Tom amended.

"You still ain't popular with some quick-trigger gents here. You blab too much with yore mouth." He lowered his voice a trifle. "Was I you I'd light a shuck."

"Right away?" Tom asked with a grin. "And get scalped by the Pachies."

"The Pachies ain't lookin' for you particular, son." The old-timer leaned over the edge of the wagon so that his whispered words would reach Tom. "You didn't claim any of them was murderers, did you?" He dismissed Fallon from his attention and spoke to the storekeeper. "I'm two barrels of flour shy but I'll make out to bring them on my next trip."

CHAPTER 7

Darkness still lay heavily over Copper Fork when Tom saddled his bay and moved down Cochise Street into the open country beyond the entrance to the gulch. It was likely that the renegade band of Apaches were by this time far back in the hills but on the chance that they were not, the young deputy wanted to cover the most dangerous lap of the journey before day broke.

The wrangler at the corral had flung after him a cheerful but sleepy farewell. "Good luck, fellow. No need to worry none about them Injuns. They've done hived off to other parts."

I'd be carefree too if I was going back to my bunk to hit the hay like Tim, the rider thought. *It's no hair off his head if the Pachies do scalp me.*

Tom wished he did not have so much imagination. Every clump of Spanish bayonet he saw in the dim light looked like the feathers of an Indian's topknot. Every rustle of a stirring rabbit in the scanty vegetation could be an ambusher lurking in wait for him. He welcomed the coming day, though he knew it would increase the danger if the small war party of braves was still in the vicinity.

The road passed over rolling hills strewn with great rock slabs, gradually descending to the desert which stretched to the far horizon. From above the plain looked level as a billiard table but the floor of it was seamed with gullies and uneven terrain. At the summit of a small rise he pulled up and swung from the saddle. A whitened buffalo skull had been set up on two rocks in the middle of the road. On the forehead was written a message: Keep your eyes skinned. Saw bunch of Pachies on Ridge Hill. Don't think they saw me.

The warning was signed Pete Maloney. Tom had met the man at Tomahawk. He owned a blacksmith shop. Probably he had been at Copper Fork to see the fiesta.

Within the hour Tom had proof that Maloney had been in error on one point. The Apaches had seen him. Tom came on the body of the blacksmith lying sprawled in a sandy wash. He had been scalped. There was evidence that he had made a desperate fight. Half a dozen shells from his .45 were scattered close to him. The trampled ground showed that a fierce hand-to-hand struggle had taken place before the trapped man was killed. A hundred yards from him lay the body of his horse. Evidently the animal had been shot first and Maloney had made a run for the shelter of the dry stream's bank.

The freshness of the footprints and the condition of Maloney's body which was not yet quite rigid told Tom that the tragedy had occurred only a short time before his arrival. His eyes swept the adjacent ground. The Apaches might be crouched behind hummocks or mesquite watching him. The roar of their guns might sound at any moment. There was nothing he could do for Maloney. His concern was to escape alive if possible. Fear crawled up and down his spine like the cold feet of mice. If the Apaches should capture him he would be tortured.

He put his horse to a gallop and raced down the road, crouched low in the saddle. Because of the Indian scare he had brought a rifle with him. Old-timers had told him that the Indians had inferior weapons and were poor marksmen. His bay could probably outrun any of the scrub horses the Apaches owned. The momentary panic that had swept over him was gone. He had ridden through blizzards and stampedes, had stood up to bullies who tried to run over him. The hard outdoor life of the frontier had toughened him. This was no time to get jittery. Presently he slowed his mount and took the rise to the summit of a small hill at a road gait.

His heart jumped. To his right, grouped in a small arroyo, his sweeping gaze fell on a group of mounted braves. A guttural shout announced that he had been seen. At a touch of the spur his bay got into motion fast. A slim breech-clothed figure jumped out from back of a boulder beside the road in front of him. A whistling bullet whipped past Tom's head. Fallon charged straight at the brave and rode him down. The bay stumbled over the prone body, staggered for a few steps, regained its stride, and dashed down the hill. The trampled man had evidently been a sentry left to watch the road. Along the slope parallel to Tom's course the raiders were strung out in a line racing to head him off before he reached a cut where the hill closed in on the trail. Most of the attackers were equipped with cheap rifles bought from traders. The rest had only bows and arrows. Already the gunmen without slackening their speed were sniping at him, flinging wild shots that threw up spurts of dust in front of and behind him. An arrow struck the horn of his saddle and tore it off. In the hands of the tribe warriors the bow and arrow

43

was a deadly weapon. The missile could tear through two strips of weathered bull's hide.

Tom reached the cut and was through it a hundred yards ahead of his pursuers. They came out of the cut fast, a pack of them bunched, one well in front and the others trailing. The brave who was leading rode a paint horse, evidently very speedy. It was no native-bred broomtail but a blooded animal stolen from some ranch. The young buck handled it expertly.

Fallon had not as yet fired a shot. Nobody on a galloping horse can fire at a mark behind him with any accuracy. A hogback ran out from the foothills into the desert, the crown of it covered by a rimrock of huge boulders. If he could reach it he might make a stand and pick off some of the renegades as they came up the narrow pass. He knew it was going to be a close race between the bay and the pinto. The Apache was gaining slowly but while he was still some hundreds of yards from the steep incline Tom saw he would make it unless he or his mount should be shot.

Looking back from the summit of the pass, Tom saw the leader of the Indians at the lower end. Fallon flung himself from the saddle back of a flat tiptilted outcropping of rock and grounded the reins. He rested his Winchester on a spur of the boulder and took sight carefully at the man on the pinto. The Apache was a showy figure in his war dress, long, lithe, and graceful. For a moment Tom thought he must have missed. It was several seconds before the rider plunged headlong to the earth.

When Tom heard the sound of wheels grating on the rubble of disintegrated quartz he did not believe it, but when he turned his head he saw the stage coming into sight from the other slope of the hogback.

Tex Scully called from his seat beside the driver, "What's going on here?"

"Pachies," Tom answered. "A whole mess of them, crowdin' up fast on the prod."

The shotgun messenger put his foot on the wheel and came down to earth. He took a look at the Indians. They were scattering for cover like a covey of quails. Their leader lay still and lifeless on the road.

"Hell's bells!" Tex exclaimed. "Hadn't been for you we

would of run into them without warning." He turned to the driver. "Mac, get Miss Faunce out of the coach and into the rocks."

A girl came out of the stage without assistance. She was pale and her dark eyes showed fear but no sign of panic. There were no other passengers.

"Are they going to attack us?" she asked.

Tex shook his head. "I wouldn't know. Not right away anyhow. This boy got one of them and that stopped their rush. Likely they will try to sneak up without being seen."

The girl looked at Tom. "Many of them?" she questioned.

"A right smart number. We can stand them off, miss."

Young Fallon did not know much about girls but he thought it was remarkable that this one's voice was low and steady. Terror must be drenching her heart, for until the past few years Geronimo's raiders had been an appalling threat in the territory. They warred without mercy.

She was the prettiest girl he had ever seen, graceful and light-stepping as a fine-bred colt. A dark beauty, sloe-eyed, with abundant black hair neatly snooded except for little tendrils that escaped, head held proudly above fine sloping shoulders. She was a picture of controlled fear.

"You won't let them—" Her lips trembled. She could not bring herself to finish the sentence.

He understood what she meant. His gaze met hers very directly. "No. Never that."

Scully's rifle blazed.

"Get one?" Tom asked.

"Don't think so. They're keeping mighty close to cover."

The driver, Bert MacIntosh, said sourly, "I got nothing but my six-shooter. Can't help a mite unless they get closer."

Tom found a protected spot among the boulders a few yards from the road. "Don't be scared," he told the girl. "You stay right here. We won't let them get you."

"No matter what happens?" She said it almost in a whisper.

"No matter what happens," he promised.

"Won't they come at us from behind?" she wanted to know. "When they find out you're not alone."

"They'll try. But we can pick them off while they are climbing the hogback."

He spoke confidently, but in his mind he was not at all sure. At this kind of fighting the Apaches had the reputation of being very skillful.

MacIntosh backed the stage into an open spot and headed it in the direction from which it had come. They might have to make a run for safety.

Tom's gaze swept the rocky slope of the hogback. "Where are they? I don't see one."

"They are there," Tex answered grimly. "Hidden among the rocks. Might be a good idea for us both to fire about the same time so as to let them know you are not alone. Might keep them from rushing us."

"When one of us sees something to shoot at," Tom added.

The Apaches were both wary and patient. It was many minutes before Scully fired at a brave dodging from one rock to another. The man stumbled and fell. As he started to crawl for cover a bullet from Tom's Winchester stopped him. He collapsed and lay still.

MacIntosh cheered. "One gone to the happy hunting ground," he exulted. "Maybe that'll learn them."

From the rocks below came a scatter of shots.

"They are crawling up the hill through the brush," Tex said. "We'll have to knock off two or three of them to stop that." He talked in an even voice, no excitement showing in it, though he knew there was a chance they would all be wiped out.

Tom, crouched behind an outcropping rock, had his eyes fixed on a clump of prickly pear. There had been a slight movement back of it. As he watched, a puff of smoke ballooned and a slug caromed from the boulder. Involuntarily Tom ducked. This was too close for comfort. He raised his head cautiously and aimed at the cactus. The sharpshooter rolled down the hill, picked himself up, and dived into a small water runway.

A moment later the stage driver cried out. "Dang it, I'm hit."

"Badly?" Tex asked.

"In the hand," MacIntosh told him irritably. "A jim dandy place for a stage driver to get plugged. Doggone it, I need my hands."

Tex thought he might not need them long but he did not say so. Far off to the left he could see an Apache crawling

46

close to the rock rim. It was a long shot for Tex. He tried it and missed twice. By that time the man had disappeared into the stone-clad crest of the hogback.

"They are coming up out of range to get in our rear," Tom said, his voice low enough not to reach the girl.

"We'd better run for it before they cut us off," Tex decided. "Can you drive with that wounded hand, Mac."

"You bet," Mac retorted. "Anyhow, I could drive better with one hand than you with two."

Tom followed the stage down the grade. Miss Faunce was inside and the other men on top. Tom had let down the leather curtains to protect the girl against arrows while Tex was flinging the baggage on the roof overboard. The body of the stage, slung on stout leather braces, rocked wildly as the driver guided the coach at racing speed along the ledge road to the plain below. They had a good start, since the Indians had to get back to their ponies before they could begin the pursuit. By skillful handling of the reins Mac brought the Concord down the hazardous trail without disaster.

They were racing across the desert floor before Tex, looking back for the dozenth time anxiously, reported that the Apaches were in sight pounding down the ledge strung out in a long line. They were flogging their ponies in a ferocious urge to lessen the distance between them and the stage.

Tom rode beside the window back of which he knew the girl must be sitting in a swither of dreadful alarm. Once she pushed aside the curtain to look back at their pursuers.

"Are they getting nearer?" she called to Tom, the color washed from her face.

"We'll reach Half Way station and get help," he promised her.

But he was not sure they would. The Apaches were drawing closer. And even if they got as far as the station there would be only one man and a boy there. Already the renegades were flinging shots at the Concord. Tex was kneeling on the top of the swaying stage, his face to the horsemen drawing nearer. He held his fire until they were within range. The crack of Mac's whip sounded again and again as he drove the horses to their greatest speed.

Arrows as well as bullets were flying now. Tom and Tex were pumping lead at their enemies.

Mac let out an exultant yell. From a gulch not a quarter of

47

a mile in front of them a detachment of blue-coated soldiers was emerging. An officer in command waved his sword and shouted an order. Troopers came up the road at a gallop. The Apaches jerked their mounts to a halt and turned in flight, the cavalry in hot pursuit.

The driver pulled his horses up. Several arrows and two bullet holes decorated the stage. Tom tore back the curtain. The girl was huddled in a corner, her trembling hands covering her face.

"You're not hurt, are you?" Tom asked. He saw she did not realize what had occurred. "A troop of soldiers saved us. They are chasing the red devils now."

Her hands dropped to the seat. She leaned against the window, her body slumping. Tom stepped inside, afraid she had been wounded. Her eyes opened in a few moments.

"You're sure?" she murmured.

"Yes. All danger past." His knees were so weak they could hardly carry his weight. He had been facing not only the peril of death but the terrible obligation his promise to her had imposed on him, to make sure she did not fall into the hands of the savages.

"It was—awful," she said, shivering at the ordeal through which she had just come. "I thought—I thought—"

He knew without words the horrible fears that had obsessed her. Many a time in nightmares she would live them over again. He stepped into the coach and sat beside her.

"It's all over now," he told her, and took her small cold hands in his.

How it came about he could not afterward remember, but she was in his arms, her head on his shoulder, clinging to him as if he were her only hope of safety, sobs racking her body. He petted her like a child with comforting words. Presently the catching of the breath subsided and she withdrew from him.

"I'm an awful baby," she said.

Tex Scully's head appeared in the window. "You all right Miss Faunce?" he wanted to know.

She nodded that she was.

"Fine. As the old saying goes, all's well that ends well. But you sure took a jouncing."

"I'm not hurt any," the girl said.

48

"Good. Uncle Sam was sure on the job this time. Looks like a few braves won't make it back to the reservation to celebrate."

For the rest of the journey Tex took the ribbons from Mac on account of the driver's injured hand. Tom rode beside the coach as before. At the first opportunity he put a question to Scully.

"Is this Miss Faunce any relation to Curt Faunce, the fellow I had the run in with at Copper Fork?"

"Daughter. She's been away somewheres at school."

This was a blow to Tom. It was hard to believe that a girl so vivid and so obviously refined could have a father so dead to decency as Curt Faunce. He did not of course know much about her. She might be selfish and arrogant. There was a look in her eyes that suggested an explosive temper. But she had an air of good breeding, which was the last thing one would expect from the daughter of such a man. In any case there was no use thinking about her. As soon as she learned that he had accused Faunce of murder she would have nothing to do with him.

At Half Way station, where they stopped to change horses and eat dinner, Nancy Faunce watched for a chance to speak alone with Tom.

"You saved our lives," she said in a low voice.

He shook his head. "No, the soldiers did that."

"You first," she insisted. "Before they came."

"Tex and Mac did most of it. We were fighting for our own skins too." He was embarrassed at her words and changed the subject. "You all right now?"

"Yes. I got terrified and acted like a baby."

"You were very brave not to break down until it was over."

. Their eyes met and held. She was not much more than a child, he thought. Maybe seventeen. But she was woman too, in some ways a good deal older than he. A primeval urge stirred in the young man's heart. His pulses stilled, then crashed to a swift clamor of the blood, moved by an emotion he had never before known. She seemed to him God's flawless product. The slender throat that carried the lovely head like the stem of a rose not yet opened typified her proud adolescent beauty. It did not occur to him that millions of other

49

men had been moved to adoration of women since the beginning of history.

He sat beside her at dinner and was fascinated by her dainty ways, though he noticed that she had a hearty appetite. That she was a practical young person he had discovered when she had helped Tex dress and bandage Mac's wounded hand. There was no nonsense in her such as fainting at the sight of blood. Her deft fingers had done a neat workmanlike job.

During the meal he learned that she lived with an aunt at Tucson and had lately returned from a boarding school at Santa Fe. She had seen very little of her father since her mother's death fifteen years earlier but was now on her way to a week's visit with him at his ranch.

The driver of the stage and Tex were of opinion that it would be better to return to Tomahawk rather than to continue the journey to Copper Fork. The Apaches might have eluded the troops and still be a danger.

While the fresh horses were being brought from the corral the returning soldiers trotted down the road to the station. The officer in charge of the detachment was a shavetail recently out of West Point. Lieutenant Archie Ramsay was a gay, good-looking young fellow whose eyes brightened at sight of Nancy. He introduced himself and showed solicitude about the shock she had endured. His command, he explained, had been sent to guard the road from the raiders. He was very happy that they had arrived in the nick of time. It had been a bad break for the Indians. The troopers had shot down three before they escaped into the hills.

"You didn't stay on their trail?" Scully asked.

The lieutenant flushed a little and answered curtly. "That job has been assigned others. My orders are to patrol the road and protect travelers."

Nancy justified him quickly. "We are very thankful that you did, Lieutenant Ramsay."

Mac looked at his bound hand. "No complaints here," he said with a grin. "Hadn't been for yore boys we would of been goners. I don't aim ever to knock the army again."

The young officer was pleased with the situation. He had been in Arizona three months and during that time had been cut off from the society of desirable young women. He was tired of dust, desert, alkali, and long days on horseback under a broiling sun. Romance was what he needed to make life more bearable, the chance to flirt with a pretty girl and make love to her on a shady porch in the dark of the moon.

Tom watched with some envy the soldier making himself agreeable to Nancy. Young Ramsay knew how to toss small talk in a light entertaining way with a charming touch of deference. He managed to convey the impression that this girl was to him the most important in the world. The others present he largely ignored, not contemptuously but with the implication that he and Nancy had contacts from which these frontiersmen were excluded. Fallon admitted to himself that this was probably true. They were talking about tennis, a game he had never seen played. Even if his relations with Curt Faunce had not been a barrier he could not forget that he was only a dusty sunburned cowpuncher. For one fierce hour circumstances had forced him and Nancy into a closeness he would never forget. Yet though her soft warm body had clung to his frantically the drive that moved her had been fear rather than any liking for him.

Since Ramsay offered to guard the stage to Copper Fork the decision to take it to Tomahawk was reversed. Tom assisted the station keeper to hitch up the fresh horses and stood back to watch the lieutenant escort the girl to the coach and help her inside. The officer murmured something in her ear that provoked a burst of merry laughter from Nancy. Both of them were enjoying themselves immensely.

Nancy almost forgot to say goodbye to Tom. It was after the stage was rolling that she remembered to look out of the window and wave a hand at him.

Mac, who had decided to stay with Tom and take the incoming stage bound for Tomahawk, summed up the matter cheerfully. "Looks like that smart Aleck has done stole yore girl, boy."

Tom was too depressed even to try a retort. Not considering Nancy, he realized that after the excitement had died down in him he was going to have a bad time. He had killed two men and wounded another. His stay in the territory had not been long enough for him to accept the pioneers' view that Apaches were pests to be wiped out like wolves. They were human beings and felt that they were fighting for the land that belonged to them. They had families—mothers and wives and children, for whom no doubt they had a deep affection. Tom had done only what he had been forced to do, but he could not escape a conviction that warfare like this was savage and barbaric. Primarily the blame did not rest either on the settlers or the tribes. Both were driven into a conflict they could not avoid.

CHAPTER 8

Tom reached Tomahawk late at night and reported to the sheriff next morning. Listening to his story of what had occurred, Dunham was not sure he had been wise in appointing him a deputy sheriff. Tom Fallon had the fighting edge an officer in this turbulent frontier needed. He had an alert mind. But he seemed to be lacking in discretion. The fight with Curt Faunce—if it could be called a fight—might have been avoided by a wise reticence. The San Simon ranchman might have killed Sheriff Fallon but Tom certainly had no evidence to prove it. Granting the possibility of Faunce's guilt, to fling an unsupported charge of murder at him was a foolish risk.

"When I left you at Copper Fork to do undercover work you promised to keep your mouth shut and do no talking," the sheriff said coldly. "Before I had been gone twenty-four hours you have a mix-up with Faunce and were lucky not to have your brains blown out. Haven't you a lick of sense?"

Tom knew this rebuke was justified. "I'm sorry. Fact is, when I found he is my father's murderer I kinda went haywire."

"You're still just guessing. He may not be."

"I'm dead sure he is," Tom answered doggedly.

"Let's say he is. Do you think he'll let it ride and forget what you said? He'll go after you certain."

"That's between him and me. Understand, Mr. Dunham, I don't aim to do anything that's not legal."

"You ought to leave the territory."

Tom diverted the talk to the robbery. "About the spy the

bandits had in camp. Tex Scully gave me a lead." The young deputy told the sheriff the reasons why he and Tex believed that Heilman was the man. Suspicion pointed at him on three counts. Tom had seen him with the bandits in Tomahawk several days before the raid. He had purposely led the posse in the wrong direction. And Tex was almost sure he had seen Heilman strangling the bandit Wheldon.

The sheriff did not reject the possibility that they might be right, though he pointed out that the evidence was less than that against Tom himself. As to the charge of strangling the dying outlaw, it seemed to him an incredibly daring and almost impossible crime for a man to commit in an open street where a dozen persons were milling around. Yet he admitted he had noticed the marks on the bruised throat of the dead raider.

"Remember the light was bad and Heilman got to the man fast," Tom explained. "He blocked Tex off so he couldn't see Wheldon. If Heilman was in cahoots with the gang he couldn't run the risk of letting the wounded man talk before he died. So he made sure there wouldn't be any confession."

"I hate to believe it," Dunham said. "I took a liking to Heilman."

"So did I, but a lot of people liked Jesse James," Tom mentioned.

"We'll probably find out the truth after we get the actual robbers," the sheriff decided. "I have learned that Dutch Frater was seen in Tuscon day before yesterday. He was gambling at the Legal Tender."

"Wasn't that a crazy thing for him to be doing, with the hunt for the bandits still hot?"

"Since he doesn't know he is suspected he might think it a smart play not to go into hiding. I'd like him watched, but I can't leave here myself. If you weren't such a trouble hunter I would send you to Tucson to find out what you can, listen to talk, hang around the gaming places."

"Nobody knows me there. I might pick up some evidence."

"I don't feel sure you won't get into more trouble," the sheriff said sourly. "Though I have had the pleasure of your acquaintance less than a week you have just missed getting killed three times."

"A streak of bad luck. You can't blame me for this fight

with the Pachies and it wasn't my fault Faunce picked me out to get hanged. I'm really a peaceable guy." Tom's face wrinkled to a boyish grin.

"I am going to give you a chance to prove that. There is nobody else I can send. Act like a run-of-the-range puncher come to town to see the elephant. Don't do anything to get people to pay any attention to you. You are not there to arrest Dutch but to check up on him. Take notice of any fellows he is running with. If he has left Tucson try to find out where he has gone. Do you think you can do that without starting a rookus?"

Tom promised to be dependable.

After a long day's ride he made a dry camp ten miles from Tucson and slept on the desert floor. He was awakened by the sun shining on his face. A few indolent minutes drifted away before he banished the hangover of sleep. Last night he had missed supper and he was ravenously hungry. While he saddled the picketed horse he spoke his thoughts out loud as men who live much alone in the open are likely to do.

"We'll be hittin' town soon, Monte, and there's a good feed there waiting for both of us. You have had some alfilaria, old hoss, but my belly is flat as an empty mail sack."

The sky was flushed with the pink and mauve tints of dawn and the porphyry range of the Catalinas held in the canyons of their slopes blue lakes of mist softening outlines that soon would be bare and gaunt. On the broad sunbaked mesa sown with cholla and prickly pears adobe huts began to appear as he approached the town, a settlement of scattered houses lying in a bowl surrounded by mountain ranges far and near.

He rode into the plaza back of Congress Street and tied at a hitch rack near the old monastery that had now become a rooming house. From a Mexican sweeping out a saloon he learned the location of the Longhorn Corral. Before he ate he saw that Monte was watered and fed, then returned to the plaza and by way of the rear entrance walked into a Chinese restaurant where he devoured three eggs, a large steak, half a dish of hashed brown potatoes, and several cups of coffee, for which he paid the standard breakfast price of twenty-five cents. His appetite did not surprise Lee Ching. He had fed hundreds of hungry cowboys and knew their capacity for food.

Tom left by the front door. He stood on the sidewalk and let his gaze drift up and down the street. This was a typical cow town with false fronts and adobes elbowing one another. Every third building was a saloon and a gambling house. Like most frontier settlements in the Southwest, it was apparently dominated by Americans though Mexicans were in a large majority. It was an untidy place. Dingy and dilapidated shacks stood next to vacant lots on which grew scraggy mesquite and greasewood. During his first stroll through the narrow streets he saw broken sheds, bake ovens, sore-backed broomtails, numberless curs, and the carcass of a dead burro that gave evidence of having been there several days. He almost stumbled over a squealing pig that ran across the road pursued by a hound.

Yet he saw too the fringe of emerald green in the cultivated stretch along the creek, the gently waving cottonwoods, the dark, waxy-green foliage of the pomegranates, and the crimson strings of pepper hanging like medieval banners along the adobe house walls. In the better residence section were pleasant thick-walled ample houses with cool inclosed patios and shaded porches from the roof of which hung ollas of fresh spring water. Some day this would be a city of which the dwellers would be proud, he guessed.

His job was one that could not be done in a hurry. He tried to fit himself into his environment, a footloose cowboy with a month's wages in his pocket come to town to blow in his earnings. He sat in the shade of an adobe corral wall for hours whittling on a pine stick. When the sun shifted and reached him he strolled into a pool hall and got into a two-bit game of stud.

After dark Congress Street began to quicken with night life. The saloons and gambling spots were going full blast. He dropped into the Legal Tender and watched the games, Mexican monte, poker, faro, chuckaluck, twenty-one, and roulette. The room was a picture of the frontier West at play. It held an oddly mixed crowd. A mining millionaire rubbed shoulders with a pigtailed Chinaman and a white-faced "lunger" from Boston out for his health. Merchants, cattlemen, saloon swampers, punchers, the town marshal, and

Mexican caballeros in costume were trying their luck at one game or another.

At the roulette table Tom spotted the man he was looking for, Dutch Frater. He was a huge fellow, broad-shouldered and deep-chested. A scar ran from the corner of his mouth across his chin. Dissipation had left its marks on his harsh brutal face. A large pile of chips was in front of him and his eyes, cold as balls of ice, were lit with the gambler's lust of winning. He was betting yellow chips.

Tom murmured into the ear of a young cowboy standing beside him, "Who is the big guy bulling the game?"

The cowboy gave him Frater's name, and added information. "He has been losing heavily until tonight."

"A regular player?" Tom asked.

"Lives in the San Simon country. Dropped into town two-three days ago. Fellow named Husky Sowers came with him."

"Sowers here tonight too?"

The range rider hitched a thumb toward the chuckaluck table. "The bird with the red bandanna."

Tom took a long look at Sowers. He was young, not more than twenty, with a good deal of interest in his own personal appearance. He wore custom-made boots, a good suit, and an expensive sombrero sat jauntily on a head of light curly hair. No evil was written on the handsome face but there was a strong suggestion of recklessness. He must be one of the lads, of whom there had been many in the West, who had slipped across the borderline between decency and crime, driven by the urge for excitement and adventure, plus the stimulus of drink. So Tom guessed him. He had seen Sowers at least once before, perhaps twice. This young man had been one of the group with Dutch Frater the first time Tom had seen the big ruffian, but he was not sure Sowers had been one of those who had ridden into Copper Fork the night of the raid.

The deputy drifted over the chuckaluck table and put half a dollar on both three and six. When the dice rolled out they showed two threes and a six.

"How do you do it, fellow?" Sowers asked. "When I pick a number it turns out a sure loser."

"Must be the life I lead," Tom told him cheerfully.

Sowers slanted a gaze at the man beside him. He saw a youngster with a lean strong-jawed face, one built to carry himself with light and graceful ease. The friendly eyes were at the moment mirthful.

"Hmp! You don't look like no sky pilot to me," Sowers said dryly. He frowned, some memory of this stranger stirring in him. "I've seen you before somewheres."

"I was in Tomahawk the day before I started for the fiesta at Copper Fork. You were coming out of the Good Grub restaurant as I was going in."

"Might be," Sowers agreed. After a moment he asked, "How was the fiesta?"

"I didn't enjoy it," Tom admitted. "After the raid I was picked for the goat and just missed getting hanged."

"Holy mackerel. Were you that guy?"

"In person. I got so scared I aim to lead an honest life from now."

"Maybe it wouldn't be polite for me to ask if you was one of the bandits." There was a dancing imp of deviltry in Sower's eyes.

"No, sir. I didn't even have the fun of sharing in the loot."

Sowers liked this insouciant character. "Let's go have a drink," he proposed. "I want to know all about this almost necktie party." He linked an arm under Tom's and led him to the bar.

Fallon was not a whisky drinker. He ordered a glass of beer. By good luck he had met casually one of the Frater gang and he hoped to knit closer this tenuous tie. It might lead to important information.

While Tom sipped at the beer, one foot on the bar rail, he told the story of the raid and the circumstances that had implicated him.

"They must have been crazy to get vengeance or they wouldn't have jumped you without more evidence," Husky Sowers commented. "These guys you saw on their way to town, would you know them again?" He asked the question indifferently as if with cursory curiosity.

Tom shrugged his shoulders. "Might be. If I did I would pay no mind. Likely they had nothing to do with the robbery. Anyhow, I don't owe Copper Fork a thing. They scared me plenty. Even had the tree picked out where they were aimin' to hang me. I got out of the jam by a narrow squeak and I ain't going to get mixed up in it any more."

"There's a big reward offered," Sowers reminded him.

"To hell with the reward. Let somebody else go after it if he feels that way. I'm not a plumb idjit. Even if I knew anything about it, which I don't, I'd be in trouble again up to my neck by buttin' in. The law would grab me sure, claimin' I was one of the bandits. Me, I'm out to stay out."

"Sounds reasonable. Look after yore own hide." Sowers reverted to the miners' trial. "Old Curt Faunce is a bull-headed cantankerous cuss. Get a notion in his head and you couldn't blow it out with dynamite. I never did cotton to him. It was like Heilman to stand up for you. He's all right."

"A friendly fellow sure enough."

"Seems like those raiders messed up the job considerable. I'd guess they must have been tanked up to start all that shooting."

"Craziest thing I ever saw. I reckon one of them got scary and started it. Or maybe some of the town folks began it."

"From the way it read in the *Citizen* it must of been some fracas," the bartender chipped in.

"I was in my room fronting on the street and it sounded like the battle of Bull Run," Tom said. "After the trouble was over the crowd milled around like a heard of fretted cows."

"Did the outlaw who was shot have anything to say before he kicked off?" Sowers inquired. His manner was unconcerned, but Tom thought he detected anxiety back of the apparently haphazard question.

"There wasn't life enough left in him to speak a word. He died almost at once."

"They say he was a cowboy from the San Simon."

"Yeah, I heard that," Tom replied. "Might be true. I don't know."

Sowers yawned. "Well, it ain't our funeral. What say we go shoot a game of pool?"

Tom thought that would be nice. They strolled out of the Legal Tender to an adjoining pool hall.

Tom spent a good many hours of the next two days with Husky Sowers. Each of them liked the other and was glad to have a companion near his own age. But the deputy sheriff was not happy about his growing friendship for Husky. He was trapped between two loyalties. On the one hand to gather evidence against the bandit raiders; on the other the fear that by deception he might be working to put a rope around the neck of Sowers. He could not rid himself of the thought that he was playing a despicable role. Yet as he came to know the young fellow better he became more sure that Husky had not been one of the Copper Fork bandits. Perhaps in trying to convict the criminals he might be doing his friend a service.

They were at the Longhorn Corral one morning feeding their horses when Dutch Frater came through the gate. Husky introduced him to Fallon.

"Tom is the lad who was mighty near hanged at Copper Fork the other night, the one I was tellin' you about," Sowers explained.

Dutch Frater's cold eyes searched the face of Fallon. He had no ground for suspicion except the fact that Tom had been on the spot at the time of the raid. If talk pointed in his direction this boy probably was aware of it.

"Spill it," Frater ordered. "The whole story."

Tom gave a deleted account of the raid and of his trial. He did not mention the later trouble with Curt Faunce on the street. The big outlaw was not much interested in the trial but he flung a dozen harsh questions dealing with the death of Wheldon, the pursuit of the bandits, and the efforts of the law officers to run down the guilty parties.

As to the last point Tom professed to know nothing. He had left for Tomahawk two days after the raid. From loose talk he had heard he gathered that Sheriff Dunham was fussing around but not getting anywhere. Nobody seemed to have any idea who the road agents were.

There were follow-up stories in the newspaper about the Apache outbreak. The band had been captured and were now prisoners on the reservation. In the account was a line or two mentioning that one young man of the attacked party was just now in Tucson. An hour after the issue was printed a boy brought a note to Tom at his hotel. It was from a Mrs. Jennie Harshaw. She was, the note said, an aunt of Nancy Faunce and she wished very much that he would call on her. She would like to have him come that night for supper.

Mrs. Harshaw welcomed him warmly. She was a good-looking widow, about halfway through her thirties, full of kindness, and human charity. She had long-lashed lovely dark eyes and the clear complexion of a girl half her age. It was Tom's opinion that if she stayed in Tucson, a town where there were ten men to one woman, she would have a dozen proposals of marriage in as many months.

"I have just had a letter from Nancy telling how kind and brave you were. She feels you saved her life," his hostess mentioned.

"Nothing to that," Tom replied promptly. "You might put it that she and the two men on the stage saved mine. I would never have got away without them. That's for certain. I don't want ever to be in a tighter jam."

"I'm the nearest to a mother that Nancy has and I love her dearly, so of course I am deeply grateful to you. It was a shock to learn of her dreadful experience."

The boy who had brought the note to Tom walked into the room. He was a freckled tousle-headed twelve year old. His worshipful eyes fastened on Tom.

"Jerry," his mother said by way of introduction, and to the boy, "This is Mr. Fallon."

"I know," Jerry answered, his fascinated gaze still fixed on the guest. "He 'most got hanged the other day."

"Who told you that?" Jennie Harshaw asked in astonishment.

"I heard Mr. Kinross say so."

"Where? In his pool hall? I told you to keep out of there."

"Yes'm. I wasn't clear inside. I sorta stopped at the door when I heard him talkin'."

Mrs. Harshaw turned to Tom. "Is this true?"

"It was all a mistake," the deputy explained. He narrated the circumstances, leaving the name of Curt Faunce out of the story.

"What an awful thing to happen to an innocent boy," she said.

"I am glad you think I am innocent," he told her gratefully. "It took a lot of persuadin' to some folks."

"They must have been blind," she retorted with decision. "Anyone can see to look at you that you couldn't be guilty of such a crime."

Tom wondered what she would say when she learned that he had accused her brother-in-law of cold-blooded murder.

60

He had an uneasy feeling that he was accepting hospitality on false pretenses.

It was a long time since Tom had sat down to so good a home-prepared meal. One did not get at a restaurant fried chicken, mashed potatoes, and rice pudding cooked like this. Perhaps it was because the food brought to mind his mother's dinners that he began to talk of his early life in Nebraska. She was pleased to learn that he had been brought up in a God-fearing home. Mrs. Harshaw liked this slender youth whose compact figure suggested rippling muscles perfectly under control. He was clean and brown and straight. In spite of his youth he had eyes steady and tranquil that reflected a spirit unafraid. In his manner was a boyish quality both shy and gay.

The house was a very pleasant one. The Harshaws and Nancy Faunce had lived in it for nine years. The furniture had come from Jennie's home in Illinois. The china used at the table was Haviland and the silverware well plated. Thick adobe walls with deep windows made for coolness in summer and warmth in winter. The patio was planted to flowers and in the center of it a fountain threw up a thin spray of water. In the parlor was a small piano and a shelf of books. Among them the visitor recognized old friends, *Ivanhoe*, *David Copperfield*, and *Tom Sawyer*.

Jerry was impatient of the general conversation between his mother and Fallon. He had fifty questions he wanted to fire at his new hero. First there was the gun battle during the raid, then the near hanging, and most important of all the fight with and flight from the Apaches. He did not want to be impolite, but he could not bottle up his eagerness. Gee whiz! A fellow did not get a chance like this more than once. Tom Fallon was better than a Henty book because his adventures were immediate and real. The boy was mentally reconstructing that wild and dangerous ride. If he had been in that Concord stage instead of Nancy that would have been something to brag about for years.

Tom was flattered but embarrassed at this youthful adoration. He minimized the incidents and mentioned that he had been scared white. Finally Mrs. Harshaw put a stopper on her son's questions.

When Tom left it was with a promise to come back again

61

after Nancy's return. He carried with him a warm feeling in his heart.

CHAPTER 9

As Tom walked along the outside upstair gallery of the Orn-dorff Hotel to his room he heard a gay voice singing a song he had often sung himself while circling a night herd of cattle sleeping after a day's drive.

> *Roll yore tail,*
> *And roll her high;*
> *We'll all be angels*
> *By-and-by.*

Tom knocked on the door of Husky's room and poked his head inside. "You sure of that, fellow?" he asked. "You ain't been converted yet."

Sowers was tilted back in a chair with his boots on the bedspread. "I have too," he retorted. "Twice. I walked down the sawdust trail for Sam Jones* when he came to Santone and I went to the amen corner when another sky pilot was revivalin' at El Paso couple of years later." He admitted reufully, "I done backslid considerable, I reckon."

Fallon sat down on the bed without commenting on this confession. Husky looked him over suspiciously. "What are you all rigged out in yore best bib and tucker for? You been gallin'."

"No such thing," Tom denied. "I was invited to supper by a very nice lady who has a half-grown son."

"Thought you claimed you didn't know anybody in Tucson."

"That's right. This lady is the aunt of the girl in the stage when the Pachies jumped us. She sent me an invite to supper."

"I get it. She wanted to thank the li'l hero."

*Sam Jones was a famous revivalist in the South during the eighties.

62

"Quit your joshin'. You know all the heroing I did was quirtin' my bronc to light out sudden."

"Hmp! Pity to waste yore glad rags on me. What say we sashay down to Levine's Garden and have a look-see at the señoritas?"

They sauntered in the velvet Arizona night to the creek where the resort was located. Before they reached the park they could hear the music of a string band and the thumping of feet on the floor. A *baile* was in full swing and Japanese lanterns lighted the grove. Cowboys in big hats and still wearing spurs were cavorting with pretty Mexican girls in rebozos and gay skirts. A tin-pan piano, two fiddles, and a guitar supplied the primitive tunes for the whirling dancers.

Husky sized up the girls quickly. "The one in the red and blue dress for me," he announced. "She's prettier than a speckled pup."

"You don't know her," Tom said.

The Texan grinned. "I'll know her right soon."

After the dance was finished he pushed his way through the crowd leaving the floor to the master of ceremonies. They talked for a minute and then crossed to the place where an older Mexican woman was sitting with the girl Husky had indicated. Tom watched the introduction and the smooth way in which Sowers devoted himself to the mother for several minutes before he made his request for a dance. He and the duenna were still exchanging smiles when he took the floor with the daughter.

Watching Husky, as the young man and his partner glided gracefully over the floor, Tom wished he had with women some of the cool audacity of his friend. He just did not have the gift of making girls admire him, he thought.

It was a few minutes later that Tom became aware of a pair of eyes fastened on him. He turned his head and saw the fat man Budge who had been so eager to see him hanged after the raid on Rosenstein's store.

Budge moved toward him and held out a hand. "No hard feelings, young man," he wheezed.

Fallon paid no attention to the hand. He did not trust the small pig eyes that looked out of the flabby face. The man was false and slippery.

Tom said coldly, "I don't shake hands with a scalawag who does all he can to hang an innocent man."

"Now that ain't any kind of way to talk," Budge protested. "We done give you a fair trial and let you off."

"You are a contemptible liar," Tom answered, his eyes flashing. "You wanted to hang me first and look at the evidence later. Don't ever speak to me again or I'll forget you are only a tub of blubber and give you the thrashing you deserve. "

The man started to bluster but changed his mind. He did not like the savage expression on Fallon's face. He turned and disappeared into the shadows of the cottonwoods. Tom, his fists clenched, watched him go.

Husky Sowers, drifting back to Tom after the quadrille was finished, heard the angry threat of his friend.

"Got yore war paint on, looks like," he commented in his slow pleasant drawl. "Whyfor, pal?"

Tom explained. It was in his mind that probably he had made a mistake in losing his temper. Budge would make it his business to let Faunce know that Fallon was in Tucson. But the fellow's barefaced impudence had been more than he could take.

The Texan shrugged his shoulders. "Maybe you'd ought to have whopped him. But I dunno. He ain't important. Just one of Faunce's jackals."

That was true, but sometimes tragedies were brought about by the unimportant fuddy-duddies who ran around making trouble to give themselves the appearance of importance. And this Sam Budge would have the added incentive of getting even with Tom and ingratiating himself with Faunce.

As they walked back to the Ordorff hours later Sowers hummed a stave of a popular song that was just then sweeping the country.

> Shoo fly, don't bother me,
> For I belong to Company G.

He was quite pleased with the impression he had made on Maria Gonzales. She was a dusky dark-eyed girl who danced feather-light in his arms and spoke broken English in a low voice that charmed him.

During the past few days Tom had been very careful not to ask any questions of Husky that might arouse suspicion, but the Texan was of an open sunny disposition and he had talked a good deal about himself. Until four or five days ago he had been riding for the C C C Ranch and had been absent only once for a few hours—the time when Tom had seen him at Tomahawk—in the past month. He had quit the ranch two days after the Copper Fork robbery. This Tom had verified. It lifted a load from his mind. He gathered that his friend had done some rustling of Mexican stock and had helped drive a herd or two across the line but outside of that had stayed within the law.

"I have the doggonedest luck," Sowers grumbled. "Just when my *dinero* is running low I meet up with Maria and get a mash on her. Looks like I'll have to go back to chasin' cows' tails through the brush. I hate to leave that gal with nobody to protect her from the city slickers but her mammy, daddy, and three grown brothers." His eyes shifted to his silent companion. "You ain't listenin', fellow. You still got that Budge on yore mind."

"Not Budge, but the wolf who owns him," Tom answered.

"Faunce ain't going to bother you any more now you've been proved innocent. Why should he?"

"You don't know all the story." Tom told of his later meeting with Faunce and how close he had come to getting killed.

Sowers grinned at his companion. "Hmp! 'Wild and woolly, full of fleas, Never been curried above yore knees.' That's you. And you got the nice look of a Sunday school kid. Whyfor do you have to go huntin' for trouble? That old bullypuss scoundrel has got a memory like an elephant. He won't ever forget you claimed he killed yore pappy. A sidewinder is real friendly beside that mean cold-blooded old vinegaroon."

"I believe you. Point is, will he come to Tucson looking for me?"

"No law against you being an absentee if and when he comes. California has a nice climate I hear."

"I got business here," Tom said bluntly. "If Faunce comes lookin' for me I'll be waitin' at the gate."

"Yeah, but it won't be that way," the Texan drawled. "A bullet will come spang outa the ark and you'll fold up never knowing what hit you. Faunce has the rep of being a cold-blooded hombre who never gives an enemy a break. If I was you I'd slope out for California and forget to leave an address."

"No, you wouldn't, not if he had killed your father."

"Then go Injun on him. Dry-gulch the bugger like he did yore old man."

"You know I can't do that. What I'd like is to get evidence enough to have him hanged."

"You can forget that. This territory is full of killers who ain't ever even been arrested. No law man is going to pick on a fellow like Faunce, with a bunch of hellions back of him as a candidate for the gallows, not unless he is loco. The only way to stop his clock is to fill him full of lead."

Tom reluctantly agreed that this was probably true. A few years earlier the fearless sheriff John Slaughter had cleaned up this corner of Arizona, but his day was past and bad men were rampant again. In the next decade Burt Mossman and his rangers were to wage relentless war on the outlaws. But that purge was still in the future.

The next day Tom dropped into the Shoo Fly restaurant for dinner. It was domiciled in a long, low-ceiled adobe building, the floor of rammed earth, the walls washed in a yellow tint. Tom sat down in a chair with a homemade rawhide seat. The waiters wore white suits with red sashes and they carried slappers which they wielded vigorously against the swarm of flies. But Mrs. Wallen's food was celebrated in the neighboring district. She served chicken, kid meat, jerked beef in stews, black frijoles, a variety of vegetables, and fine oranges from Mexico. Always on the bill of fare was the famous Pete Kitchen ham, made from pigs that might have known the sting of Apache arrows.

Sowers joined Tom at the table. They were nearly finished when Dutch Frater walked into the restaurant. He stopped abruptly at sight of the young men, anger flaring in his eyes.

"Thicker than thieves," he growled.

Tom said amiably, "No objections, I hope."

"What you stickin' around here for?" Frater demanded stridently. "You're too big for yore britches. When Faunce comes along he'll bump you off certain."

Apparently Sam Budge had been getting in his spite work already. "It's a free country," Tom suggested.

"Free? You bet!" the outlaw jeered. "So free that inside of a week you'll turn up yore toes to the daisies. Curt Faunce will eat you alive, and if he don't I'll handle the job. No tenderfoot can come snoopin' around me." He turned to Sowers. "Want to see you, fellow."

Sowers did not like his peremptory tone. "You see me," he said coolly.

"Not here," the big man snarled. "Be at the Longhorn Corral waiting for me after dinner."

The Texan let a moment slip away before he replied. His curiosity was stronger than his resentment. "I'll be there," he nodded.

The young men stopped outside the Shoo Fly while Husky lit a cigar. "He is sulky as a wounded bear about something," Sowers said between puffs. "I reckon I'm going right soon to find out why. Maybe I've got to let him know he don't own me."

Tom thought but did not put it into words that there must have been a leak somewhere. The bandit suspected him of being a law man.

Husky Sowers was drowsing in the small office of the corral, his hat over his eyes, when Dutch stamped into the room.

The bandit came to the point at once. "I won't have you runnin' with this fellow. Cut it out."

There was no movement of Husky's head or body but his eyes slid around to take in the scarred brutal face of the huge bully. He cut his reply to a monosyllable. "Why?"

"Because I say so," Frater snarled. "That's reason enough."

"You been appointed my nursemaid?" Sowers asked softly.

Dutch slammed a ham-size fist on the table where the young man's feet rested. "If you must know, he's a spy. Budge saw him at Tomahawk coming out of Dunham's office."

Husky picked up a quirt lying on the table and examined it while he considered this new angle. "Might not mean a thing, even if Budge isn't lying. Dunham helped keep Fallon from being hanged so when the kid gets to Tomahawk he draps in to say thanks."

"You talk like a chump. He rode on the posse after the Copper Fork holdup. If Dunham helped him it was because

he knows the fellow is some sort of officer. Fallon is playin'
up to you to get at me. A fool could see that."

This might be true, but Husky did not want to believe it.
"He hasn't made any play along that line. But I'll keep my
eyes open and my mouth shut."

"No. He's too slick for you. I'll take care of him."

There was a blaze of anger in the big man's shallow eyes.
Husky read murder in them. "How?" he asked.

"Never mind. Keep away from him. That's an order."

"I don't take orders from you, Dutch." The Texan had not
raised his voice, but his steady gaze held fast to the furious
eyes of the other.

Dutch swept the spurred boots from the table and dragged
the Texan to his feet. "You'll do as I say, damn you." His
strong hairy fingers bit into the shoulder muscles of Sowers
like prongs of steel.

Husky rammed forceably the heavy loaded end of the
quirt into the stomach of Dutch. The giant let out a grunt of
pain. For an instant he relaxed his grip, then jerked the cowboy to him and wrapped him in his bearlike arms with a
terrific pressure. To Husky it felt as if a narrowing steel
band was squeezing the life out of him. He was helpless, his
arms pinned to his sides. Only his legs were free. His feet cir-
cled the great legs of Frater. They dug the spurs deep into
the calves of the man and raked them up and down. The
sharp points of the rowels ripped gaping wounds in the flesh.

Dutch gave a yelp of agony, tore Sowers' body from his,
and flung it from him. Husky hung breathless against the
wall. He sucked air into his lungs during that short space of
time before Frater charged. The reprieve had been just long
enough to let him get control of his muscles. He slid to the
right, ducked under the arm slashing at him, and went out of
the room like a streak of cat before a bulldog. As he raced
through the corral entrance a bullet slammed into the adobe
wall close to him. With the protecting wall between him and
his attacker he ran along it, his body crouched, until he was
out of range.

CHAPTER 10

"How did it go?" Tom asked.

He was sitting on the top fence rail at the shipping pens rolling a cigarette.

Husky's answer was less than friendly. "He told me to lay off runnin' with you. Maybe that is good advice. He claims you are a law man."

"Budge put that idea in his head. First the fat scalawag was crazy to have me hanged as a bandit. Now it suits him to have me a peace officer. He can't have it both ways, Husky."

"You rode on the posse after the Copper Fork holdups."

"Sure I did. Any decent man would have. I didn't make any secret of it." There was no warmth in Tom's steely eyes. "It won't hurt my feelings any if that bunch of killers are caught and hanged. If things had shaped a little bit different that night when I was tried I would have been a victim of the outlaws just as much as if they had shot me during the robbery."

"That's not the point. Far as that goes I wouldn't lift a finger for them myself. You and I have hit it off fine, but if you are using me as a tool to find out what I know I'm through with you for good."

"Search your mind and answer that yourself. Have I tried to worm any information out of you? You are in the clear. The day of the holdup you were seventy miles away on the C C C range chasing cows. What could you know about it?"

The suspicion planted in Sowers was not yet banished. "All right. Answer my question. Are you a sheriff's man or ain't you?"

"I don't like your manner, Husky," Fallon said. "That's my business and not yours."

"You've done answered," Sowers retorted curtly.

He turned on his heel and walked away.

Unhappily Tom watched him go. The friendship that had been growing between them was blotted out. He could not blame Sowers for feeling that he had been imposed upon by deceit. Since he was a reckless untamed young fellow his reaction might drive him back to the outlaw gang he had been cutting loose from.

Later in the day the news reached him that Frater had fired several shots at Husky. This disturbed him. He had no doubt that Frater's savage anger had flared up against the cowboy because he had stood up for Tom.

Toward evening Tom sauntered down to the depot to meet the incoming train. Its arrival was still enough of an event to draw a daily group of idlers. Fallon found himself by chance standing beside Husky Sowers. The Texan moved away from him without speaking, then changed his mind and came back.

"I reckon I had better tell you, Mr. Sheriff's Man, that Dutch Frater is on the prod and means to get you," he said, his voice coldly hostile. "Not that I give a damn, but I don't like to see even a law man shot in the back."

"Much obliged, Husky," Tom replied. "I'd like to explain how—"

"Nothing to explain," Sowers cut in sharply. "You play yore hand and I'll play mine."

He turned his back on Tom to watch the train coming into the depot.

Half a dozen passengers descended from it, among them Lieutenant Ramsey. He stood beside the steps of the car and gave a hand to help Nancy Faunce to the platform. Mrs. Harshaw had come to meet the girl and they went into each other's arms for a kiss. Nancy introduced the young officer to her aunt. Tom heard him explain that he was stationed at Fort Lowell just outside of Tucson and just happened to be on the train. That last Tom rejected with sardonic disbelief. The two had arranged to make the railroad trip together. When Jennie Harshaw invited the officer to join them at dinner it did not increase Tom's pleasure. Nancy was a proud and ambitious girl. The glamour of this dashing West Pointer no doubt attracted her greatly. Outside of his personal charm he stood for all the social advantages that a frontier country denied her. Tom had come from a family of well to do pioneers with some education but he did not feel that he could compete with what Ramsey had to offer.

He started to leave just as Nancy turned. Their eyes met and her slight body stiffened. The girl's face set in a refusal

70

to recognize him. He knew at once the reason. She had been told that he had charged Curt Faunce with the murder of his father.

The voice of Mrs. Harshaw held a warm friendliness. "How nice to meet you again, Tom," she exclaimed. "Now that Nancy is home you must come and see us soon."

Ramsey broke an embarrassed silence. "Not so grim an hour as the last time we saw each other, Fallon. That was nip and tuck."

"Yes, we were in a tight when you came to the rescue, Lieutenant." To Jennie Harshaw he said: "Afraid that is a pleasure I must deny myself."

She answered, surprised, "But—I don't understand."

"Miss Faunce does," he replied dejectedly. "If you will excuse me I won't spoil this happy reunion."

Tom bowed and walked away. Mrs. Harshaw's eyes followed him in astonishment.

"What in the world has got into him?" she asked.

"I'll explain it later, not here," Nancy said with cold anger.

Her aunt looked at her quickly. "You too. What silly nonsense is this? You haven't seen him since you wrote me a letter saying how grateful you are to him."

"If you can't wait I'll tell you," the girl broke out. "He accused my father of murdering his a great many years ago."

Mrs. Harshaw stared at her niece with wide astonished eyes. "Good gracious! Are you sure?"

"Yes. One of the boys at the ranch told me and I asked Father. He did not want to talk about it but I kept after him. Finally he admitted it was true. Tom Fallon was crazy mad because Father investigated evidence that he was one of the Copper Fork bandits, so he cooked up this silly charge. He deserved the whipping Father gave him."

"I am sorry," her aunt said. "Tom seemed to me such a nice boy."

The explanation Nancy had given her did not satisfy Mrs. Harshaw, though she did not say so. She knew Curt Faunce much better than his daughter did. He had been a bad husband to Jennie's sister from the first after she married him in Iowa. Soon after moving to Arizona Mollie had died and the Harshaws had taken the only child Nancy to live with them. Since that time she had never seen her father until this visit. Jennie did not know why Faunce had left Nebraska but she had always suspected that he had fled under a cloud. He had changed the family name from Fenwick to Faunce. There was evil in the man. His sister-in-law was sure of that. He had not only a violent temper but a bitter cruel nature. When his letter came a few weeks earlier ordering his daughter to pay a visit to the ranch there was nothing Jennie could do but let the girl go, yet she had seen Nancy off with deep misgivings.

In Jennie's heart lay a fear that the accusation Tom had made might be true. She made up her mind to have a talk with young Fallon. In her opinion it was not in character for him to make a groundless charge out of resentment. Moreover, unless he was a fool he must have known how dangerous it would be.

Her chance came next day while she was in a store buying groceries. Tom walked in to get some smoking tobacco. She told him that she wanted to talk with him. At the moment they were alone, the clerk at the other end of the store getting her a pound of Arbuckle's coffee.

Tom said in a low voice, "I don't think we had better. It won't do any good."

"That's for me to judge," she answered sharply. "I'll meet you in ten minutes at the old plaza."

"I'll be there," he promised.

When she came around the corner of the old convent into the plaza she found him waiting there. Three or four cow ponies were drowsing at hitch racks back of the Congress Street stores. A burro with a jag of mesquite stove wood tied to its back was being driven down the road by a barefoot Mexican boy. Two youngsters were playing marbles at a far corner. Otherwise they had the plaza to themselves.

Jennie's gray eyes looked directly into those of Tom.

"I want the truth," she said. "Have you any proof that Curt Faunce killed your father?"

Tom was unhappy that this situation had arisen. If he stood by his charge he would be greatly hurting this fine woman. That is, if she believed him. And the shame of it would have to pass on to Nancy too.

"Maybe I made a mistake," he replied.

"I don't want an evasion. That is no answer. You had some reason for saying it. What is it?"

72

He found it difficult to meet her searching eyes. "I just sort of jumped to that conclusion."

"On what evidence?"

"Well, mighty little, come to think of it."

Jennie knew he was covering the facts to spare her. She tried another approach. "In what Nebraska town did you live?"

"In Hastings."

"What year and month was your father killed?"

Reluctantly he told her. The date was a blow to her. It was at this time her brother-in-law had left Nebraska. His wife and daughter had followed him a few months later.

She forced out of him the manner of his father's death, that he had been shot in the back at night by a criminal he was about to arrest.

"Did you ever hear of a man named Carl Fenwick?" Jennie asked.

"Let's not go on with this, Mrs. Harshaw," he begged. "I said that maybe I was wrong."

"You have said too much or too little. Was that the name of the suspected killer?"

"The evidence was circumstantial. No witness was on the spot. Put it that I meddled in something without a good reason. Please forget all about it. I won't trouble you any more." Tom's face was a map of distress.

She had no doubt of her brother-in-law's guilt. It was better not to press the issue any further. Publicity would be very harmful to Nancy. She had questioned Tom in the hope that she could convince herself of Curt Faunce's innocence. That hope was gone.

"This is very distressing to Nancy and me," Jennie said. "If you have any consideration for us you will withdraw your accusation, since the crime occurred many years ago and there is a doubt as to the killer."

"I want you to know this, Mrs. Harshaw," Tom explained. "At the time I was chump enough to tell Curt Faunce he was my father's killer I had never met you or Miss Nancy. He was crowdin' me hard and I blew my top. It wouldn't make it better to back down now. He's got it in for me."

"You could leave the territory."

"Yes, ma'am. I could do that—and all my life I'd hate myself for runnin' away. There are some things a fellow can't do. He has got to go on living with himself." He added ruefully: "What I've said is done said. If he comes lookin' for me I've got to defend myself."

She shook her head. "You don't know him, Tom. You wouldn't have a chance. I don't like to say it of my brother-in-law, but he is a hard cruel man and—treacherous."

"I'll look out for myself," he promised.

Jennie turned to go. There was no use arguing with him. A wilful man must go his own way. She could only hope that Curt Faunce, having beaten up the boy, would be content with that.

Tom watched her go, moving with light grace, a woman young for her years, with a fine animal vigor inspired by a spirit free and generous. Someday her warmth and vitality would meet response in a man worthy of her. By evil chance he had lost the friendship of her and of her niece. It made the day dark for him.

Jennie too was unhappy at the situation. Her brother-in-law was a man dark and vindictive. If it was true that he had killed Sheriff Fallon he would not hesitate to destroy the son if he became dangerous. As she had told Tom, she knew too much or too little. She could not rest without learning the facts. She wrote to an old schoolmate who had lived many years in Hastings and asked her to send her all she could about the death of Sheriff Fallon. A week later a letter came that told her the whole story.

After Mrs. Harshaw had left Tom he saddled and rode up the Santa Cruz valley along the fields of the Papago Indians to the San Xavier Mission. He wanted to be alone to try to work out some solution of the difficulty in which he was involved. The scene was restful as a Sunday morning in a peaceful New England village. Across the fields the mellow tones of the bells in the mission tower came to him like healing music.

The padre who took Tom through the charming building told him the story of San Xavier. It had been built in 1797 and the priests living there had known war against the Spanish rule, Apache raids, water shortage, blighted crops, and outrages from both Mexican and American ruffians. But the padres had remained faithful to their charges through the years. Neither the Spanish cavaliers nor the more recent American settlers were of such heroic character as these zealous propagators of their faith. After long stretches of patient service they had died far from civilization, many of them slain by their own parishioners.

CHAPTER 11

Tom's ride to the mission had brought to him no solution of his problems but it had given him for the time at least more peace of mind. Perhaps he was wrong not to leave the territory as all his friends had advised. It might be only a silly pride that was keeping him here. Yet he knew it would take more moral courage than he had to go to Sheriff Dunham and tell him he was about to walk out on the job he had undertaken. His mother would have told him that what he lacked was Christian humility.

Darkness was falling when he reached town. He unsaddled at the corral and was carrying his saddle into the stall when a bullet tore through the wooden casing. The slug had missed him by not more than a few inches. He dived into the shed and found cover behind the oats bin.

The voice of Johnny Adler, the owner of the Longhorn Corral, yelped out a protest, "Hey, what's going on here?" Tom judged that the sound of the shot had brought him to the door of his office.

"Keep yore trap shut, Adler," a harsh command warned. "You're not in this."

Dutch Frater talking, Tom decided. The fellow must have learned that he had ridden out of town and have slipped into one of the stalls to wait for his return.

A third speaker cut in with a question. "You get him, Dutch?"

Tom could see the man's narrowed eyes peering over the boarded side of an ore wagon, but he made no sound to betray his own position. Crouched on one knee, his finger on the trigger of a .45, he remained motionless. The next move was up to his enemies. For the moment the advantage lay with him. In the semi-darkness of the shed they could not spot him. Any attack they made would have to be a frontal one.

"Wounded him, I reckon. Maybe he's lying in there dead." Frater's next words were addressed to Fallon. "If you're alive come outa there with yore hands up or we'll fill you full of lead."

Tom did not accept the rasping invitation. Dutch Frater was an impatient ruffian. He did not consider the lad in the shed a dangerous foe. If it came to a battle of nerves he might choose to close in and end the affair rather than play cautious, especially if he believed Fallon was wounded. In that case there would be a second or two when his big body would be clear against the outside light and Tom would be protected by the gloom of the interior.

The man in the wagon raised his head and fired twice. One of the shots hit the bin. Tom noticed that he was wearing a red bandanna.

After that there was continued silence. Tom listened, his nerves tense, for any rumor of sound. He heard a stirring in the gathering darkness that resolved itself into soft footfalls. Frater was changing his place from the stall where he had been stationed.

Another streak of fire came from the wagon and that bullet too plowed through the box frame into the oats. Red Bandanna was trying to keep their victim's mind occupied while Frater drew closer. So Tom thought, and knew he was right when a pebble rolled beneath a heavy boot to warn him. Frater was getting near the entrance to the stall and probably meant to rush him.

Tom almost held his breath, the pistol pressed against his side. It would not be long now. Red Bandanna was out of the wagon and moving forward cautiously on his toes. Tom still held his fire. The more immediate danger was Frater.

The big body of the bandit slid into sight. The roar of Tom's .45 filled the shed. Frater swayed on his feet, backward and then forward. The bullet from his .44 plowed into the ground as he plunged down.

For a long moment Red Bandanna stood rooted in his tracks. Tom blazed at him. He turned and ran, not for the gate but for the adobe wall which was nearer. He clambered over it fast, using both hands. The revolver slipped from his fingers but he did not stop to pick it up. His hurry to get away obsessed him, for Tom's gun was barking at him.

Warily Adler came out of the office where he had taken refuge. He stared at the huge body lying on the ground. "My God, you've killed him."

Tom was kneeling beside his fallen foe. He slipped a hand under the cotton shirt and felt the heart. It was still beating. The young man looked up at Adler. "He's alive. You had better get a doctor quick. Maybe we can save him."

"What for?" the owner of the corral asked bluntly. He knew Frater and his record. In his opinion Dutch was a man better dead than alive. "If you wanted him to live why did you shoot him?"

"You know why," Tom answered. "You saw him ambush me. It had to be one of us. I had the luck."

"You played yore hand better I would say. If you want a doc go get him. I'll stick around here."

Tom looked regretfully at the prone figure lying there with arms outflung, all the bearlike strength stricken out of it. "I had to do it," he said to himself, almost in a whisper.

"Sure you had to," Adler answered impatiently. "Don't blame yorself, boy. The damned killers figured not to give you a chance."

Before Tom left to get the doctor he asked a question. "Do you know who the other fellow is, the one with the red bandanna?"

"A bird called Todd—Rufe Todd. A no-account bummer."

Doctor Clifford found two bullet wounds in Frater. One was in the man's side and another in the thigh. He thought the patient's chance was slight. After the doctor had given first aid Tom helped carry Dutch on a stretcher to the place where he was lodging.

As soon as he could Tom gave himself up to the Sheriff. Adler was with him. The owner of the Longhorn had collected the revolvers of both attackers and brought them along as evidence. The sheriff listened to the stories they told and said he did not see any blame at all attaching to Tom. He asked them both to write an account of what had taken place and leave the papers with him. If Todd had not left town he would arrest him.

CHAPTER 12

Since Tom had come to Tucson he had written two letters to Sheriff Dunham giving an account of his activities. He now wrote a third.

> *Dear Mr. Dunham:*
>
> *I reckon you will cuss me good when I tell you the trouble I have got into. But I don't see how I could have helped it. Looks like I'm just unlucky. In my last I told you how Frater acted kind of suspicious of me. Well, along come that fellow Budge and told him I was seen with you at Tomahawk. Frater blew his top for sure. First off he ordered Husky Sowers to lay off running with me. Husky is quite a guy and he must of told Dutch where he could get off at. They had a rookus and the big fellow took a couple of shots at him. No damage done. But Husky and I had a falling out because he doesn't like law men.*
>
> *Well when I was unsaddling today at the Longhorn Corral Frater and another bird called Rufe Todd tried to dry-gulch me. I got a break and come out all right. Frater got shot up bad. The doc doesn't think he will make it. Todd lit out like the heel flies was after him and is now under arrest. He is one of the men I saw with Frater at Copper Fork the day of the robbery. Maybe if we work on him he will squeal on his pals.*
>
> *This is all for now. Maybe you want me to turn in my badge. The officers here string along with me.*
>
> Tom

Fallon did not enjoy the notoriety he had to face after the fight. Dutch Frater had so bad a reputation as a bully and bad man that the sentiment of the town was wholly in his favor. When he walked down the street small boys followed him admiringly and spoke about him in awed tones. Business men congratulated him on having rid the territory of one of its worst killers. The *Star* praised him editorially. If Dutch Frater died he would always carry the brand of a killer. He would be marked for life as the man who had shot this desperado. This was very distasteful to him. He did not want to be placed in the category of a gunman. Yet all his attempts to minimize what had occurred were laid to modesty and increased his prestige.

When Husky Sowers met him the Texan fell into an attitude of profound respect and mockingly called him Mr. Slaughter, a reference to the famous little sheriff John Slaughter who had a few years earlier ordered bad men to get out or be killed and had effectively made good his threat.

"Cut it out, Husky," Tom snapped. "You know I'm just a guy who happened to be lucky."

"Oh no, Mr. Slaughter," Husky jibed. "How can I help marveling at one who cut down the deep-dyed villain who sent me skedaddling out of the corral a mile a minute?"

"Go jump in the Santa Cruz," Tom told him with a grin.

"Anything you say, Mr. Slaughter."

When Tom thought of this later he was pleased. He could see that the edge of Husky's hostility had been blunted. The young Texan was not ready yet for a renewal of friendship but in spite of his scoffing approach he approved mightily of Tom's victory over Frater.

Tom hoped his enemy would get well but not too fast. He did not want to be haunted by a regret for having taken another life, yet he had no wish to meet Frater again with blazing guns. He realized that he had escaped the trap with his life only because he had outmaneuvered his foe by deceiving the man into thinking he had been killed or badly wounded. The only comfort he got out of the encounter was the satisfaction of knowing that after the first moment of shock he had reacted with cool and steady nerves.

Since the rumor was already prevalent that Tom was a law officer he decided that he had better explain his real status to Sheriff Marshall. The sheriff was a big rawboned Westerner who had served with the Union troops during the Civil War and had been interested in raising cattle until he was elected to office. He was honest as a silver dollar and had no use for the riffraff engaged in lawlessness.

"So you're one of Dunham's deputies," he said after Tom

had finished telling his story. "I reckon you know you have no standing in Tucson. You can't make an arrest here."

"That's right. My orders are only to gather any evidence I can."

"And Dutch Frater got on to what you are doing?" The sheriff added grimly: "Then you had to stop his clock."

"Doc Clifford says he just might make it. I hope so."

"I hope different," Marshall disagreed. "He's got to be killed sometime. Better have it happen before he has sent any more men to the graveyard."

"What I came to see you about was this other fellow," Tom explained. "This Rufe Todd. He's one of the men I saw riding into Copper Fork with Dutch Frater."

"That is not proof he was one of the bandits. You don't know for sure that Frater was one."

"The robber who was killed, that Bob Wheldon, was another of the party that passed me on the outskirts of the town. If he was guilty—and he was—I'd say the others are too."

"That would look reasonable," Marshall agreed. "What have you in mind for Todd?"

"Well, I thought we could bring pressure on him. He is not a strong character. Down at the corral he lit out fast when Frater went down. He might turn state's evidence."

"He might." The sheriff after consideration decided to say more. "Seeing you are one of Dunham's men I might as well work with you. We found seventeen hundred dollars on this Rufe Todd. Three weeks ago he was bumming his drinks. Where did he get this *dinero?* Frater had about four hundred on him. The rest he had lost at roulette. Both of them were in that Copper Fork raid certain. But what we know isn't enough to stand up in court."

"Unless we could get a confession out of Todd," Tom suggested.

"Yeah, and why would he confess? He would sure be hanged. With Frater ready to kick off and Wheldon already dead there's only one of the bunch left beside Todd. He could not sell a confession in exchange for his life."

"I reckon not," Tom agreed. "But there is an off chance he might spill something."

Marshall lifted his broad shoulders sceptically. "All right. Hop to it, boy. He's all yours."

Todd was a long lank man with shallow light blue eyes set too close together. They gave his ugly long-jawed face a shifty look. It wore an expression crafty and unfriendly. Tom judged him a callous man, one who might kill with no sense of guilt, but at bottom weak and cowardly.

He was lying on a cot when Tom came into the cell. At sight of his visitor he rose hurriedly, plainly perturbed. "Get out of here," he snarled. The sickening dread was in his mind that Fallon had come to kill him.

"Take it easy," Tom told him. "I'm not going to rob the gallows."

"I got nothing to say to you. Nothing at all."

"You said it all with that gun you dropped when you shinnied over the wall," Tom scoffed, and sat down at the foot of the bed. "You're going to hang, Todd. That gun was the same one that killed Marshal Pollock."

"No—no! I wasn't there. You can't prove it."

"Several witnesses will identify you. You are not cut out for a bandit. You panic too easy. Dutch Frater made a bad choice when he picked you. It wasn't necesary to start the firing but you got goosy. Later you were forced to kill Pollock. I'm surprised Frater didn't bump you off later for messing up the robbery."

"It wasn't me who started shooting." The prisoner stopped as if the words had been jerked out of him. "I—I wasn't there."

"Oh yes, you were there," Tom corrected. "Remember? I saw you riding into town beside Wheldon and Frater." He spoke with light assurance, a damning certainty in his manner.

Tiny beads of perspiration had broken out on the outlaw's forehead. A wind of fear swept through him. He was trapped. The attack on Fallon yesterday would be counted as corroborative evidence against him.

"You're aimin' to frame an innocent man," he charged. "Look, mister. I done wrong when I let Dutch Frater force me into siding him down at the corral. But I didn't shoot to hit you. When he got his I was plumb glad. That's an honest-to-goodness fact."

"You were an innocent bystander," Tom replied ironically. "I ought to apologize for taking a couple of shots at you. But you are barking up the wrong tree. They won't hang you for using me as a target but for killing Pollock and Barrows."

"I'll give it to you straight," Todd pleaded. "I met up with these fellows and rode into Copper Fork with them. I was aimin' to see the fiesta. Soon as we hit the camp I separated from them. I dunno what they did after that. I was dog tired and after supper I went straight to bed."

"Where did you sleep?"

"Why, I dunno the name of the place. I'm a stranger to the town."

"What fellows did you say you rode in with?"

"Why, those birds we were talkin' about—Frater and Wheldon and—" Todd cut off his sentence just in time.

The deputy nudged him along. "The other man, Todd. Who was he?"

"Never met him before. Seems to me they called him—Andy."

The name was so palpably an afterthought that Fallon grinned. "Or Bill—or Phil—or Zeke. Any one will do, won't it?"

"You got me stumped. Maybe it was Art." Todd was sweating fear. This lean-loined boyish chap with steel-barred eyes had got him so mixed up he did not know how much information he had given away. It was a cinch that if he ever came to trial he would be convicted. He ought never to have come to this town. Mexico was where he ought to be right now. Instead of lighting out he had let Frater bully-rag him into that fool business at the corral. If he ever got out of this jam he would keep traveling fast and not stop this side of San Francisco.

Tom rose to go. "You can't lie yourself out of this," he said coldly. "Might as well come clean."

"Just what I've done, but you're all against me," the man whined. "I ain't even got the makings for a smoke."

The deputy tossed on the bunk a sack of tobacco and a book of cigarette papers. After all the poor devil was coming to the beginning of his last crooked mile. Tom could not help feeling sorry for him.

CHAPTER 13

Jennie Hershaw was rolling the dough for the top crust of a wild plum pie. She worked automatically, her mind busy with the news she had heard an hour earlier at the grocery store. If it had been her brother-in-law who had made this attack on young Fallon she would not have been surprised, but she knew of no reason why this notorious ruffian Dutch Frater should try to kill him. From the account she had been given this bad man and an accomplice had attempted to ambush the boy and by some miracle he had been able to shoot down Frater and drive the other gunman away. The clerk in the store did not know the cause of the trouble.

She was worried for Tom who no sooner escaped one danger than he ran into another, and she was depressed by a lurking fear that Curt Faunce might be back of the assault. There was in the man a sullen savagery. He had the reputation of nursing an injury until he had paid the offender back in full.

As Jennie cut the overlapping dough from the edge of the pie plate she heard Lieutenant Ramsey and her niece come into the house. He had ridden in from Fort Lowell to see Nancy, as he did nearly every day, and they had gone for a walk to have a look at the Papago village at the edge of town. Their cheerful voices and little bursts of laughter came to her from the parlor. She wished she knew how strong the officer's feeling for Nancy was. It would be too bad if her affections were involved more deeply than his. Jennie admitted prejudice, since the girl had been like a daughter to her for so many years, but she thought a man exposed to Nancy's charm must have blood of ice if he did not respond intensely. Her beauty was like quicksilver, so swift and mobile.

There was to Jennie a certain poignancy in the girl's eagerness to snatch at life. She seemed sometimes like a slim gay sprite dancing on the shifting sands of fate. The older woman had learned by experience that the years move fast and take with them that first bloom of rapture. Was it Shakespeare who had written, "Youth's a stuff will not endure?"

Ramsey followed Nancy into the kitchen. Already he felt quite at home in the house.

"Archie bought some Indian pottery at the village," Nancy told her aunt. "It's not bad, though of course not so good as what the Navahos do."

"Did you hear the news about the trouble at the Longhorn Corral?" Jennie asked.

"No. When I got in from the Fort I came straight here," Ramsey said. "What kind of trouble?"

"Two ruffians tried to murder Tom Fallon last night. One was Dutch Frater. Tom shot him and drove the other away."

The shock forced the color from Nancy's cheeks. "Was Tom hurt?" she said in a low voice.

"They say not. Frater is still alive, but Doctor Clifford thinks he can't live."

"Good riddance," the lieutenant pronounced curtly. "But I never saw such a troublemaker as this Fallon. He's hardly old enough to vote yet he is always in a difficulty."

"I don't suppose Tom asked these desperados to kill him," Jennie said sharply. "Before I condemn him I'll want to know why these men ambushed him."

Mrs. Harshaw was a woman of decision. She set out that afternoon to find why. At the upper end of Congress Street she stopped at a small brick building in front of which hung a sign. It said:

James Saunders
Attorney At Law

On the other face of it, for the benefit of Mexican clients, the announcement was in Spanish.

DESPACHO
De
James Saunders, Licenciado

Jennie was wearing one of her more attractive dresses, a figured dimity patterned with spring flowers that set neatly to her fine figure. Before entering the office she patted her hair

84

gently to make sure the breeze had not disarranged it. The man she was about to meet had become important in her life and might soon be more so. He had asked her to marry him and though she had not told him that she would her mind was moving in that direction.

Saunders rose from his chair behind a desk, a glad surprise showing in his eyes. She had never been in his office before.

After the first words of greeting Jennie discovered that she was embarrassed. Perhaps it was not a ladylike thing to have come here. She poked at a crack in the floor with the tip of her parasol.

"It is about that boy Tom Fallon," she said, raising her eyes to his. "I like him. He's such a nice young man. I am interested in him partly because he helped Nancy through that dreadful experience with the Apaches. Can you find out for me the truth of that fight yesterday at the Longhorn Corral? I know the ruffians attacked him, but I would like to find out the reason why."

The lawyer was a tall slender man in the early forties. He was notable for the quiet reserve and courtesy of his manner, but there was no self-restraint in the eyes of the scholarly face that worshiped her. Jennie knew a man looks at only one woman that way.

"What you want to know is that the young man was not at fault," he said. "I can tell you now. Sheriff Marshall confided to me that Fallon is a deputy sheriff from Tomahawk. He was sent here to get evidence that Dutch Frater is one of the bandits who recently robbed the Rosenstein store at Copper Fork. Frater tried to kill him because he is getting too close to the truth. Marshall thinks that Fallon is an unusually fine young man."

"I'm so glad to hear that, though I was already convinced of it."

Jennie rose and smoothed down the flaring skirt along her thighs. "I hope I didn't interrupt your work," she said.

"You always interrupt my work," he replied. "I get busy reading a deed and suddenly it is you I see."

She looked at him, a smile breaking on her lips. "Dear me, we must do something about that," she told him.

Her voice, with its undertone of friendly mockery, stirred in him a heat of recklessness. "I think so," he agreed, and took her in his arms.

Breathlessly she drew back from the long kiss. It was their first. A rich color had run into her cheeks. Her heart was hammering with an excitement she had not known for years. "You are impetuous, sir," she said, her eyes luminous.

An unspoken message passed between them. It told him that Jennie had come to a decision. She knew what she wanted, and she caught herself wondering at her emotion—a world reborn because a man was going to walk the coming years with her.

"It was time," he answered, the words rough and urgent. "A fire burns in a man. He keeps it pent up until it is a torment. All his years he had been master of his life and keeps it in an even current. Then he meets one woman, one out of the hundreds he has known, and he is enslaved by his love for her. She is in all he does and thinks."

Somehow she was in his arms again. "Why?" she asked. "Why me? I'm not so wonderful. You're just trapped by an illusion. But I am so glad you are," she added.

He held her close. "Why? There are no words for it. The turn of your head. The sound of your voice. The light grace of your walk. But love runs deeper than all that. It's what a man feels about the inner light in a woman that never dies in her because she is what she is."

"You make me proud and a little frightened, James. I'm a woman not an angel. You'll see me flare up impatiently. I'll be unreasonable sometimes. You'll find flaws in me. But if you keep on loving me I'll make you a good wife. You'll have to settle for that."

"I'll settle for you whatever you are," he promised exultantly.

Nancy looked at her aunt with a thoughtful scrutiny. "What's come over you?" she asked. "You go out wearing that new dress that is such a love. You come home with your eyes aglow looking so pretty a man would want to eat you. That letter you started this morning you sit down to finish, but you jump up and leave it to go to the piano and sing 'Annie Laurie.' What have you been up to?"

"It's such a lovely day," Jennie said lamely.

"No different from yesterday," Nancy declared. "Or any day this week. It's you that has changed. Who did you go to see when you left the house?"

"I went to find out the truth about why those ruffians attacked Tom Fallon."

"What did you find? And who told you?"

"Tom is a deputy sheriff from Tomahawk employed to run down the Copper Fork bandits."

"But he's so young," Nancy protested.

"He's twenty-one," her aunt replied. "In this part of the country boys become men early."

Though Nancy had turned a frozen face on Tom at their last meeting, she was more interested in him than she admitted to herself. Her mind recurred often to that desperate half hour when she could hear the wild yells of the Apaches and the drumming of their horses' hoofs behind them. In spite of her terror she had relied on the promise of the slim straight-backed rider racing beside the coach to save her from the savages. The gaiety and devotion of the lieutenant had never wiped out her feeling for Tom. It was likely that she would marry Archie Ramsey if he asked her, but even while she admitted that to herself she realized that Tom was the stronger man.

"Why did he have to say that terrible thing about my father?" she asked abruptly. "I don't see how I can be his friend now. But I daresay he doesn't want me to be."

Mrs. Harshaw was tempted as she had been many times before to tell Nancy the whole truth about her father, but she knew that it is a serious thing to destroy a child's faith in her parent. The shock would have to come someday, yet Jennie hoped not through her. Perhaps her reticence was a mistake. She guessed that Nancy already had doubts. She knew that Curt Faunce had treated her mother very badly and that he was an indifferent and negligent father. Since her visit to the ranch she had begun to ask questions about the past. Jennie had softened or evaded the facts in her replies.

"Tom would like very much to be your friend and there is no reason he shouldn't," the older woman said. "When Tom made that charge against your father he thought it was true. People make mistakes."

"But he must have had some evidence," the girl answered, puzzled.

"Don't forget that he was excited and that your father was bullying him. Best forget the affair."

"I'd like to." Nancy's mind jumped back to her unanswered question. "You haven't told me yet who you went to see."

"I called on James Saunders at his office. I thought he might know. He told me Tom fought only in self-defense."

Nancy's eyes grew wide with surprise. A deeper color was beating into the cheeks of her aunt. The girl gave a small whoop of delight. "So that's it. You're going to marry Mr. Saunders. I'm so glad, darling. He is the best of the lot of them."

Jennie agreed with that verdict, but protested there were not a lot of them. Her niece ticked off on her fingers five names of men eager to change the name of her aunt. "You're the prize package in this town," she said stoutly.

They went into each other's arms as women do.

CHAPTER 14

Tom met Sheriff Dunham at the depot. While they were still shaking hands the eyes of the deputy caught sight of another passenger descending from the car. In a low voice Tom said, "Look who is here."

Dunham did not turn his head. "I know," he answered. "Saw him on the train."

An icy grip clutched at Tom's stomach. The hard malevolent gaze of Curt Faunce was fixed on him. The showdown might be now.

"So you are here, shaking hands with a sheriff, after murdering a friend of mine," Faunce accused, anger flaring into his harsh face.

The deputy said, his words hard and crisp, "Frater isn't dead yet, and if he dies it is his own fault for trying to ambush me."

"That's your story. I don't believe your lies." Faunce turned on the sheriff savagely. "You throwin' in with killers, Dunham, instead of arresting them?"

"This boy isn't a murderer, Curt. He shot Frater in self-defense. All Tucson knows that. Dutch was caught in his own trap." Dunham spoke with quiet earnestness.

"Were you there when it happened?" the ranchman demanded.

"No, but I have talked with Sheriff Marshall and read the papers. It can't be any other way. Before you are here an hour you will know that."

Faunce brushed Dunham's explanation aside. His fury settled on Fallon. "I told you to get out of this country or I would fill you full of lead. That still goes. If you ever cross my path again you are through. For a dollar Mex I would rub you out right now. Light out from here sudden, damn you." His hand rested close to the butt of his gun.

A dozen men on the platform heard the threat. Neither Tom nor his enemy paid any attention to them. The palms of the deputy's hands sweated, but the eyes looking into the stormy visage of his foe did not falter. He was watching the man very steadily.

"You can't drive me out," he said, his voice low and even. "This is a free country, and I'm as big as you back of a gun. Don't forget that there is law in Arizona. If I am shot in the back your threats will be remembered."

The bystanders on the platform were moving fast to get out of the line of fire. Tom saw them scatter, though his eyes did not shift from Faunce. Dunham stepped between the foes. He knew he was taking a risk, but if he did not interfere guns would smoke in another moment.

"Hold it," he ordered sternly. "In the name of the law. There will be no shooting here." His .45 had jumped from its holster swiftly. His gaze was fixed on Faunce, knowing the danger lay with him.

Men held their breaths in the long silence that followed. It was as if a whisper of death was in the air. The strange stillness lasted long enough for the stationmaster to come out of the baggage room, sense the situation, and cry "Holy smoke!" as he dodged back.

Then the tension lifted. Faunce spoke, a jeer in his voice. He had made his choice. "Have it your way, Dunham. I've got plenty of time. Baby-nurse your killer and see what it will get him in the end. What I said still goes." He turned his back and strode down the platform, the thump of his heavy boots clumping sharply.

The sound of excited voices filled the air when he had gone. Tom's relief expressed itself in studied lightness. "Gent on the prod," he said.

"Nothing to joke about," the sheriff reproved. "You just missed death."

"Or he did," Tom amended. He was putting on a front to conceal how worried he had been.

The two men walked up town to Sheriff Marshall's office and reported what had occurred. Marshall showed concern. He knew the reputation of Curt Faunce and realized that the danger had been only postponed. His opinion was that the ranchman had not come to town looking for Fallon but had been drawn to Tucson on account of the trouble at the Longhorn Corral. Both Todd and Frater belonged to the group he dominated and he had to protect them.

Dunhan felt that the two reasons tied together. Todd had to be got out of jail and Fallon must be destroyed. Both were strong motives. Todd had to be released before he was coerced into telling what he knew. Tom Fallon was a danger not only to the Copper Fork raiders but to Faunce personally.

"I'm going to send you back to Tomahawk," Dunham announced to Tom.

"Why?" Fallon asked. "I wouldn't be any safer there. Faunce means to see this through to a finish. I can't run away from it. Fact is, I am better off here where I have made some friends. In Tomahawk I don't know a soul who would lift a hand for me."

"Something to that," agreed Marshall, "though the plain truth is that Tom won't be safe anywhere unless he lights out for the Pacific coast."

News of the arrival of Curt Faunce and the scene at the depot swept through the town like wild fire. The reputation of the cattleman as the leader of the wild bunch of night raiders in the San Simon made him a notable character, though no specific crime could be charged against him. He stayed in the background and let others operate for him and themselves. Those participating looked to him for defense when the arm of the law was long enough to reach them. More than once he had arranged prison breaks if other methods failed.

Faunce stayed at the Russ House, a rooming place near the depot. He had no intention of calling on his sister-in-law or seeing his daughter. Long since he and Jennie Harshaw had come to a parting of the ways. She had made it clear that she would have nothing to do with him. This did not distress him, since he had no place in his life for good women.

The day after his arrival a neighbor dropped in to talk with Mrs. Harshaw. A confirmed gossip, Matilda Bartells wanted to know how Jennie would react to Curt Faunce's declaration of war. She was disappointed, for her hostess took the news with apparent polite lack of interest, back of which was a touch of frosty reserve.

"He is kin of yours, isn't he?" the self-invited visitor asked.

"No," Jennie answered curtly.

Nonetheless she was much disturbed, and as soon as she had got rid of the busybody set about finding where Faunce was staying. She tried the Orndorff. There were three men in the lobby in addition to the clerk. One of them, she noted idly, was a curly-headed cowboy. In answer to her question the clerk shook his head. Faunce was not staying there. He suggested two other hotels as possibilities. And of course there were four or five rooming houses.

The curly-headed range rider followed Mrs. Harshaw to the street. He lifted his sombrero. "Excuse me, ma'am. I heard you ask where Curt Faunce is stopping."

"Yes. Do you know?"

He was, she thought, good-looking and evidently had spent a good deal on his clothes. His manner was prepossessing.

"I saw him go into the Russ House. I reckon that's where he is puttin' up."

"Thank you very much." A notion flitted through her mind. "Are you by any chance Husky Sowers?"

His eyes widened with surprise. "Sure am. But how come you to know my name?"

"Tom Fallon told me about you. You are his friend, aren't you?"

He hesitated. "Well, I ain't his enemy." The words came rather reluctantly.

"He's a nice boy," she said.

"Yes'm, I expect he is." He started to say more, then decided against it.

His puzzled eyes followed her as she moved up the street with the easy grace that marked her movements. He wondered what this nice well-dressed woman, evidently a lady, could want with that ruffian Curt Faunce. She could not know what kind of man he was, that only a few hours ago he had come near killing Tom Fallon. He toyed with the thought of warning her and abruptly yielded to the impulse.

She heard the click of his high-heeled boots behind her. A few moments later he was beside her and his hat came off again.

"Excuse me, lady," he apologized. "I'm buttin' in. But maybe you don't know that man Faunce. If not, I'd say he's a hard tough character. A few hours ago he came mighty nigh killin' a man."

"I know how bad he is," she told him. "That's why I'm going to see him."

That did not make sense to Husky. "Maybe I'd better go along with you—just in case," he volunteered.

She gave him her warm and friendly smile. "That's the nicest offer I have had for a long time. But I don't need you. I have to do this errand alone." As an afterthought she added: "If you want to help, get Tom to keep away from this man."

That was one thing Husky could not do, though he did not tell Mrs. Harshaw so. Tom was a grown man and he had to make his own decisions. Out in this frontier land you could not call the police to help you out of a difficulty. A man had to fight his own battles.

As Jennie walked up the short path to the porch of the Russ House she saw three men in a group at one end of it. One was Curt Faunce. The other two were disreputable and shabby cowboys, one about forty years old, the other scarcely more than a boy. The cold eyes in the vicious leering face of the younger man fixed on the woman.

"We got a visitor," he said. "I speak for her."

Jennie thought, *with that flat head he reminds me of a cobra.*

Faunce turned to look at her. "What are you doing here?" he demanded.

"I came to talk with you," she said.

"Forget it," he flung at her harshly. "I don't want to hear it."

She ignored his rudeness. "You are going to listen," she told him, quietly determined.

"Any time I meet you it is bad news," he snarled. "Let me alone and I'll do as much for you."

92

"That will suit me—after I have had my say today."

"Then get through with it," he ordered.

Jennie glanced at the other men. "This is something you won't want discussed before others."

He glowered at her, a mulish stubbornness on his heavy face. "Damn it, spit it out and get through."

"If you prefer. I'm going to talk about the time you left Nebraska."

Anger flared into his face. If her eyes had not met his so steadily he would have struck her. He fought down his savage urge to beat her. She had put a finger on the vulnerable spot in his pachydermatous hide.

He swung round on the younger cowboy. "Pull your freight, Jeb. You too, Yeager."

Jeb Purdy grinned lecherously. "Any time you'd like a private talk with *me*, lady, I'll be waitin' at the gate."

He and Yeager stepped down from the porch and disappeared around the corner of the house.

"Well, unload it," Faunce snapped.

"You're going to let that boy Tom Fallon alone. If you lift a hand to him again I'm going to have you arrested for the murder of his father."

"Have you gone crazy?" he stormed. "I didn't kill him, and if I did I'd stop you from blabbing certain. Anyhow you haven't got a lick of proof."

She laid the evidence before him. He had been in a saloon drunk the night of the murder and had boasted that he was going out to kill the sheriff. Within a quarter of an hour two shots were heard and Fallon was found dead, two bullets in his back. Curt had been seen running from the scene with a rifle in his hands. That night he left town leaving no address. Three months later his wife heard from him with instructions to join him in Arizona. She told nobody in Hastings where she was going when she and the baby left. But later, just before she died, she had written to her sister Jennie to come and get the baby. She was in great distress, for her husband during a quarrel had practically admitted to her that he had killed Sheriff Fallon. She knew she was not going to live long. Her concern was for little Nancy.

Faunce was both alarmed and furious. It was a pack of lies. He never had told his wife any such thing. Not at any time. Where had she picked up that stuff about his movements the night of the killing? None of it true. Nobody had seen him running away. How could anybody on a dark night like that?

"So you remember it was a dark night," Jennie mentioned.

He slammed his heavy fist down on the railing of the porch. "You always were a meddlesome vixen," he said with a savage curse. "Keep out of my business or I'll take care of you. No woman can tell me what to do."

"I suppose that is a threat. Perhaps I had better tell you that I have written out the whole story and left it with a trustworthy man to be opened if any harm comes to me." She had not, but she had just decided to write such a statement and leave it with James Saunders. "In it I wrote that nobody but you had any reason to injure me."

He glared at her, his fists doubled. No other woman had ever stood up to him and defied him so coldly. The urgent desire was in him to hammer her face until it was a bloody mess, but he knew he dared not do it. He poured bitter invective at her.

When he stopped she said, very quietly, "If you kill the son as you did the father I shall see that you are either hanged or shot down like a wild beast."

"I can take care of myself," he boasted. "And I can take care of my daughter. She is going to the ranch with me. I won't let her stay with a woman who is willing to blacken the name of her father."

"No," his sister-in-law told him firmly. "She is going to stay with me. You have forfeited your right to her."

"We'll see about that," he retorted. "The law doesn't say so. You can't hold her."

"If you stick to that you will force me to tell all I know."

"Tell it. Nobody will believe you. All you have against me is scraps of slander, lies you have invented because you hate me."

"I haven't told you half of what I have against you. How will you explain changing your name to Faunce when you fled to Arizona? Or that you left your wife and child without a dollar, though it is known you had several hundred dollars when you lit out in the darkness to save your hide?" She added, resolution in her chill voice, "You ruined my sister's life, and I'm not going to let you do that to Nancy's."

He was a man violent and cruel but except when his passion slipped the leash of self-control he moved with sly and crafty caution. It was his custom to stand back and use others as his tools. There were plenty of reckless drifters in the country to serve as cat's-paws for him, scoundrels like Jeb Purdy who would dry-gulch a man for a fifty-dollar bill. But just now was a time for caution. He hated to let himself be dictated to by Jennie Harshaw, both because he hated any interference with his plans and because he considered women inferiors and despised them. But for the moment she had him in a cleft stick.

"You want to rule the roost," he sneered. "I'll show you about that. Keep that tinhorn deputy away from me if you want him to stay alive." He spat out a vile epithet at her and stamped into the house.

Jennie Harshaw knew the man well enough to be sure that she had stopped him only temporarily. His threat to take Nancy from her was disturbing. She decided it was time to tell the girl the whole truth about her father.

Nancy took the story very quietly. She did not ask any questions after Jennie had finished but rose white-faced and went into her bedroom. Though she was shaken by the knowledge that her father was a murderer, the news did not surprise her. She had always felt that the father she did not know was not a good man and since she had been with him at the ranch the conviction had grown that he was callous and not to be trusted. She had neither loved nor respected him, but it was a shock to know that she was the daughter of a cold-blooded killer. Her pride was hurt and she had the sense of being cheap and unclean.

An hour later she came out of the bedroom and said to her aunt, "Let us never speak of him again."

When Lieutenant Ramsey rode with Nancy that afternoon he found her distrait and unresponsive. In her talk there was none of her usual gay give-and-take.

Presently he asked her, "Have I offended you?"

"No, it's not that." Her voice was not quite steady. "Please, Archie. I—I don't want to talk about it today."

The words were hardly out of her mouth before Curt Faunce walked from a restaurant and caught sight of her. He raised a hand in a gesture to stop the riders. Nancy rode past him, her eyes straight in front of her. His yelp of anger she disregarded.

"Who is the fellow that tried to stop us?" Ramsey asked.

"His name is Faunce. He is my father."

The lieutenant made no comment. The tone of the girl's voice told him that the subject was closed.

CHAPTER 15

Tom waited as directed on the bank of the creek a hundred yards below Levine's Garden. He had been greatly surprised when Jerry Harshaw had brought him the note from his cousin asking him to meet her there. Her desire to see him must have something to do with Curt Faunce, he guessed, but he had no idea what it might be.

When she was still some distance from him he saw her coming through the cottonwoods wearing a figured print that fitted snugly her lissom body, as fine-lined and graceful as that of a two-year-old registered colt. He thought her the most exquisitely feminine creature he had ever seen. On the cattle ranges where he had been brought up even the pretty girls did not have this spirited look of pride that enwrapped Nancy Faunce. It did not occur to him that the difference was mainly a matter of clothes and opportunity.

Though her eyes met his directly, there was a touch of embarrassment in her manner. She was not so sure of herself as she had been when he last saw her, but had a shyness that was almost humility.

"I've come to ask to be forgiven," she blurted out. "I've been an ungrateful girl." She hurried on to explain. "It was what you said about my father. But now I know it was true. I'm the daughter of a murderer."

He could see that she was flogging herself with a whip of self-scorn. "It doesn't matter what he is," Tom said gently. "You are like your aunt and she is the finest lady I know. It is because you are loyal that you stuck up for your father. Nobody can blame you for that."

He held out his hand and she gave it a warm little pressure.

"We're friends again," she said happily, a lilt in her voice. "I'm so glad you've forgiven me for being horrid."

There was a song in his heart. "I'm mighty glad too," he assured her. "If there's ever anything in the world I can do for you please let me know."

"I'll begin now," she told him, her face dimpling to a smile. "We shall see how much you mean that. Don't have any more trouble with that man. Keep away from him."

"I'll do that if I can," he promised. "At first I meant to see that he is punished for what he did to my father. But I've given that up because I can't do it without hurting you and Mrs. Harshaw. The difficulty is that he won't let me alone. He is very stubborn and—well, stubborn."

"And vindictive, as you started to say. You needn't try to save my feelings. I know he is an evil man, even if he is my father." There was an accent of despondency in her words, as if the wickedness in him must be reflected in her. "But you could leave here—get clear out of Arizona."

"Yes," he agreed. "I may do that, as soon as I have finished a job I am on. I do not like to go, since I came here to live."

"You might come back in a year or two," she suggested.

"Yes. After you are married to Lieutenant Ramsey." His impulsive words shocked him. "I oughtn't to have said that," he added quickly.

"No, you shouldn't," she replied. "Unless he has asked you to be his John Alden." The color in her cheeks had deepened and in her voice was the sting of a small whiplash.

"It is a pity I can't mind my own business," he said.

"How right you are."

But at sight of his downcast mien her manner of an outraged young Portia collapsed into giggles of mirth. "If you could see how mournful you look. The world won't come to an end even if Lieutenant Ramsey doesn't ask me. I won't be an old maid for two or three years yet."

"You won't ever be one," he blurted.

She gave a little curtsey. "Oh thank you, kind sir. I won't have to worry since you are so sure."

He did not mind being laughed at, for it was a sign that he was pardoned. On the way back to her house he discovered that it was easy to talk with her. He began to see that she was not a young goddess but a girl. She would like him more if he were less lamblike and more impudent.

Mrs. Harshaw was in the garden watering flowers. The sound of their laughter told her that the dissension between them was healed.

"I'm glad to see you again, Tom," she said.

"He has been giving me advice, Aunt," Nancy explained. "He wants me to marry Archie Ramsey if I can get him."

"I didn't say any such thing," he protested.

Jennie smiled. "I don't suppose you did. I know this young lady quite well. What did you say?"

Nancy answered for him. "He said he was going away and that he wouldn't come back until after I had married Archie."

"She's fibbing, Mrs. Harshaw. She knows that is not what I meant."

Jennie picked the essential fact from what her niece had said. "I am so very glad you are going away, Tom. We've been worried."

"I didn't say I was leaving right now," Tom corrected. "As soon as I've finished a job I'm on."

Mrs. Harshaw slanted a long deliberative look at Tom. Back of his smiling youth she sensed that he was very much a man. She thought of Curt Faunce, implacable and pitiless, fighting to keep the power he had so carefully built up through the years; of the desperate villains who would move into action when he spoke the word, such men as Yeager and Jeb Purdy and Dutch Frater if he lived, as now seemed likely. Tom Fallon was no fool. He knew how ringed about with enemies he was, that next time the attack might come in the night from behind as it had on his father, yet he showed no signs of panic or fluttery nerves. More than once she had seen in his eyes the steely coldness of a stark fighting spirit in him that only death could extinguish. There were men like that. The records of the frontier showed many such, some good and some bad, but all with a fire in them that could not be snuffed out while life was in them. Because she liked Tom the breath of fear stirred in her.

"What is this job that nobody else can do?" she asked.

"Now Mrs. Harshaw I didn't say that," he corrected with a grin. "It just happens to be my job."

"Won't Sheriff Dunham release you?"

"Yes, but I can't walk out on it. Some people still believe I was one of the Copper Fork bandits. I can't let that ride all through my life."

"I think you are foolish, Tom. Nobody who really knows you thinks you were one of the robbers. How can you pin the crime on the guilty men when you are not sure who they are?"

"Since you are asking for the lowdown I'll say this. Dutch Frater is the leader. One was killed in the raid. Another is in the jail here. I am almost certain I can name a fourth. That leaves only one still unknown."

"If you have done the spade work surely our sheriffs can be trusted to clean up the thing and arrest the bandits."

"I'll make a promise, Mrs. Harshaw," Tom said. "If the holdups aren't caught inside of a week I'll quit."

That was the only concession he would make.

Jennie was not happy about the situation. She thought of the three hard crafty scoundrels she had seen at the Russ and it was strong in her mind that his smiling confidence was no match for the evil in them. It was likely that he did not have a week to spare.

"Why don't you get that nice boy they call Husky to stay with you and never leave you for a minute?" she asked.

"To ride herd on me like a nurse does with a baby." He shook his head. "I won't throw down on myself for certain, Mrs. Harshaw."

The women's eyes followed him as he walked jauntily up the street, spurs jingling and hat tilted at a debonair angle.

CHAPTER 16

Curt Faunce sat beside the bed where Dutch Frater lay. Doctor Clifford had just told him that the wounded man would get well unless complications arose. The San Simon ranchman did not care whether Dutch lived or died. His only concern was that the fellow did not let himself be pressured into betraying secrets.

The big bandit let his suspicious eyes rest on his visitor.

"So I fooled you after all," he jeered. "I'm not going to kick off. You traveled quite a ways to make sure I wasn't going to make one of those deathbed confessions."

Faunce's cast-iron face did not disclose how close the other had come to the truth. "I came to make sure you were getting good care," he said. "If there is anything you want that you are not getting just let me know. I'm not a fool, Dutch. I know you'll clam up. For two reasons. Because you've sand in yore craw and wouldn't let anybody bully you into talking and because you couldn't blab without putting a rope around yore neck."

"And around yores too," Frater retorted sullenly. "Don't ever forget that and try to throw me to the wolves."

"That's crazy talk. I'll go through for you to a finish. But I am worried about Rufe Todd. He is soft. I've got to get him out of jail before he rats and sends himself and you too to the gallows. I tried to get Sheriff Marshall to let me go bail for him. Nothing doing. But he did let me talk with Todd alone. Rufe is scared sick. I pumped some heart into him by promising to get him out certain."

"How?"

"I brought Jeb Purdy and Cad Yeager with me. I'll find a way."

"Soon as I get on my feet I aim to settle the hash of that two-bit deputy who shot me," Frater announced savagely.

"If he is still around," Faunce amended. "I got plans about him myself."

"Leave him for me," Frater demanded.

"I would if he wasn't too dangerous." The rancher rose and gave the wounded man what was intended to look like a friendly grin. "Be seeing you, old-timer, soon as you are fit to travel. The San Simon will sure throw a big welcome for you."

Faunce walked back to the Russ House and went into a close huddle with Purdy and Yeager. "We are going to be busier than heel flies in July," he said. "First off, we have to get Todd out of jail before he spills the beans. There mustn't be any hitch about that. And we have to rub out Fallon. He knows too much. That will be yore job, Jeb."

Purdy's flat head slid forward and his beady eyes narrowed. "Guess again, Curt. I kill my own rattlers, not yours."

"Think straight, Jeb." Faunce did not raise his voice but

there was a rasp of anger in it. "This Fallon aims to bust the Copper Fork raid wide open. Right now he is mighty close to the truth. He already has Frater and Todd spotted. It's a mighty little jump from them to you. Soon as he sets eyes on you he'll recognize you as one of the men who rode into the camp that night with the others. If he lives to testify in court you're a gone goose."

"He's sure got you whipped," Purdy sneered. "A kid not dry behind the ears."

The cold dead-fish eyes of Faunce rested on the youth with the seamed leathery face and the rippling muscles of an athlete. He thought, *Some day I'll have to put an end to this insolent devil.* But the words he spoke were no reflection of this intent.

"Face the facts, Jeb," he said mildly. "When Dutch and Rufe tried to ambush this kid, as you call him, he put two bullets in Dutch and made Rufe run for his life. If you are the snake-stomper I hear you are I would advise you to get this sidewinder before he strikes."

"You get him," Purdy mocked. "You've been making war talk against him. Maybe you can do better than Dutch."

"That's the reason I can't go after him," Faunce explained patiently. "I'm known to be his enemy. The law men would figure I did it. But if I have an alibi that would let me out."

"And let me in," jibed Purdy. "Wouldn't that be nice?"

"You are not looking at this right, Jeb. If you do a smooth job you will never be suspected. I'm willing to pay a reasonable amount."

"Why didn't you say so? How much?"

"Well, it oughtn't to be hard. Catch him alone after dark. Time it right and you would have no trouble."

"If it's so easy hop to it yoreself. No use wasting two hundred dollars hiring my gun. You know how you squeeze a two-bit piece till the eagle screams."

"Two hundred dollars!" Faunce yelped. "You're doing this for yoreself more than for me."

They wrangled over the price ten minutes before coming to terms.

"Maybe I could get into a rookus with Fallon and have to gun him in self-defense," the young desperado suggested.

"If you could make it look good," Faunce answered doubtfully. "I don't care how you get the tramp, but my idea is

101

that after dark would be better. We've got to move fast on both jobs."

"That's right," agreed Yeager, "especially if Rufe Todd is as jumpy as you say."

"We might slip up on that jail break," Purdy said, and proposed callously an alternate method. "If we called him to the window and riddled him we would know he wouldn't do any blabbing."

Faunce vetoed this. "Two killings would be one too many. This town is unfriendly to us because of Dutch. It thinks we're tied up with him. We can get Todd out. After we reach the San Simon you can take care of him if you think it necessary."

Yeager nodded agreement. "We don't want to bite off more than we can chew."

"I'll have to get two more horses. I had saddles shipped in. They are at the depot."

"Why two more, Curt?" Yeager inquired. "Seeing that Jeb and I have ours here at the Longhorn corral."

"You don't need two," Jeb said. "Take Dutch Frater's sorrel. You can buy a cheap broomtail for Todd."

"That's a good idea. But I'll still need two. My daughter is going back with us to the ranch."

Purdy's small eyes shone with an unholy light. "That will be fine. Quite a surprise. Thought she didn't like it there."

"It doesn't matter what she likes. It's my say-so."

"Have you told her yet?" Purdy wanted to know.

"I'll let her know when it is necessary," Faunce said curtly.

"None of my business, but I'm kinda wondering." The young scamp grinned impudently at his boss. "That gal has quite some temper. Wouldn't surprise me if she said no thanks."

"You are right," Faunce told him bluntly. "It's my business, not yours. When I say she's going that's all you need to know."

"No kick here. Yore ranch needs the refinement of a lady's society—even if you have to kidnap one."

Faunce swallowed his annoyance. This was no time to quarrel with Purdy. He said: "Might as well get this straight. At her age my daughter is under my authority. It's quite legal for me to take her regardless of her whims."

"I certainly spoke out of turn," Purdy replied with a humility his devil-may-care eyes refuted. "Knowin' you, I feel sure you wouldn't do anything not legal."

The ranchman ignored that and outlined his plan for the jail break. It would be better, he thought, to pull that off before Jeb snuffed out Fallon. The others could be on their way home when Jeb rubbed out the deputy and he could join them later.

Purdy did not object to that but he took pains to gibe at Faunce and let him know that he understood the reason for Curt's timing.

"You always play yore own hand, don't you?" he sneered. "With you twenty miles outa town nobody could accuse you of having a thing to do with the killing of Fallon. If anybody gets stuck with it the guy will be Jeb Purdy and a hell of a lot you will care."

Curt Faunce liked to use a rough tongue but not to be on the receiving end of one. He was both violent and arrogant, but when his plan demanded it his words could be softer than butter though war was in his heart.

"I'm trying to do what's best for all of us, Jeb," he said reproachfully. "We're in a tight and have to work our way out. What's past is past, but it's only fair for you to remember that if you boys hadn't gone hog wild and started shooting at Copper Fork that night this trouble would not have developed. Soon as the town folks looked at Bob Wheldon suspicion fell on you and Dutch. The job was sure bungled."

"I won't take the blame for that," Purdy retorted promptly. "Rufe Todd got goosy and began the fireworks. I wasn't responsible for his being one of us."

"Well, the least said about that the better. We don't want to have any hard feelings among us. This situation will clear up all right if we pull together."

"Suits me," Purdy said derisively. "Cut the cackle and tell us how we're going to bust that jail open."

Faunce explained his plan. It was a very simple one.

CHAPTER 17

The jail stood near the river on an isolated spot outside the business district and apart from the residence section. There was no other building on the block. The jailor, Sam Downey, was a bachelor and slept on the lower floor in a room adjoining the kitchen where a Mexican came from his home every morning to prepare the meals for the prisoners.

Sam was snoring comfortably with his mouth open when a voice broke into his dream. At first he disregarded it, but the persistence of the call awakened him. He heard the sound of his own name and struggled from a tangle of blanket and sheet to his feet still drugged with sleep. Wearing his night-shirt he stumbled to the window. It was dark in the street but he made out three figures in front of the door. One of them had his hands tied together in front of him.

Knuckles knocked on the panel and a man called "Hi, Sam! Wake up. We've got a prisoner for you."

"Cripes' sake!" Sam protested. "Do you have to wake me in the middle of the night? Who is it anyhow?"

The name given was Walt Taylor, the town marshal. "Got a greaser here who cut a guy in a saloon rookus."

Downey was a rather dull-witted unsuspecting man. "All right," he answered. "Be out soon as I've got my pants on."

"Take yore time. No hurry. Sorry we had to wake you, Sam."

After he had unlocked and flung open the door Downey started a grumbling complaint. "If this is a twenty-four-hour position—"

The rest of the sentence died on his lips. He stared at the men in black astonishment. They were masked. The one who seemed to be bound tossed away the rope from his wrists. Three revolvers covered him.

He cried, "Goddlemighty, boys, what is this?"

The leader, a big heavy-set man, ordered him back into the building and closed the door behind him. "So we can do our business without any interference," he said.

"W-what business?" Downey asked.

"Light a lamp and get yore keys," the spokesman of the intruders told him.

The jailor did as directed.

"How many prisoners do you have?"

"Six right now."

"We'll go upstairs, open the cells, and turn them loose."

"But we can't do that," Downey demurred. "I'm responsible for them. The sheriff would raise hell."

The big man jammed his pistol hard into the ribs of Downey. "Stop beefing and get going," he growled.

The jailor led the way to the second story, the others at his heels. A Mexican was in the first cell and a Negro in the second. One said "Gracias" and the other "Thanks, Boss."

"No talking," the big fellow commanded.

Rufe Todd was in the third cell and was bid to shut up when his joy began to explode in words. The remaining prisoners were released. All of them were allowed to leave with the injunction to stay off the streets and to keep their mouths shut. Todd remained with his rescuers. They tied up Downey securely, gagged him, and left him locked in a cell. Outside the building the masks of the jail breakers were flung away.

Four horses were tied in the cottonwood grove bordering the creek. As the men swung to their saddles Yeager said, "Worked slick, didn't it?"

"So far," Faunce agreed grimly. "We're not through yet."

They followed the bank of the creek until they could see the lights of the Japanese lanterns at Levine's Garden.

"This is near enough," Faunce said, and dismounted.

A *baile* was in full swing. They could hear the sawing of the fiddles and more faintly the thumping of the dancers' feet.

Faunce gave explicit directions to the others. Yeager would remain with the horses. Purdy and Todd would move forward with him and crouch in the darkness outside the circle of light. He would leave them there. How long it would be until he returned he could not say. Perhaps a few minutes, perhaps half an hour. It depended how long he must wait to see his daughter alone. He might be forced to bring back her escort, Lieutenant Ramsey, with the girl. If so, they must be ready to club him into unconsciousness before he made an outcry. But on no account was he to be killed. At the right moment he would slip the gag into his daughter's mouth to keep her from screaming. Only with perfect timing could they get away leaving the dancers unaware that anything unusual had occurred.

Curt Faunce walked cautiously out of the complete darkness to the shadowy penumbra at the edge of the lighted amusement resort. Others were watching the *baile* but they paid no attention to him. His gaze searched the scene and presently found the lieutenant and Nancy on the dance floor doing a polka. When this was finished the proprietor clapped his hands for silence and announced a recess for refreshments. The food was served from a long table behind which were several Mexican waiters.

Ramsey left Nancy on a park bench while he went to line up with a score of others to be served. Faunce saw that this was his opportunity. The officer would not be back without food for them both.

Nancy became aware that a man was standing in front of her and looked up to discover that he was her father. She rose with the intention of walking away. He blocked her path.

"Wait, my dear," he said. "I want a few words with you."

"No," she answered. "Leave me alone. I don't want to have anything to do with you."

"If you feel that way I can't help it," he replied, and gave her his friendliest smile. "I have to accept yore decision, unfair though I think it is. But this talk is important. It won't take five minutes." His voice became pregnant with meaning. "If you love yore aunt you will listen to me."

His words disturbed her. "Very well, I'm listening," she told him.

He glanced around at the crowd and noticed that Ramsey was now fourth in the line from the table. "Let us get out of the mob where nobody can overhear what I have to say."

She hesitated, then fell into step beside him. "Though you may not realize it I am greatly concerned for your happiness," he said, his voice smug and cheerful. "If you are interested in this young officer I hope he is a good man."

"What is it that you want to say to me?" Nancy asked coldly.

106

"Something confidential about yore mother and yore aunt." They were passing into the shadows beyond the light. "It is time that you but nobody else should hear it."

"I won't believe anything you say that is insulting to them," she retorted angrily.

"I have nothing but good to say of either of them," he said gravely. "Though I have had differences with Jennie I respect her."

"This is far enough."

He made no attempt to force her. Not once had he even touched her. "Just a few yards farther, to make sure we are not overheard."

She moved with him, a little reluctantly. Yet she was curious to find out what he had to say. It did not occur to her that she was being tricked.

Nancy stopped when they came to the cottonwoods. "Well, what have you to say?" she said sharply.

For a large man he moved with extraordinary swiftness. One arm encircled her waist and snatched her to him. The gag in his left hand cut off her scream as it was thrust into her mouth. She was lifted from her feet and carried along the bank of the stream deeper into the darkness of the cottonwood grove.

Nancy fought furiously to escape. She almost freed her mouth of the bandanna that was being used as a gag but before she could cry for help her father's strong hand thrust it again between her teeth. She became aware that other men had come out of the gloom to join Faunce.

"If you can't handle the li'l vixen, Curt, let me take over," one of them said with wanton flippancy. "It would be a pleasure."

The ranchman paid no heed to the offer. "Knot this handkerchief back of her neck, Jeb," he ordered. "Make sure she can't shout."

After tying the ends of the bandanna Purdy patted her cheek softly with the palm of his hand. "Yore li'l wildcat is pretty as a spotted pup, Curt," he declared.

"Keep yore hands to yoreself," Faunce snapped testily. "And bring the roan over here, Yeager."

Nancy was hoisted astride the horse.

"Take the reins," her father bid the girl.

She did not touch them. Her hot eyes looked down at him with anger and contempt.

"As you please," he told her brusquely and flipped the bridle reins to Yeager. "Lead the horse. Let's go."

Nancy was not afraid. She was furious and humiliated. They had tossed her into the saddle as if she had been a sack of corn and were treating her with a callous brutality that shocked her sense of decency.

Jeb Purdy did not travel with them. "Be seeing you later," he promised, his ribald eyes slanting toward Nancy. "I know you'll miss me, but they say that absence makes the heart grow fonder."

They followed back streets through the town until they struck the road to Tomahawk. After they had passed the last scattered houses Faunce removed the bandanna from his daughter's mouth.

As soon as she could speak she flung at him blazing defiance. "I hate you and I always will. A man like you cannot know how terribly degrading it is to have for a father a lying cheat and a cold-blooded murderer."

His heavy hand struck first one cheek and then the other. "Keep a civil tongue or I'll use a quirt on you."

They rode through the long hours of the night until the sky began to lighten with the coming day. From his saddlebags Faunce took a cheap dress he had bought in Tucson. He lifted Nancy from the saddle and gave it to her.

"Take off that thing you are wearing and put on a decent dress," he bade her.

She was very weary and stiff. Her muscles ached and she no longer had the will or the strength to fight back. Behind a mesquite she changed from her pretty dance dress to the dull ill-fitting garment he had given her. The reason why he had brought it she understood. The other frock would stir comment among any people they might meet. On a long ride a girl did not wear clothes so gay.

"You think of everything, don't you?" she told him bitterly.

"You had better understand me," he said. "You are my daughter, under age, and I am taking you home. If you make trouble on the way you'll taste the whip. Yore aunt spoiled you. My ideas are different. I advise you to behave."

"You have always beaten women, as you do your dog and

108

your horse," she charged. "I'm not afraid of you. But it wouldn't do any good for me to ask strangers for help. I'll have to be your slave until I get a chance to escape."

"The law is on my side. Remember that. You'll be treated all right as long as you deserve it."

"I'm sure I shall be. Tonight's experience makes me certain of that," she countered bitingly.

Nancy's accusation was true. He had to be top dog and to prove it to himself he had to bully others. No dog or horse he owned could expect kind treatment. In dealing with women this sadistic urge was particularly dominant. They were to be servants of his will and if they resisted he must break their spirit. It was because Jennie Harshaw had never let him lord it over her that he hated her.

They camped in a hill pocket near Tomahawk. Faunce sent Yeager into town to buy food for the party. Next morning they by-passed the county seat and headed for Copper Fork. The long desert trip to the mining camp exhausted Nancy. She so dreaded another cold night in the open that when her father proposed a lodging in town on the condition she would promise to make no attempt to escape she gladly accepted the terms.

A young woman named Mary Landon was the owner of the rooming house where they stopped. She was not more than two years older than Nancy, a shy girl with a low lovely voice and an eager warmth of manner. Her heart went out to this weary saddle-worn child who looked so desperately unhappy. To be the daughter of Curt Faunce was in Mary's opinion reason enough for being sad. Nancy did not look at or speak to him unless it was necessary and then only in a tone chill and hostile.

Mary gave Nancy her own room because it was more homelike. She filled a tub with hot water for a bath and arranged with Faunce to give his daughter supper in the room so that she would not have to go out to a restaurant. This suited him very well, since the fewer public appearances Nancy made the better.

After the bath and hot supper Nancy felt much refreshed. The girl was older, Mary saw, than she had thought at first, a beautiful young creature close to womanhood. They talked for a few minutes before Mary left her tucked up in bed.

"Aren't you the girl in the stage that the Apaches attacked?" Mary asked diffidently.

Nancy told her that was correct.

"Then you met Tom Fallon."

"Do you know Tom?" Nancy answered her own question. "Of course you do. You must be the one he told me about who saved him from being hanged."

"I was a witness for him. My little brother was wounded by the bandits and Tom ran into the street and brought him into the house. It was a brave thing to do in all the shooting."

"I wonder if you would do something for me. Tom is in Tucson staying at the Orndorff Hotel. Will you write and ask him to tell my aunt that my father kidnapped me and is taking me to the ranch in the San Simon country? I made a promise not to write until we reached his place."

Mary said she would write at once and get the letter off on the stage next day. As she tiptoed out of the room Nancy was already falling asleep. She was wondering drowsily how much Tom and Mary meant to each other.

After he had eaten, Curt Faunce dropped into Heilman's Crystal Palace. He nodded casually at the proprietor and said, "How, Harry?" without stopping. At the roulette table he stood watching the game, then ordered a beer and carried it to a small table near the rear of the room. He had bought a newspaper on the street and was reading it when Heilman drifted back greeting customers cheerfully on the way. Faunce looked up when he reached him and said, "I read here in the paper that Dick Pearce aims to run for Sheriff. Make a good officer I'd think."

Heilman slid into the seat opposite him. "Why, yes. A game man. Rides tall in the saddle."

The glance of Faunce swept the room to make sure nobody was near enough to overhear him. "I reckon you know the Tucson news," he murmured.

"I know about the Fallon-Frater shooting. Is Dutch going to make it?" Heilman too spoke in a whisper.

"Looks like it. We've been underestimating that Fallon kid, Harry."

"Not me. I knew by the way he took it the night of the trial that he would go through to a fighting finish. Bring me down to date. What happened after you got there?"

"I broke Todd out of jail. He's around here somewhere.

110

Not worth a hill of beans. Soft as mush. But I couldn't leave him there to squeal on us."

Heilman waved a friendly hand at a passing Cornishman. "Is Fallon going to make us any trouble?" he asked softly, back of a hand to deaden the sound.

"Not if Purdy does a better job than Frater."

"Oh, it's like that. Purdy is still in Tucson then?"

"In Tucson or on his way back." Faunce still kept his voice low but it held a sharp edge of anger. "If I had known how badly the fools were going to bungle it I never would have let them tackle the pay roll here. They couldn't have done worse if they had been trying to get into trouble. I think we're all right now, but I had to work fast."

"I see you brought your daughter back with you."

Faunce snapped a "Yes" for answer. His reasons were private and personal. "I'm leaving for the ranch tomorrow morning. Soon as you get any news from Tucson send it to me right away. You ought to hear soon if Purdy is on his toes."

"You taking Todd with you? We don't want him running around loose where he can be picked up again."

The eyes of the men met in a long understanding look.

"I'll take him to the ranch," Faunce said. "*He won't be running around anywhere.*"

He rose to go and spoke audibly for the benefit of anybody within hearing distance.

"Sure I'd support Pearce. Dunham is a politician who sits around doing nothing most of the time. Well, so long Harry."

The San Simon ranchman passed greetings with one or two acquaintances as he walked out of the hall.

CHAPTER 18

Tucson was a leisurely small town just emerging from its status as a sleepy Mexican village. One sunny day followed another lazily. Time was marked more by notable events than by the calendar. It was easier to remember "The week

111

before Jim West was scalped by the Apaches" than to pinpoint the date at June 17. So in later years citizens used as a milestone the night of the jail break and the kidnapping of Nancy Faunce. These combined spectacular events stirred the old town from its lethargic calm.

At first nobody in Tucson except Jennie Harshaw and Jeb Purdy thought of the two pieces of news as having any connection any more than they tied up with them the overnight disappearance of Curt Faunce. All they knew was that masked men had freed six prisoners and that Miss Faunce had vanished during the dance at Levine's Garden.

After Lieutenant Ramsey reported to Mrs. Harshaw that Nancy could not be found they went to Sheriff Marshall with the tidings. Their call wakened him from a sound sleep but he got into action quickly. The grounds adjacent to the resort were searched and a handkerchief with the initials N F was found in the clump of cottonwoods. This Jennie Harshaw recognized as belonging to her niece. Not far from the spot there was evidence to show that horses had been stationed near during the past few hours.

"This is her father's work," she told the sheriff. "He is stopping at the Russ House. Unless he has taken Nancy away you will find her there with him."

Faunce was not at the Russ House and investigation showed that the two horses he had bought the day before had been taken by him from the Longhorn Corral early in the evening. Nobody remembered having seen him in the past few hours. Jeb Purdy was questioned and said he had not the least idea where Curt Faunce was.

The sheriff was in a dilemma. If Faunce had taken the girl there was nothing he could do about it. Since he was her father he was within his legal rights. But there was a chance that somebody else had abducted Nancy.

The jail break was not discovered until morning. When Sam Downey was questioned, after he had recovered from the effects of a night spent in great discomfort, it became clear that he could not identify any of the masked jail breakers. The only clue he could offer was that the big man who seemed to be a leader had called one of the others Jeb.

This brought Purdy back into the picture. Sheriff Marshall in the presence of Dunham interrogated the San Simon

112

cowboy. Purdy was insolently cynical. He half sat and half leaned on a corner of the office desk while he rolled a cigarette, lit it, and slowly sent into the air a fat smoke ring before replying to the official's request for information.

"I don't seem to remember breaking into any jail," he drawled. "Mostly I break out of them."

"One of the men in this jail break last night was named Jeb," Marshall mentioned.

"Like to help you but I don't know any Jebs around here —except me," he jeered.

"Do you know where Curt Faunce disappeared to in such a hurry?" Dunham asked.

Purdy looked him up and down coolly. "Ain't you takin' in too much territory, Mr. Lawman? Why not look after the criminals in yore own county? Seems to me I heard tell of a big holdup at Copper Fork and none of the villains arrested yet."

"They will be," Dunham retorted curtly.

The scoundrel grinned at him derisively. "I'm kinda bettin' they won't," he differed.

"Since you are so particular maybe you will tell *me* where Mr. Faunce went and why in such a hurry," Marshall said.

"I'd sure like to oblige you, Sheriff," Purdy explained. "But the fact is that Mr. Faunce didn't tell me where or why."

"Were you with him when he left?"

"No, sir, I wasn't. I reckon if he knew you was going to worry about him he would of told you."

Sam Downey walked into the office. "You sent for me," he said to Marshall.

"Yes." The sheriff indicated Purdy with a wave of the hand. "Did you ever meet this young man, Sam?"

"Seems like I've seen him around somewheres," the jailor said.

"Recently. Last night for instance."

Downey rubbed the palm of his hand over his unshaven chin to help him to think. He shook his head slowly. "Not far as I know." His dull eyes lit. "You think maybe he—but I wouldn't be sure."

"You're not helpin' the boss the way you should, Sam." Purdy told him impudently. "Take a good look at me. He

113

wants you to say I was one of the guys that busted into yore jail last night."

"I'll go this far," Downey said indecisively. "You've got the build of one of the guys. But, holy smoke, so have forty other young fellows in this town."

"Can't arrest them all, can you, Sheriff?" Purdy inquired jauntily. "How about getting the other thirty-nine in and having us shake dice for it?"

Marshall refused to share the young scamp's smile. He said coldly, "I think the one I want is in the room right now, but I can't prove it."

Purdy rose from the desk with the slow lithe motion of a cat on the prowl. "If you're not going to put me in the jug I reckon I'll be driftin'. Be seeing you in church."

He stopped to roll and light another cigarette before he sauntered to the door.

CHAPTER 19

Tom Fallon was eating breakfast at the Can Can when Husky Sowers walked in from the plaza by the back door. After a momentary hesitation he stopped at Tom's table.

"You're a hell of a lawman," he said amiably. "Whyfor ain't you out lookin' for Miss Faunce?"

The deputy looked up at him, startled. "I don't get it, Husky. Unless you are joshin' me."

"Haven't you heard she is missing?"

"Missing? Is this straight goods?"

Husky took the seat opposite Tom. "Y'betcha. She was at the *baile* with that officer Ramsey and she disappeared."

A chill wind blew through Tom. "Maybe she had a quarrel with him and went home."

Sowers shook his head. "Not the way I got it ten minutes ago. Her aunt and the lieutenant went to the sheriff. They have been hunting for her all night. Marshall found her handkerchief in the cottonwoods by the river."

"Do they think somebody took her by force?"

"Nobody knows. Looks like it."

A terrible unreasoning fear gripped Fallon. He thought of Apaches. Yet his judgment told him it could not be an Indian raid. Renegades from a reservation would not dare come into a town the size of Tucson.

He pushed back his chair and rose. "I'm going to see Mrs. Harshaw."

"Mind if I go along?"

"No. Let's get going."

They found Nancy's aunt at home. She had not slept all night and was almost sick with worry. When she mentioned that the sheriff had cut sign of shod horses in the grove Tom was relieved. The ponies of the Apaches did not wear shoes. He realized now that his first wild guess had been foolish.

"How could anybody have snatched her away without being seen while she was at Levine's Garden with a hundred other people?" Tom asked.

Jennie Harshaw explained that Lieutenant Ramsey had left her to bring back refreshments and that she must have been enticed to stroll away from the lighted park. "I know who did it," she said. "At least I'm almost sure. Curt Faunce."

Sowers' forehead wrinkled to a puzzled frown. "I heard yesterday he is her father. But if that is right why the grandstand play? Did they fix it up together?"

"No. She was very much ashamed of being his daughter." Jennie picked her words carefully. "He had to take her by force if at all. I know the reason for it, but I can't tell you what it is."

Tom understood that she could not denounce Faunce for fear he might take his revenge out on Nancy.

"I don't suppose he will do her any harm," Sowers said doubtfully. "He is a sure enough bad hombre, but he wouldn't hurt his own daughter."

"He has no feeling whatever for her," Jennie replied bluntly. "He might force her into a marriage with some one of the scoundrels that hang around him." She lifted her hands in a helpless gesture. "What can I do about it? He has a legal right to take her."

An idea was prodding at Tom's mind. "We have an illegal right to snatch her back," he suggested.

The eyes of Sowers lit. He was a hardy reckless scamp

ready to undertake any adventure. "Why not? Say I drop in, a puncher lookin' for a job. Curt and the ranch boys know me. Seeing I'm on the chuck line, I'm welcome as the flowers in May to stick around long as I like even if he doesn't hire me. Some night Miss Nancy and I light a shuck out of there. What's the matter with that?"

"The only matter with it is that when Curt Faunce finds out what you are up to he won't hesitate a minute to kill you," Jennie said. "No. Even if you got away he would follow and catch up with you."

"Wait a minute," Tom interrupted. "I think Husky has got something. But it is a two-man job. We could maybe pull it off together."

Sowers shook his head. "Boy, you're talkin' through yore hat. Soon as a Circle C F warrior sees yore phiz you would be gone. You are just one guy who can't show up there."

"I don't have to show up. I stay in the brush till I am needed."

"I'm not going to have you two boys killed trying to get Nancy out of that country," Jennie said decisively. "It's a crazy idea."

"Ma'am, we are bullheaded as a government mule," Husky explained with his boyish grin. "We've done made up our minds. You better write a letter to Miss Nancy for me to take so she'll know I'm on the level."

He was gay as a youngster starting on a picnic but Jennie was not deceived. It was more than possible that they might not come out of this alive.

"I'm frightened," she said. "I ought not to let you take such a risk. I know Curt Faunce. He's a terrible man."

"Don't you be scared," Husky comforted her. "We're a pair of tough guys, me and Tom, and we sure don't figure on laying down on ourselves."

Tom said cheerfully, "You fix up a nice dinner to celebrate when we come back with Nancy."

"Curt may be holding her at the Russ House," Husky guessed.

"No. He left in the night. Yesterday he bought two horses. One must have been for Nancy to ride. Both horses have disappeared from the Longhorn Corral."

"I reckon you're right, Mrs. Harshaw," Tom agreed. "Faunce pulled this off."

116

He was more sure of it when he learned half an hour later of the jail break. The masked men had freed all of the prisoners to cloud the fact that the one they wanted was Rufe Todd.

There was no great need to hurry. They decided to take a pack horse with them loaded with supplies. Tom might have to camp out in the brush for a week or more after they reached the Circle C F. To prevent any suspicion of their destination they gave out that they were going on a hunting trip.

During the day they made their preparations. It was close to two when Tom came out of a grocery store carrying a sack containing provisions. Three men were moving down the sidewalk toward him. The one in the middle stopped and with a gesture of his left hand held back the others.

He stood crouched a little, head thrust forward, cold eyes venomous. "So you're going hunting," he said. The words were not merely the statement of a fact. They were a jeer, almost a challenge.

Caught by surprise, Tom was silent. He recognized the man, though he did not know his name. Twice he had seen him. Once in Tomahawk with Frater and his companions, again on the summit of the hill from which the road descended into Copper Fork.

Tom said quietly, "Why not?"

He knew that trouble had come looking for him. It was written in the eyes of the man. But he could not know that the outlaw's plan to murder him that night under cover of darkness had been foiled by his impending departure, that what this gunman had intended to do secretly must be done in the open. What Tom did realize was that he had made a vital mistake. After he had learned that Faunce had left town he had put his pistol in the table drawer of his room at the Orndorff.

"This is it, fellow." The words came almost in a whisper from the thin lips of the killer. "End of the trail for you."

Tom's stomach seemed packed with ice. Fear crawled up his spine. But in his steady gaze none of this could be read. He folded his arms to make it clear he was not going to reach for a weapon.

"I'm not armed," he said.

"Don't pull that. You're crawfishin' because you haven't

117

the guts to go through after spreadin' lies about me, claimin' I'm one of the Copper Fork holdups."

"How could I claim that when I don't even know who you are?"

"You've been sneaking around like a polecat trying to build up lies to frame me. Dutch would of rubbed you out if he hadn't been a blunderin' fool." The man's vicious anger boiled over and he poured out a stream of obscene abuse, working himself up for the kill. His fingers slid around to the butt of the .45 at his side.

"Hold it, Purdy," one of the men beside him cried.

As the desperado's gun came out the man's arm knocked the barrel aside and the bullet smashed through the store window. Before Purdy could fire again Tom's fingers closed around his wrist. They struggled for the gun. Both of them were strong and active, Tom outweighing the other by fifteen pounds. He drove Purdy against the wall and slammed his gun hand hard to the bricks. The revolver clattered to the sidewalk.

Tom stooped for it but Purdy was swarming at him like a wildcat. They went down together and tossed to and fro, each trying to pin the other down, a tangle of flying arms and legs. Purdy was a wiry tough athlete but Tom's poundage made the difference. On top, he spread his legs to hold the advantage and hammered his foe's head on the wooden sidewalk. Purdy relaxed, for the moment out as well as done.

Fallon scrambled to his feet, his breast heaving from the violence of his exertions. His glance swept the ground for the revolver. It was safely in the hand of the man who had saved him from the bullet that had shattered the window.

The man holding the gun said, "What's the matter with the fool? We meet him in the Silver Dollar for the first time half an hour ago. We walk down the street with him, everything nice and friendly, then he blows his top."

Purdy's eyes were open, glaring at Tom. He rose slowly and snarled, "Gimme that gun."

The stranger who had it shook his head. "Not just yet, my friend. You just missed making a bad mistake. If you had killed this unarmed man you would have been hanged before night."

The outlaw moved toward him with his catlike tread. "Don't try to keep my gun from me, fellow."

The stranger shrugged heavy powerful shoulders. "All right. You get your gun." He broke the weapon, emptied the shells into his hand, and handed the .45 to its owner.

Purdy turned his smoldering eyes on Fallon. He spoke, still softly, almost biting his words off. "Before night you'll be dead." He wheeled around and his high-heeled boots tapped the warning in his sinister retreat.

Tom asked the name of his friend in need. Told that it was James Faulkner, he said it was a name he would remember.

Faulkner waved aside his thanks. "Better get your mind on this fellow Purdy. Don't forget the last words he said. Make arrangements to save yourself."

The other stranger spoke. "Was I you I'd cut my stick and light out of this town. No point in waiting for him to shoot you."

"Good advice," Tom said.

As he walked back to the Orndorff he thought he had better take it. He was pretty sure that Purdy would make another attempt to kill him. The man had been wounded in his most vulnerable spot, his vanity. His reputation as a bad man he must protect at all costs or lose face.

Luck had ridden on Tom's shoulder several times during the past few weeks. Without it he would not be still alive. But a chap's luck was bound to run out if he pushed it too far. He had heard a good deal about this Jeb Purdy and he did not like what he had been told. The man was a cold and callous killer, one who did not fear man or God. Since he was also the best, or at least one of the best, shots in the Territory there was no sense in letting himself be a target for the gunman's marksmanship.

Tom had another reason for avoiding this showdown. He was pledged to attempt the rescue of Nancy Faunce. Nothing must be allowed to interfere with that. Even if he survived an encounter with Purdy he would probably be held in town several days by legal formalities. This last was a valid motive for side-stepping Purdy but Tom knew that it was not the predominant one. He was afraid of the man. Again he felt a chill drenching him as he had in those moments when death had hovered so close to him. This boy with the reptilian eyes was an expert at snuffing out life.

After he had buckled on his belt he tested the pistol several times to make sure it could be drawn from the holster easily.

The hour set for him and Husky to leave was four and the sun was already far past the meridian. There were preparations still to be made. Husky was getting together the camp equipment. They were to meet at the corral where they would pack their supplies on the spare horse before saddling.

He could not stay hidden in his room. The chance of meeting Purdy had to be faced. He walked through the lobby of the hotel carrying the sack of supplies in his left hand. A cowboy lounging in a chair with his feet on another wished him good hunting. Another rider of the range, wearing a rattlesnake skin for a band to his hat, flung a careless question at him.

"Where's yore gun, fellow? You going huntin' without one?"

"My gun!" Tom was startled for an instant. "Oh, my rifle. It's down at the corral."

It was in his heart to envy these lighthearted sons of the saddle. They had not a thing to worry about. A killer was not lying in wait to fling bullets into them.

He had a few more articles of food to buy before he went to the corral. These he bought at a small store off the main street. He glanced behind him uneasily to make sure no shot would come from the rear. It was a mistake not to have arranged for somebody to follow him and give warning if necessary.

His gaze took in the sawtoothed Catalinas shining in the untempered sunlight and it came to him that this might be the last time he would look at them. It would be soon now, if it was to come at all. His mind was more settled. Strangely, a verse from the school reader flashed to his recollection and he found comfort in it. He spoke the words aloud and they gave him a lift.

> *Cowards die many times before their deaths;*
> *The valiant never taste of death but once.*

A man passed him and in his eager eyes Tom read that the news of the killer's threat had been broadcast. Turning into Congress Street, he caught again in men's swift glances their expectation of impending tragedy.

Then other thoughts vanished and all his being focused on

one issue. Jeb Purdy had come out of a saloon and was walking toward him. Tom dropped the sack and advanced slowly
to meet him. All his fear had gone. One factor was in his
favor. The sun was shining in his enemy's eyes. Later, when
he had time to think of it, he wondered that the killer had
overlooked such a disadvantage, and the only explanation he
could find was that the man had been drinking.

Purdy did not hurry. Men watching him from doors and
windows noted his smooth waving pantherlike tread. He
looked confident as a hunter stalking his prey. Though his
eyes were pinpointed on Fallon he did not move a hand toward his weapon till he was within striking distance. There
was pride in his easy swagger.

Tom had stopped. His eyes did not leave the figure
paddling along the sidewalk with soft footfalls that made no
sound. He knew that even slow approach was meant to shake
his nerves, to cause him to fling shots wildly before his
enemy came too near.

Purdy's arm swept up, the pistol in his hand. The wind of
the bullet brushed Tom's coat sleeve. A second slug whipped
past Fallon before his weapon smoked. He saw Purdy stag-
ger. The man's knees buckled. He made a tremendous effort
to keep his feet and succeeded in firing another shot before
he sagged down. He pushed his body from the ground to fire
again. Tom's second bullet caught him in the throat. He lay
prone, the pistol still in his hand.

As Tom moved closer he kept the still figure covered with
his revolver. But before he had taken three steps he saw it
was not necessary.

A few seconds earlier the street had been deserted except
for the two. Now a dozen men were pouring into it from saloons and stores. The sound of their excited voices filled the
street.

Tom looked down at his enemy so swiftly stricken from
life. A thin trickle of smoke rose from the pistol held in the
still hand.

"The sun in his eyes saved me," he said.

Men thumped him on the back and told him how pleased
they were at the outcome. He did not answer. There was no
pleasure in this for him, as yet scarcely any sense of relief,
though that would come later.

He heard the slap of running feet and Husky Sowers pushed through the gathering crowd. Husky glanced at the dead man and then at Tom. He had not known of the meeting between the two an hour earlier.

"Hell and high hinges!" he exclaimed. "How come?"

"He shot at me an hour ago," Tom told him. "He served notice I wouldn't live till night. I armed myself. He fired first."

Faulkner was among those present. He corroborated what Tom had said and added that except for his interference Fallon would have been killed at their first meeting.

Sheriff Marshall arrived and listened to the story of Purdy's death. He was satisfied that Tom Fallon was in no way to blame but he thought it better to hold an inquest in order to make the release of Tom legal. The jury did not leave its seats. There was five minutes of informal talk after which the foreman announced that the deceased had come to his death while attempting to kill an officer. He added informally that the unanimous opinion of the jurymen was Fallon ought to be given a medal.

CHAPTER 20

Night covered Copper Fork when Tom Fallon and Husky Sowers rode into the wagonyard near the mouth of the canyon. After watering and feeding the horses they walked up Cochise Street and dropped into the Denver Chop House for supper. The waiter who came to their table to serve them showed startled eyes at sight of Fallon.

Tom grinned at him amiably. "Business been good lately, Mr. Silliman?" he inquired.

Silliman had read the newspaper accounts of the battle at the Longhorn Corral in Tucson. He hoped this dangerous young man was not too much annoyed with him on account of his testimony at the miner's trial.

"Why, pretty good, Mr. Fallon," he said.

"No more bandits been in trying to find out where the pay roll is kept and how to get at it?"

"Now, Mr. Fallon, any man can make a mistake once," he protested.

"So he can. Don't make one this time. My friend and I want thick steaks covered with onions and plenty of hash brown potatoes. That is, if you don't think there is anything suspicious about that order."

After the travelers had eaten they separated. It was better that they should not be seen together much lest word reach Faunce that they had traveled in company. They had arranged the time of meeting next morning at the wagonyard to leave for the San Simon country.

Tom dropped in to see Mary Landon. A young man was with her in the parlor. He was a slender clean-cut youth with a frank and honest face. Mary introduced him as Mark Scully.

"If he is any kin to Tex Scully I'm for him," Tom said as they shook hands.

"Younger brother," Mark informed him.

Mary showed a shy embarrassment. It was plain that Mark was in love with her and that she liked him. But her gladness at seeing Tom shone through her diffidence. Fallon had a renewed sense of her loveliness. Her eager expressive face missed prettiness but when she smiled one would never notice it. Her beauty lay deeper—in a fine spirit that found expression in her charming personality.

"But you can't have got my letter yet," she said.

"Did you write me?"

"Nancy Faunce asked me to have you tell her aunt she was being taken to her father's ranch by him. She spent the night here. She was very tired and unhappy. They left this morning early."

"I'm here to help her if I can."

"How can you help her?" Mary broke out. "You surely aren't going to the Circle C F."

"I might do that, without their knowing I was there," Tom answered.

"I'll side you if you go," Mark said quickly.

Tom shook his head. "This won't be a raid on the ranch. If we try to force we'll never make it. By the way, I'd like to talk with Tex. Is he at home tonight?"

Mark said he was.

Before Tom left he accepted Mary's offer of a room for

123

the night. He had not gone a dozen yards from the house when he met Heilman. The man was standing under the lighted lantern in front of a saloon. Though he recovered quickly, Tom saw shock in the handsome face. He thought, *Founce planned it for Purdy to kill me and Heilman knew it. He was jolted to see me here alive.*

Heilman tucked an arm under Tom's elbow and walked with him to the Crystal Palace. "This calls for a drink on the house," he said. "How have things been going with you?"

Tom took a beer. "Oh, I've been rocking along," he replied. "Nothing exciting."

"What do you call exciting?" Heilman asked, with his facile pleasant smile in evidence. "You mighty nigh got scalped by the Pachies, you had a run-in with Curt Faunce, and you put two bullets in Dutch Frater to teach him manners."

"Dutch and Rufe Todd jumped me," Tom explained.

"I'm not blaming you, boy. Dutch asked for it. What I'm concerned about is your safety. Seems to me you're always sitting on a keg of powder. San Simon isn't more than a hop, skip, and a jump from here and Frater's gang roosts there. I'll lay it on the line, Tom. If they learn you're here they will figure you are lookin' for trouble and they are quick-trigger lads."

"I'll be moseyin' along tomorrow morning," Tom said.

"You shouldn't have come back." Heilman laid a hearty hand on Tom's shoulder. "Take my advice, son. Light out. Pull your freight. And *pronto*."

"You bet. I'll do just that." Tom wondered whether back of Heilman's friendly manner his mind was figuring on a plan to get rid of him more finally. "California looks good to me."

As if by an afterthought Heilman tossed a casual question at Fallon. "By the way, did you happen to see in Tucson anything of a young scamp named Purdy? He slickered me out of twenty bucks."

Tom answered this guileless question with a face blandly innocent. "Yeah, I saw him a couple of times on the street. Well, I'll be drifting, Mr. Heilman. It's the sack for me. Much obliged for the warning. I'll keep my eyes peeled certain."

He walked up the trail to Tex Scully's house. Nora opened the door. She called over her shoulder to her husband, "It's that shootin' terror of the hills Tom Fallon." After which she put her arms around him and kissed his cheek.

Scully jumped up in mock alarm. "Hey, what's going on here?"

"Don't shoot!" Tom cried, and flung his hands up.

The shotgun guard pounded their visitor on the back. "Boy, we're sure enough glad to see you. Sit down and spill the story of what's been happening to you."

"I got into some trouble if that's what you mean."

"Not the way we heard it. The paper says you 'most stopped Dutch Frater's clock, and a fellow who came in on the stage says he saw you stand up to Faunce at the depot when he got rambunctious."

"Correction. It was Sheriff Dunham who stopped Faunce from massacreeing me. I did have some luck with Frater, mostly because he got in a hurry and played his hand badly."

"We want the whole story. From the time I saw you last at the Half Way station after our run-in with the Pachies."

Tom sketched it for them, omitting private details and the meeting with Purdy.

"So they broke Todd out of jail," Scully said. "He got in here yesteday with Faunce. I wondered how he came to be free. The fellow on the stage said Jeb Purdy was in Tucson with Faunce. Yeager was with the others when they showed up at the Fork. And Curt's daughter. Maybe Jeb stayed in Tucson."

The pause that followed seemed to Scully significant. His eyes searched those of his friend. "How about that, Tom?"

"Yes, he stayed there." Tom's voice was low and troubled.

Tex made a guess. "Curt left him there to bump you off."

"It looks like that."

"But you slipped out of town and fooled him."

"I might as well tell you. He got to me before I could leave."

"And then?"

"I couldn't help myself. I had to kill him."

"You poor boy," Nora murmured softly.

He told the Scullys how the fight was forced on him and how the position of the sun had given him a lucky break.

"Glory be!" cried Tex. "I'll say you had luck. Purdy was the top killer in this corner of Arizona."

Presently Nora asked a question. "Why did you come back here—to see Mary Landon?"

Tom smiled. "To see another girl," he said.

"What other girl? I didn't know you had met any other here."

"She isn't here. She is at the Circle C F. Nancy Faunce."

"Have you gone crazy?" Nora wanted to know.

Fallon told them the story of the kidnaping and what he and Husky Sowers had in mind.

"Can't be done," Tex announced. "Nobody but a pair of harebrained kids would try it."

Tom thought it could. Faunce had no reason to distrust Sowers. Husky was smart and game. Nancy would not be held a prisoner in her room but would have the run of the ranch. Why couldn't they get away?

Nora watched her husband and guessed what he was thinking. "No. You're not going with them, Tex," she let him know sharply.

"Now, Nora, I didn't say a thing about going with them," Tex reproached her. But there was guilt in his grin.

"He couldn't go if he wanted to," Tom assured Nora. "This is a two-man job. Our idea is to get Nancy away without gun smoking." He explained it in more detail.

Nora warmed to the plan. "If you get her this far bring her into town at night, right to this house. We could keep her hidden a week if necessary."

She flung a parting shot at him. "I was hoping Mary Landon was your girl instead of this Miss Faunce."

"Mary has got another fellow and so has Nancy Faunce," he said. "Me, I'm sitting out in the cold."

"Then they are both lucky," she retorted saucily. "How could a girl live comfortably with such a pepperpot?"

Cochise Street was dark as Tom walked up the lower end of it. He was passing an adobe harness shop when a bullet whipped past his head and sent a spatter of dirt from the soft brick. As he crouched low and ran the gun roared again. He dived into the darkness of an alley, dashed down it, and raced along the back of the buildings close to the wall of the gorge.

He knocked on the back door of the lodging house and Mary pushed back the bolt to let him in.

"Anything the matter?" she asked, surprised at the haste with which he bolted the door.

"Somebody doesn't like me," he explained. "Took two shots at me."

Mary locked the front door and pulled the blind down in the kitchen. She made him a cup of coffee before she asked him who had done it.

"I'm only guessing but I think it was a man who told me an hour ago how concerned he was for my safety," he answered dryly. "Name of the gentleman is Heilman."

He could see how troubled she was. That was natural, he thought, because they were friends. It did not occur to him that she was more emotionally involved than he, that he alone woke dreams in her heart.

When he came down from his room next morning he found breakfast ready for him. Mary had heard him moving about as he dressed. He was stirred at her kindness and when he looked into her lovely long-lashed eyes the urge was strong in him to kiss her. But some instinct warned him that he had better not. His goodbye was a handshake.

Darkness had not lifted when the two young men rode out of the gorge. Husky knew this country well and they left the road to strike into the hills. They made a long day's ride of it, avoiding both small settlements and ranch houses. It was important that Faunce should not learn Fallon had companioned Sowers on the journey.

Behind the jagged mountain range the sun was setting when Husky mentioned that they were on the Circle C F range. It was a rough country of deep washes, heavy brush, and gorges that led to hidden hill pockets. Down in the valley the ranch house lay, a huddle of buildings surrounding the one in which Faunce lived.

Husky led the way through prickly pear and cholla covered flats to slopes where yucca and ocotillo flourished. Above these were great tumbles of rock flung up a million years ago by earth upheavals. They wound in and out among the boulders to a cove where a small mountain stream emerged from a gorge on its tumultuous way to the flats below. Here Husky swung from the saddle.

"This is it," he said.

They picketed the horses, unloaded the kyack, built a fire of brush, and cooked supper. After which Husky resaddled.

Tom felt a momentary regret that he had involved his friend in this dangerous enterprise. "Play it close to yore belly," he warned. "If Faunce gets a notion you're tied up with me you'll be a goner."

"This is gonna be duck soup," Husky answered as he swung to the saddle. "I did a li'l business with Curt once, driving some rustled longhorns from Sonora. He'll figure me still one of the boys."

The night was chill, but Tom had brought blankets with him. He rolled up in them and with his saddle for a pillow fell asleep almost at once and did not awaken until the rays of the sun slanted over the boulders and hit the floor of the cove.

He watered the horses and picketed them in another spot where they could graze on uncropped grass. For breakfast he had leftovers from the night before. In the daytime he could not light a fire lest the smoke be seen. After the sun had warmed the cove he bathed in a pool of the creek and lay for a time undressed to let the heat beat comfortably on his relaxed body.

Life in the open had taught him patience. He had to wait, probably for several days, until he heard from Husky. There was no use fretting. Later he would catch two or three fish that he would cook after darkness fell. From a pocket of his saddlebags he brought a book, *Oliver Twist*, and settled himself against a flat boulder. He had not finished high school when he left the classroom for a more active life, but he had a sense of values in his reading. He felt that though Dickens was a great writer he would have been better if he had not hammered so hard to get his effects. He was, Tom thought, a tear jerker.

CHAPTER 21

Husky jiggled at a road gait along the lane leading to the yard of the Circle C F. Tired though he was, he had a sense of pleasurable excitement in this adventure and he gave it expression by humming an old Hoosier folk tune.

Chicken in the bread pan,
Pickin' up a-dough;
Granny, will yore hen peck?
No, chile, no.

The ranch yard was an untidy clutter of disorder. Rusted farm machinery, a rimless wagon wheel, a wornout Mexican saddle, a broken-down buggy with its upholstery stuffing gaping, the equipment for shoeing horses, all littered the place and made it an eyesore. Evidently Faunce took no pride in the appearance of his ranch.

A man was standing in the doorway of the bunkhouse when Husky swung from the saddle. "Hi, Tennessee," Sowers sang out cheerfully.

"Doggone if it ain't Husky," the man exclaimed. "Ridin' the chuck line, I bet."

"You done said it, fellow," Husky agreed. "I was scrapin' the bottom of the barrel when I left Tucson."

"Couldn't raise two bits for a square meal at the Shoo Fly, I reckon."

The foreman, Ed Shell, came to the door. He was a big man, rough and weathered, with cauliflower ears. There was temper in his beady eyes. His cantankerous disposition had led him into many rough and tumble fights. Since he rode his men hard they did not like him. He had nothing against Husky, but his voice held a snarling note.

"Curt know you're here?" he demanded.

"He hasn't that pleasure yet," Husky admitted lightly.

"Well, go tell him. He decides who stays and who doesn't."

Tennessee said, "I'll take care of yore broomtail, Husky."

"Leave it stand till you hear from Curt," the foreman ordered. "Husky may have to start traveling again."

"Betcha I won't," Sowers replied.

Stiff-legged from the long ride, Husky walked to the Big House* and knocked on the door. Nancy Faunce opened it.

"You want to see Mr. Faunce?" she asked.

He told her that he did. Curt's voice boomed a question. "Who's there?"

_____
* The home of the ranch owner was often called the Big House to distinguish it from the bunkhouse.

129

"One of the men," she answered.

Husky set her right. "No, Miss Faunce. Husky Sowers."

Faunce came to the door. "Thought you were in Tucson," he said curtly.

"Left there Tuesday."

It occurred to the ranchman that he might be the bearer of news. He walked with the young man to the end of the porch.

"Anybody send you here?" he snapped.

"No, sir. I'm on the chuck line and just drifted this way. Thought I might get a job of some kind."

"Anything happen in Tucson after I left?" Faunce inquired, his hard eyes fixed on those of the cowboy.

"Yes, sir. Afraid I've got bad news for you. Jeb Purdy got himself killed."

"What!" The shock of this unexpected news showed in the startled eyes of Faunce. They were filled with incredulous amazement.

"He got in a gunfight with that lawman Fallon and was rubbed out."

"By Fallon?"

"That's right, sir."

"Are you sure? Were you there?"

"I heard the shots and saw the crowd but didn't get there till after it was over. Purdy was lying dead on the ground."

Faunce could not understand how Purdy had allowed himself to become the victim in the battle. He had the advantages of skill and of choosing the time and place. The rancher poured questions at Sowers angrily until he had drawn from him an account of the fight and also the information that the coroner's jury had freed Fallon.

"Sure," Faunce stormed. "He's Marshall's pet. I reckon he's strutting around bragging how big a man he is."

"No, sir. The fellow lit out right away. He must of known it wasn't healthy for him here. Folks think he has gone to California."

"And Jeb didn't even wound the scoundrel?"

"Not a scratch." Husky enjoyed rubbing in the gunman's failure, though his voice held dutiful regret at what had occurred. "Looks like poor Jeb was careless. He got caught with the sun in his eyes."

130

The ranchman cursed Purdy for a fool. He could not hide his bitter disappointment. Knowing Purdy's reputation, he had counted on Fallon's death as certain.

Finally he waved Husky away impatiently. "None of you are worth a damn when the chips are down. But stick around. I may have use for you. Tell Shell to fix you up in the bunkhouse."

Husky was awakened from deep sleep by the gong next morning and dressed hurriedly to eat with the ranch employees. He did not ride with them that day since the boss had not yet told him he was on pay. That suited him very well. He made himself useful about the place without raising the question of wages. Wood for the cook's stove was low and he snaked in at the end of his rope dead trees which he cut into suitable length. He mended broken harness and shod horses at the outdoor blacksmith shop. All the time he was waiting for a chance to deliver to Nancy Faunce unobserved the letter from her aunt.

His happy-go-lucky manner was an asset. He did not show any unusual interest in the girl nor make any opportunity to meet her. Nobody must suspect that any talk between them was more than casual.

He was greasing a wagon the second day after his arrival when she walked past him on her way to the corral where a lad was breaking a three-year-old chestnut gelding to the saddle. At Tucson when he had seen her at the depot he had been impressed by her warmth and gaiety but now all her good spirits had vanished. The girl's unhappiness was apparent from her stricken face and listless step.

Out of the corner of his mouth he said in a low voice, "On your way back stop and watch me work for a minute."

Nancy gave one swift glance at him without losing step. His words set her heart to beating fast. This was the young fellow for whom she had opened the door the other night. She could not be sure of him. He might be only a brash cowboy trying to pick an acquaintance with her. But she did not think so. There had been something urgent in the way he had spoken.

She was back as soon as she could come without seeming to be in a hurry. Except for the cook bringing potatoes from the roothouse nobody else was in the yard.

Nancy said, "I never saw a wagon greased till now."

He pointed to the dauber and to the hub of the wagon as if he were explaining how it was done. "Pick up the magazine in that old buggy and take it with you," he told her.

Nothing more was said. Nancy noticed that her father had come to the porch from inside and was lighting a cigar. She moved toward the house, stopping only to pick up the magazine.

Curt Faunce looked down at her as she came up the steps. "Still sulking?" he jeered.

"That's your word for it," she answered, and moved past him into the house.

His gaze followed her angrily. He resented the contempt for him she did not take the trouble to disguise. At times he was tempted to take a whip to her. He was sadist enough to enjoy the thought of lashing her lovely legs until she begged for mercy but there was a cautious streak in him that made him realize it would be wise not to drive her feeling against him as far as bitter hatred.

Nancy went to her bedroom, bolted the door, and took from the magazine a letter written by her aunt. It told her that Husky Sowers had come to help her escape and that she could trust him entirely, and that Tom Fallon was hidden somewhere on the ranch ready to assist at the proper time. They were taking a great risk and she must be careful not to let her father suspect there was help at hand for her. This letter she ought to destroy at once after reading it. In every line she felt Jennie Harshaw's anxiety and deep love for her.

In her room was a fireplace where dead ashes had gathered. She burned the letter and with a poker stirred the ashes so as to conceal what she had done. A weight was lifted from her heart. She had friends working for her escape. One of them was Tom Fallon. He would see that no harm came to her. She had such confidence in him that she was sure success in getting away was only a matter of time.

The news of Jeb Purdy's death had been told the men in the bunkhouse by Husky the morning after he reached the ranch. It had excited great interest. Jeb had lived here with them but had been one set apart on account of his record as a killer. They had been respectfully wary of him, careful not to offend. Now they talked of him at every meal. They wanted to know what kind of fellow this Fallon was and all about the trouble that had caused the fight. It appeared that Husky hardly knew the deputy. The fact that he had shot down Dutch Frater had brought him considerable notoriety. Probably he would be considered a sure enough bad man after knocking off Purdy. He did not look so gosh awful tough to Husky. Just a run-of-the-range cowpoke who had got himself appointed a lawman.

Tennesee chipped in with an opinion. "I seen him at the fiesta when Curt was fixin' to get him hanged. He was plenty game, but I wouldn't say he looked like any Bill Hickok."

When Nancy joined her father at breakfast the day after receiving her aunt's letter Curt noticed that her attitude did not seem so stiffly hostile. She even joined in conversation with him.

"Decided to make the best of it?" he asked her.

"I might as well," she replied. "It doesn't do any good to stay mad."

"All it does is make it harder on yourself." He put a question to her abruptly. "Did you ever meet a fellow who calls himself Tom Fallon?"

She was instantly on guard. "Yes, he was with the stage when the Apaches attacked it," Nancy said.

"I didn't know that. Well, I can give you some news about him. The day after we left Tucson he killed another man and pulled his freight for California."

Nancy stared at him, big-eyed with surprise and shock. "Who did he kill?"

"One of my boys—Jeb Purdy."

"But—why?"

"A killer does not need any reason. It is his nature."

The girl inquired for the particulars but made no attempt to defend Tom. She apparently accepted Curt's account of the affair. It was important that her father should not suspect she had any interest in the man he hated. She could wait and get the truth from Husky.

As they rose from the table she asked if she could take a ride. He told her she could ride to the Four Corners with one of his men to get the mail. She hoped her guard would be Husky but in that she was out of luck. The man Curt selected was Yeager.

"Take mighty good care of her," Faunce instructed him with obvious double meaning. "She is my only daughter."

"I won't let her outa my sight, boss," the man promised.

Though Nancy was disappointed, she was no longer unhappy. To canter over the mesa in the pure sunlight of Arizona surrounded by the mountain spurs reaching into the desert like great fingers was a delight to quicken young blood. She could forget the gross hulk of the man riding beside her. Somewhere in these hills, perhaps looking down on them at this very moment, was the friend who had come to rescue her.

She worried about him. This man Purdy had been her father's gunman. Curt Faunce wanted Tom killed and it was likely he had left the man to destroy him. She felt sure the story he had told her was not true, that Tom had lain in wait and shot without warning. But if one of the Circle C F riders discovered him in the hills and reported this to his boss there was no doubt in her mind that Fallon would be hunted down like a wolf.

Nancy put out a feeler to test the story Faunce had related.

"My father tells me Jeb Purdy was killed the day after we left Tucson. Do you know how it happened?"

Yeager shifted the cud of tobacco from one cheek to the other. "Didn't he tell you how?"

"Only that a deputy sheriff named Fallon did it."

The cowboy grinned. "I don't reckon any of us will go into mourning. Jeb wasn't popular. Too quick on the trigger. Always lookin' for trouble. Well, he certain found it this time."

"I suppose they must have had a quarrel about something."

"I dunno about that. Jeb could work up a fuss for no reason at all. He just picked on the wrong man this time. I ain't heard no regrets. Fact is we was plum tired of him." It occurred to Yeager that he was talking too much. "Not that any of us wished him any harm, y'understand."

"He was with you that night Father snatched me at Levine's."

"That's right. If someone had told him he would be dead inside of twenty-four hours he would of thought the fellow plumb crazy. Jeb figured there wasn't a man in the world could outgun him. It just goes to show."

What it went to show he did not explain.

"Father says that this Fallon lay in wait and ambushed Jeb," she said casually.

He slid a sly grin at her. "If Curt told you that I reckon he must of known what he was talkin' about."

When they returned to the ranch steading Husky sauntered forward to meet them. He said to Yeager, "I'll take care of Miss Nancy's horse if you like."

That suited Yeager. He liked to slide out of work when he could. He led his mount to the stable, unsaddled, and turned the animal loose in the pasture.

Husky took his time unfastening the cinch.

"You burned the letter?" he asked.

She assured him she had.

"How close does Curt watch you?"

"All the time. Except when I am in the house I am never out of sight of some one of his men."

"Do you think we could fix it for me to take you on yore ride?"

"Not a chance of it. If I asked for you he would be suspicious at once."

"Could you get out of yore room at night unnoticed?"

"I don't see how. The door is locked on the outside and the window is barred."

Husky explained that the escape must be arranged to allow them as much time as possible before their absence was discovered. Tom Fallon would join them when they reached the hills but he could not lend any help at all until then. It might be possible to surprise her guard and make a run for the mountains but that would not leave them enough time to get away. If she did not return to he ranch when due Curt would cut off the passes and comb the country for them. A plan must be worked out that was likely to succeed.

They talked for only a minute or two while Husky unsaddled the horse. They dared not stay together any longer.

Husky told her not to worry. Their chance would come. Curt would get a little careless and the bird would fly out of the not so gilded cage.

She gave him a long warm look of gratitude. He was doing all this for her because she was a girl who needed help, with no thought of any gain for himself. It lifted her heart to know that there were men like that in the world.

135

Her father stopped Nancy on the way to her room. "We're going to have a man for supper tonight that I want you to meet," he told her.

"Why do you want me to meet him?" she asked.

"It is time you were getting married. This man would make a suitable husband. He has one of the best ranches in the valley, a large herd of cattle, and money in the bank. You couldn't do better."

Her eyes sparked with anger. "If he had a dozen ranches and a million cattle I wouldn't marry him."

"That's no way to talk. You haven't seen him." His heavy voice bore down harshly on her. "If you are thinking of that la-de-da army lieutenant you can forget him. He'll never have a dime over his salary. I'm going to see you marry well."

"When I marry it will be to please myself not you," she said defiantly.

"I know what's best for you and you'll take the man I choose. Don't forget that I am your father and won't put up with any nonsense from you."

She faced him, her slender body straight and stiff. "I'll never marry a man you choose no matter how much you beat me."

Nancy walked into her room and shut the door.

Faunce and the stranger were seated at the supper table when Nancy joined the men there. Neither of them rose.

Her father said, "Meet Jasper Pike, Nancy."

"Glad to meetcha," Pike said.

Nancy bowed very slightly.

Jasper Pike was a stocky man, heavy-shouldered and square-jawed. He had the dry weathered face of leather that years in the untempered sun gives. His eyes were marble-blue and cold as ice. Throughout the meal they drifted to Nancy often. The girl ate in silence, her gaze never touching his.

The men talked of ranch matters and of politics.

When they had finished eating Pike spoke to Nancy for the second time. "I'll be seeing you often," he said.

She knew that her father had discussed the marriage with Pike. The smirk on the man's face told her so. He was taking her for granted as already his. Anger stirred in her again.

"A cat may look at a king," she said.

She thought for an instant that Faunce was going to hit her. He restrained the impulse. "She has been badly brought up by her aunt, Jasper," he said. "A little discipline will change that."

Pike grinned. He was of the same opinion. "I'll be moseyin' home now. We don't have to rush this, Curt. Give her a little time."

He walked heavily out of the room followed by Faunce.

CHAPTER 22

In his life as a range rider Tom Fallon had learned to spend days far from the sight of other humans with no sense of loneliness. This solitude at times filled a need in him, gave him an escape from the world of people into the peace of one where he was alone with the sun and the eternal mountains and the far stars at night.

But he did not find this rest now. It chafed him to be tied to this spot with no information of what was going on at the Circle C F. He could not help being worried. He was letting Husky take the post of danger. Already their plan to rescue Nancy might have blown sky-high. Faunce could have learned that he and Husky had traveled together. Or Heilman have sent word to the ranch that he had been back in Copper Fork. In the long empty hours his imagination became active with forebodings.

Much of the time he spent lying on a flat rock searching the valley below with field glasses. Occasionally he saw a rider moving about the business of the ranch. Often the glasses picked up bunches of cattle grazing, and twice he caught sight of a file of antelope crossing a hill slope. Once he sighted a man and a woman on horseback. Since he understood that Faunce employed only men on the Circle C F, he guessed that the woman was Nancy. Her companion was probably the girl's father or one of his men sent as a guard.

On the morning of the fourth day he was fishing the little

brook for trout when a faint sound brought him to attention. He laid down the stick he was using for a rod. What he had heard was the breaking of a dry branch, perhaps under the weight of somebody's foot.

He crouched behind a boulder, his senses tuned to wariness. A man came into sight on the rock rim above. He stood looking down into the miniature mountain park below him. What he saw evidently surprised him. Two picketed horses. The ashes of a campfire. Blankets, supplies of food, a saddle. Presently, very cautiously, he tiptoed down through the rock outcrop, then stopped to search the park with shallow light blue eyes set too near together in a crafty face.

He was a long loosely built man wearing a red bandanna. In his hand was a pistol, held close to his body, just above the hip. Evidently he had a sense of insecurity, though he thought the camper probably was a casual hunter.

Tom rose from behind the boulder. "Nice to see you in circulation again, Mr. Todd," he said.

The outlaw's long jaw dropped. His instant thought was that the deputy had come to drag him back to jail. He had a gun in his hand and Fallon did not. But a .45 hung in a holster at the young fellow's hip within easy reach. Why had he not drawn it before he showed himself? Maybe he was not alone.

"I got friends the other side of the rim," Todd ventured. "If I holler they'll swarm over here and git you."

Fallon thought that improbable. Only one rider would be sent to comb this rocky region where cattle seldom grazed. He played his hunch. "Let's hear you whoop it up real loud."

His bluff called, Todd tried another approach. "No sense you and me having a fuss, Mr. Fallon. Thing to do is talk this over reasonable."

"Why not?" Tom agreed lightly. "Start off by putting that gun back where it won't go off accidental."

Todd holstered his weapon reluctantly. This might be a trick. "You couldn't ever get me off the ranch, Mr. Fallon," he said. "You'd be seen and bumped off sudden."

Though Tom did not show it, he realized he was in a dilemma. If Todd went back to the ranch and reported that he was camped here the best Tom could hope would be to get out of the district alive. There would be no chance of rescuing Nancy. He must prevent Todd from getting in touch with Curt Faunce. He could not kill the man. That was not in his nature. To keep him a prisoner would be very difficult. Yet that was what he must do.

He sauntered forward. "You have put me to considerable trouble by lighting out from jail the way you did," he said affably. "Might have known I'd come after you."

Todd felt unhappily that he had jumped from the frying pan into the fire. Before he had walked out of the jail he realized that his partners in crime distrusted him. On the way down to Levine's Garden Purdy had said with savage scorn that he was a menace to them and ought to be destroyed. The news of that young ruffian's death had been a relief to him, but he was aware that Faunce was of the same opinion as Jeb. He knew it by the way Curt's cold eyes watched him. Before reaching the ranch he had made an attempt to leave the party and had been brought back before he had gone a mile. Since then the fear in him had ridden his thoughts day and night.

He had not known which way to turn. To make a getaway to Mexico would not be good, for Colonel Kosterlitzky of the *Rurales* had him in his black book for raiding cattle from the ranches of Sonora. But certainly he did not want to be dragged back to Tucson or to Tomahawk with the gallows facing him.

"I dunno why you've got it in for me," Todd whined. "I never done you any harm."

"Not for want of trying," Tom reminded him. "But this isn't personal. I'm paid to run down bandits."

Todd stepped back. "I ain't going with you. A minute ago I could of cut you down certain. You quit crowdin' me." In the man's words was a threat but in his eyes panic.

"You're under arrest," Tom told him. "Take it easy."

The outlaw retreated another step. His heel caught on the stirrup *tapedero* of the saddle and he went over backward. Fallon anticipated the man's next reaction and moved fast. A heavy heel crushed down on Todd's wrist as his hand closed on the butt of his pistol.

The fallen man let out a yelp of pain and nursed the injured wrist in supporting fingers. "Goddlemighty, you've busted my arm," he wailed.

Tom relieved him of his pistol. "You are sure a curly wolf," he chided. "I get so scared I play rough."

"I was only aimin' to cover you so I could get away," Todd complained.

Tom grinned. "You should have explained that before you started to draw."

Fallon took pains to show no hostility. There was even a touch of friendly warmth in his voice. His prisoner was no hardened villain like Frater or Faunce but a cowboy with no rock-bottom principle in him who had fallen among thieves and followed the line of least resistance. It was in Tom's mind that after the situation had eased Todd could be led to give him information.

"Let's have a smoke," he said. "I don't want to make this too hard on you. Since we've got to be together for two-three days we don't need to act like strange dogs bristling for a fight."

Todd agreed that this was a good idea. He thought that if his captor relaxed his vigilance there might be a chance to escape. He was the type of man who has to tell his troubles and seek sympathy. Presently he was pouring out to Fallon the fear hanging heavily over him, that Curt Faunce had him marked for death at a convenient time.

"They're scared I blabbed a lot of stuff to you when I was in jail," he said in explanation.

"Who else as well as Curt?" Tom asked.

Todd did not fall for that innocent question. "Why, nobody else now. I was thinking of Jeb Purdy. When I heard you had settled his hash I was plumb tickled certain."

By a natural shift Tom diverted the talk to the Circle C F ranch. He learned that both the owner and the foreman were unpopular with the hands. Ed Shell was a hard boss and never had a pleasant word for anybody. Faunce was both mean and bad-tempered.

None of this was news to Tom but it led to a mention of Nancy. Todd told the story of her abduction. She was now virtually a prisoner, he said, though she was allowed to wander about the yard and to ride with one of the men Curt could trust not to let her get away. At night the door of her room was locked and the window was barred. A sour grin flitted for a moment over the outlaw's face. "Keeps the gal in and the men out," he leered.

140

They shared the small camp tasks such as moving the three picketed horses to fresh grazing grounds and preparing dinner after darkness fell. Todd protested against being roped at night but his grumbling did not reach the point of active resistance. He knew he was physically no match for this broad-shouldered youth so tough of body and mind, even if he had the hardihood to stand up to him. Fallon tied him securely hand and foot with one end of the reata fastened around his own ankle to give warning of any jerking at the lariat. The deputy was a light sleeper and he knew that any attempt to escape would awaken him.

CHAPTER 23

Curt Faunce scowled at the letter in his hand which a rider had just brought to him from Copper Fork. It was signed "A Friend," with a postscript below, "Burn this at once." The text of the letter read:

I got bad news, Curt, for you and me both. It has come to me straight from Tucson that Jeb Purdy got himself killed by your enemy Tom Fallon. This was a surprise that sure jolted me. Seems they fought it out in the street and Purdy went down.

But that ain't all. Fallon was here in town yesterday. First I knew he was still alive was when I met him. We had a talk. I slid in a question about whether he had seen Jeb in Tucson. He came back at me cool as you please that he had met him there. Not a word about having killed him.

Fallon claimed he was going back to Tomahawk and was then heading for California. That didn't listen good to me. He left today. But Alabam came in on the stage today and tells me they did not pass Fallon on the way. Alabam is now a guard on the stage and would know if this lawman had been on the road.

He has got as many lives as a cat. A friend of yours

took two shots at him last night with a .45 but it was too dark to see well and he got away.

I don't know where Mr. Sudden Death headed for but it looks to me we ought to find out and fix it sure so he won't still be on our necks.

Faunce did not burn the letter as directed. One who called himself a friend today might be an enemy tomorrow. He put it into a small tin box which he locked. This would give him a hold over the writer. Heilman was an independent fellow who more than once had challenged the leadership of Faunce.

Nancy passed through the room as he was locking his desk. The tin box was inside. "If you are going out tell Shell to send back to the house the boy who brought me a letter just now," he ordered her. "Slim Hardy is his name."

He waited on the porch for the messenger. He was in a savage mood. The lad had been starting to the stable with his horse but he turned the animal over to Husky and returned to the house.

"You got this letter from Heilman three days ago," Faunce snarled. "Where in the hell have you been all that time?"

"Why, I stopped off a couple of days at the Bar Double V. Mr. Heilman didn't tell me there was any hurry. He said it was about a bull you was thinkin' of buying." Slim Hardy's explanation was offered in an apologetic voice. He saw explosive rage in the cold slaty eyes of the ranchman.

"So when you are sent with a message to me you decide whether it is important and waste two days fooling around with that redheaded girl at the Bar Double V." With no warning Faunce smashed his heavy fist into the boy's face and walked back into the house.

Young Hardy was out cold. Sowers brought from the pump half a bucket of water and sloshed it over his face. The youngster looked up and with some help scrambled to his feet. He swayed dizzily.

"I sure got a lollapalooza," he said. "My head feels like a hammer hit it." He added with futile anger: "What business he got hittin' me? I don't work for him and I came out of my way to bring him a letter. He acts like he thought he was God Almighty."

"You're right, kid," Husky said. "He's a hellraisin' mean

142

bad hombre. But say it soft around here so nobody can hear you. Some of the ranch boys will do to take along when the going is rough but a few are Faunce's jackals."

Slim had intended to spend the night at the ranch but the welcome he had been given changed his mind. He mounted his sorrel and jiggled down the lane. But before he left he voiced a hope.

"When Curt Faunce gets his comeuppance, as he sure will soon, I hope I'll be there to lend a hand in the job."

After supper Ed Shell walked to the big house to make report. The boss and his daughter were still at the table. What he had to tell was that one of the riders had caught sight of a camp in the hills. He had seen two men there and three picketed horses. His first impulse had been to drop down to the camp and investigate but he decided since they had not seen him to leave unnoticed and give the news to the foreman.

"Bring the man up here," Faunce ordered. "I want to talk with him. Who is he?"

"Cad Yeager. I'll get him."

Nancy felt the heart die under her ribs. Yeager must have discovered the camping ground of Tom Fallon. They would come on him without warning and kill him.

Yeager said that he had not been within two or three hundred yards of the camp, not close enough to recognize the men, but one of the horses looked like the white-splashed bronc Rufe Todd rode.

"What would Rufe be doing up there?" Shell wanted to know. "Come to think of it he didn't ride with us today."

"He wasn't in the bunkhouse last night," Yeager said. "I sleep next him."

"If he is runnin' out on us what's he stickin' around there for?" Shell asked. "And who is the other man with him?"

Faunce slammed his great fist down on the table so hard the dishes jumped. "That killer Fallon," he shouted. "Roosterin' up there waiting for a chance to get me."

Nancy felt a faintness run through her. She caught the edge of the table for support. The room swam before her. Then the wave of dizziness passed. "That's nonsense," she said. "He's not a fool. He daren't come within fifty miles of here."

Her father looked at her angrily. "What do you know

143

about what he would do?" He rose, in sudden decision. "Rout out the men. We're going after him."

He stamped out of the room, Shell at his heels.

Nancy stared at the looking glass hanging on the wall. She saw a white-faced girl with fear-filled eyes. From that palsied terror she woke to swift action. The cook looked in surprise at her as she raced through the kitchen and out of the back door. She had to find Husky without her father knowing it. To cross the yard in the open would not be possible without being seen by half a dozen men. She ran close to the fence behind the roothouse and the wagon shed. Already the night was filled with the stir of movement. Men were pouring out of the bunkhouse flinging surprised questions at one another. Her father's voice snapped out orders to run the *remuda* up and saddle.

A young man came round to the side of the bunkhouse to pick up his saddle from a rack on which it hung. He was a boyish friendly lad whose eyes she had more than once seen resting on her.

"Pete," she called softly to him.

He looked around, surprised, and his glance found her.

"Will you do something for me?" she asked. "It's very important."

"You bet I will," he answered.

"Find Husky Sowers and tell him to meet me here at once." Her voice was low and there was a pleading urgency in it. "Hurry—hurry, please! And don't let anybody else know."

He laid the saddle back on the rack and disappeared into the gathering darkness. It seemed to Nancy that she waited hours, though it could not have been more than a few minutes. Hurried footsteps, the creak of saddle leather, excited voices. The sound of them reached her as she stood close to the shadowed wall.

She moved out of sight behind the corner of the adobe building when a man brought a horse to the rack to get a saddle. The animal jerked its head up nervously and the man muttered, "Damn you, stand still." He fitted the blanket into place, threw a saddle over it, and tightened the cinch, then tied the bronco by a slipknot to the cross pole of the rack. This done, he disappeared.

Nancy recognized the horse. It was the chestnut her father usually rode. She guessed it had been in the corral. Most of the horses had not yet been run up from the pasture.

A man appeared so suddenly beside her that she was startled. The man was Sowers.

"Father has found out where Tom is camping," she told him breathlessly. "He is going now to—to kill him."

"So that is what all the fuss is about," he answered. "I had a notion it must be something like that. I'd better get a move on me."

"You must save him," she cried, scarcely above a whisper. "Tell him to forget about me and get away from here."

"Don't worry. I'll reach Tom's camp before they do." His eyes lit with impish glee. "Nice of Curt to leave his own mare saddled here for me."

He swung to the saddle and grinned down at her. "Get back to the house before Curt misses you and *don't go to bed*."

Husky turned the horse from the yard and followed the way that Nancy had come from the house to use the buildings as a protection from observation. He started at a walk and held to that speed until he had passed the house. Presently the girl heard the faint rumor of galloping hoofs.

She went back to the house and stopped in the kitchen for a word with the Mexican cook. "It would be nice if you forgot I left the house in case Father asks," she said, and gave him her warmest smile.

"Si—si, senorita, Pedro forget," he promised.

Nancy had no thought of going to bed. How could she until she had learned whether Tom escaped the trap? But she wondered why Husky had told her to stay up.

She heard her father's strident voice demanding to know what had become of his horse. There was commotion for a time, stirred up by Curt's anger. It died away. From her window she saw the mounted men start to move. they jogged down the lane at a road gait. Soon the night was silent except for the lonesome bark of a coyote. But there would be no peace in the heart of Nancy until her father's explosive anger brought her the good news that he had failed to find his enemy.

In Curt's eagerness to catch Tom he had forgotten to lock

up Nancy. It was in her mind that this was an opportunity to escape she ought not to overlook. Yet she did not feel sure she had better try to saddle a horse and leave. Probably she would not get far and to go was a desertion of her friends.

Still uncertain of what she would do, she walked to the front porch. A man was sitting on the top step smoking a pipe. He was wearing a sagging belt equipped for business.

"Pleasant evening, Miss Nancy," he said maliciously.

The man was Ed Shell.

She went back into the house and stood for a moment in front of her father's desk. In his haste he had forgotten something else. The key was in the lock. She waved aside her scruples and unlocked the desk. A tin box lay on a shelf. Several times she had seen Curt put papers in it which he evidently wanted to keep secret. The box was locked and she could not open it. She suddenly made up her mind and took it to her room.

CHAPTER 24

Though Tom Fallon kept a close eye on his prisoner, he was of opinion that even if Rufe Todd escaped he would not return to the Circle C F. Faunce would want to know where he had been and no story the cowboy told would satisfy him. If he mentioned that he had been at Fallon's camp the rancher's fear of betrayal would become sharper. Todd would not risk that, Tom thought. But it was a chance he could not take.

The two campers ate their meals together with no apparent hostility. After the sun set they risked a fire to cook their supper. The hot coffee, fried ham, and corn bread were satisfying after the cold leftovers they had eaten for breakfast and dinner.

A man's voice from the rim of the park startled them.

"Hello the camp!" it called. "Save some of that grub for me."

Tom picked up the rifle that lay close to him. "Better

come on down," he invited. "Keep your hands on the horn."

His eyes watched warily a horseman pick his way down to the floor of the mountain pocket.

"It's Slim Hardy," volunteered Todd.

The visitor dismounted and came forward to the fire. He was a boy of not more than eighteen years with a pleasant disarming grin.

"Talk about finding a needle in a haystack," he said. "Tell me I'm welcome. My belly is flat as a mashed pancake."

"What brought you here?" Tom asked.

"I'm headin' for the pass to get me down to the Bar Double V," he explained. "Saw yore smoke and drifted over."

One of the boy's eyes was swollen almost shut. From questions Tom learned that he had carried a letter from Harry Heilman to Faunce and had been knocked cold by the latter because he had taken his time on the way. At present he was not employed by any ranch but was riding the chuck line. He had no idea what was in the letter yet was dead certain that it did not please Faunce.

The news did not make Tom happy either. It was possible that Heilman had learned he and Husky Sowers were traveling together and had said so in the letter. If so, Husky would be in trouble.

Hardy watered and picketed his horse before he himself sat down to food. He had decided to spend the night there rather than go on in the dark. Tom accepted him at face value as a chance guest and not a spy. His story rang true.

They were settling for the night when a shout brought them to their feet. A rider came at a canter straight to the camp fire. "Husky Sowers," he called to forestall a shot.

He flung himself out of the saddle. "Hell's poppin'," he told Tom. "Faunce is headed this way with a dozen riders. We got to get out fast."

The first thing that Tom did was to free Todd of the rope that bound him. "You're on your own," he said. "Saddle your bronc and light out in a hurry."

Already a germ of a plan was in Tom's mind. He wanted Todd out of the picture. To young Hardy he said, "We'd better saddle too."

"How much time have we got?" Hardy asked.

"Enough. They were running up the horses from the pasture when I left," Husky replied. He walked with Tom to Fallon's picketed horse. "There can't be more than three or four men left at the ranch. It's our chance."

Tom nodded. "My thought too."

After he had saddled and cinched Hardy joined them. "You two are cookin' up something. Whatever it is, I'm in it."

Fallon said, "You'd better hit the trail for the Bar Double V, Hardy."

"You think I'm a kid," the boy objected. "Me, I wear mansized boots and I want a crack at Faunce."

Tom explained that their mission was dangerous and let it ride at that. A third man in the party might be useful.

Rufe Todd had already disappeared into the hills. None of them ever saw him again. Years later a rumor reached Arizona that he had been killed in Sonora by the *rurales* while resisting arrest.

Husky led the way down to the valley. They took with them the pack horse but left on the camp ground the kyack and what food remained. It was likely that when they departed from the ranch they would be in too much of a hurry to be encumbered with baggage.

They did not approach the ranch by way of the road. Sowers brought them to the rear of the pasture where they cut the fence wires and moved into it. He left the others in the brush and went forward on foot to reconnoiter. Another saddle was needed. It would be better to get one and have the spare horse saddled before making any attempt to contact the girl.

Through the back door he entered the stable. His nostrils warned him that somebody was not many yards distant smoking a pipe. Husky's groping fingers found the horn of a saddle that was lying on the oat bin. He lifted it very carefully to make sure the stirrups did not drag along the top of the box. Before turning he stepped backward to avoid scraping the bin and his foot struck a tin pail and knocked it over.

The smoker came into the stable. "Hey, who's there?" he asked.

"Only me," Husky drawled. "I allowed to fix my saddle girth."

"Thought you went with the others."

"No, Yorky. The old man hasn't said a word yet about hiring me. No reason why I should go along on a man hunt for him." He had dropped the saddle and was sauntering toward Yorky.

"That's funny," the man said. "I ain't seen you around since the others left." There was a dawning suspicion in his voice.

Husky's right fist traveled very fast to Yorky's chin and his left followed to the body. The back of the cowboy's head struck the door jamp and he sagged limply to the ground. Sowers dragged him into the stable and to a stall. From the man's bandanna he made and fastened a gag, then found a rope tied to a saddle and bound his hands and feet securely.

"I hate to do this to you, Yorky, but maybe it will learn you not to butt in at the wrong time," he apologized to the unconscious man.

The saddle he carried into the pasture and left it behind a clump of greasewood. Crouching low, he moved along the fence trying to discover how many men had been left at the ranch. Through the kitchen window he saw Pedro the cook. There must be more but he did not see them. He returned to the place where he had left the saddle, picked it up, and zigzagged back among the cactuses to his friends.

"All quiet along the Potomac," he reported. "Too quiet. I didn't see anybody but Yorky and Pedro. Had some conversation with Yorky but he went to sleep."

Tom was busy saddling the pack horse. He slewed his head around. "You didn't—?" His eyes asked the rest of the question.

"Gagged and tied him. That's all. But maybe you were asking did I see Miss Nancy. The answer is no. There's a light in her room."

"Let's go," Tom said. "Some of the men might be coming back."

They led the horses through the brush and tied them fifty yards from the house. In single file, crouched low, they went forward with Husky in the lead. When they reached the pasture fence Tom used clippers on the strands, his bandanna wrapped around the cutting end to prevent any sound. The back of the house lay in front of them, two rooms lighted.

Husky touched Tom on the shoulder. "The corner one is Miss Nancy's," he whispered.

149

Tom crept on hands and knees to the barred window and tapped gently on it. Nancy was pacing to and fro. She came at once to the window and lifted her fingers to her mouth lest her exclamation of gladness be overheard. Her murmured words did not reach Tom. He shook his head to let her know this. She went to a table and wrote something with a pencil. The paper she pressed against the window pane. Tom lit a match to read it. The words were:

No way out of here but through the parlor. Ed Shell and another man are sitting in it.

He nodded understanding and drew back to rejoin his companions. They decided that they must try to surprise the Circle C F men. There was a chance they might get away without firing a shot.

They edged along a wall to the front of the house, Tom now the lead man. He took the porch steps very carefully but his boot trod on and crushed a clay pipe lying on the top one. The break sounded sharp as a pistol shot if not as loud. Tom plunged through the doorway, knowing the men inside must be alerted. No surprise was possible now.

Shell was already halfway to the door. "What in the hell —!" he began, astonished at this inpour of men.

Before his .44 was clear of the holster Tom closed with him. Fallon's charge drove him back and down to the sofa where he had been sitting. He floundered on the slick horsehair, his feet struggling for a footing, Tom astride of him trying to knock the foreman out with the barrel of his pistol. The muscular arms of Shell shielded his head, then closed around his assailant. They rolled from the sofa to the floor, still in a wild tangle of flying arms and legs.

Even in the fury of the fight, as they rolled over and over each trying to pin the other down, Tom was aware that others too were engaged in battle. He heard shuffling feet, a savage oath, then the roar of a gun. To his surprise the great body of Shell collapsed in his arms. He had been shot.

Tom rose, breathless from his efforts, and recovered the weapon that had been knocked from his hand. Sowers and Hardy were still grappling with the other Circle C F man. They had him down but one of his arms was free, a smoking .45 in his hand. Tom pistol-whipped his head. He lay lax and still.

"Look out," Husky shouted.

Shell had managed to draw his pistol and was trying to raise himself to an elbow to take aim. Hardy flung himself on the wounded man and spreadeagled him on the floor. Tom tore the weapon from his hand. He sank back, no energy left in him to fight.

Tom unlocked the door of Nancy's room. Her cheeks had lost their color. Her voice shook. She came toward him trembling. When her eyes fell on the two men on the floor he thought she was going to faint. "Are they—dead?" she asked.

His arm around her waist supported her. "It's all right. Both of them will live. One of them shot the other by accident in the fight. We must not lose any time in getting started."

The color slowly beat back into her face. "I'm all right now. I knew you would come." She held in her hand a tin box. This she gave to Tom. "Keep it please. It may be important."

Shell lay on the floor helpless. His pistol had been taken from him and he was too feeble to interfere with their escape. But his hard beady eyes challenged Fallon.

"You'll never make it," he snarled. "Curt will get you certain."

Tom made no answer. They could not stop to give him first aid. But his companion, already showing signs of returning consciousness, would take care of him.

They crossed the cut wires of the fence into the pasture to the saddled horses. Tom helped Nancy mount. He had already adjusted the stirrup length. She rode astride like the men.

Since Husky knew the district he led the party. It was rough broken country slashed by dry washes, small gulches, and hill slopes. They avoided roads and took short cuts, sometimes in heavy brush and sometimes over barren wastes. The vegetation varied but all of it was spiny. Their way led across ghostly groves of saguaro, over bleak stretches strewn with greasewood and occasional patches of bisnaga, through thickets of cholla and prickly pear clutching at them with barbed savage claws.

Nancy's stockings were torn to shreds and her legs were

bleeding but she did not make any complaint. She was relieved when they drew up from the desert to the uplands where plant life was scarce. After a few hours she was weary and dropped in the saddle.

Tom fell back to ride beside her.

"Tired?" he asked.

"A little, but I don't want to stop," she answered.

He looked up into the dark sky. "Looks like the stars have all gone to bed. Maybe that's lucky for us."

"Do you think he'll catch us?"

"We'll get to Copper Fork before him. He'll waste hours hunting for me before he gets back to the ranch."

"But Copper Fork is his town. I mean he is important there and we are not. Do we have to go there?" The girl's voice showed worry.

"Wherever we go there is some danger, but look at it this way. I have friends there who will hide you. We'll get in while it is still dark. Your father will think we won't be so foolish as to stay there. He'll stop, make inquiries, and hurry on to Tomahawk."

"But you and Husky will be seen by somebody in town."

"Not if we are lucky. We won't be there more than half an hour. Our hide-out will be a hut on an abandoned mining claim up in the hills. My friends will keep us in touch with you."

Tom sounded a good deal more cheerful than he felt If Nancy had not been with them it would have been much safer. The men were inured to days and nights in the saddle with little rest but already she was showing signs of fatigue. They would have to take the journey to Tucson in short stretches and Faunce would certainly post riders in the hills to look out for them.

"I know you are awfully tired," Tom said, and promised that it would not be much farther.

"This saddle doesn't fit me, but I am all right," she answered. Presently, in a small voice, she repeated what she had told before, "I knew you would come for me."

"You can thank Husky. He took the risk and helped you more."

"Yes, Husky too. I can't thank you both enough." She

reached a small hand toward him and he took it in his strong grip.

He did not know how much her gesture meant but a warm elation pulsed through his body. He was riding knee to knee beside her and he knew that love had trapped him. For better or worse he held her in his heart and this moment would live with him a long long time.

Darkness was still heavy over the hills when they rode into the gulch to Copper Fork. Near the entrance they separated, Tom and Nancy to take the ledge trail to the house of Tex Scully, the others to wake Sam Rosenstein up quietly and buy from him provisions enough for several days.

Nora came to the door in her nightgown, freshly roused from sleep, her Irish voice warm with welcome. She left them in the front room for three or four minutes while she and Tex dressed, after which she made coffee and fried some slices of ham. Tom explained that he had to get out of the canyon with the two horses before the town woke. He stayed only for a cup of coffee and took with him a sandwich.

He asked Nora to get Nancy to bed as soon as she had breakfasted and let her have a long sleep. To Tex he explained where they would be camping and the shotgun messenger promised to have his brother Mark keep in touch with them.

Nancy followed him to the door. She begged him to be careful.

"We'll be all right and so will you," he told her. "Nobody will know you are here. You can trust Nora and Tex absolutely."

She said, "I'm sure I can," but there was wistfulness in her troubled voice. She was afraid to have Tom leave her.

He took both her hands in his and looked into her lovely eyes.

"It has to be this way, dear, but I won't be far away and it's not for long."

"I know," Nancy said. "It's just that I'm a fraidy-cat."

She smiled, tremulously. Afterwards he was not sure whether it was the forlorn smile that did it. He took her in his arms and kissed her.

Nora clapped her hands softly.

Amazed at his own rashness, Tom opened the door and

shut it behind him. As he rode down the trail he thought, *That was a crazy thing to do.* But there was exultation in his heart. She had clung to him as if she could never let him go.

CHAPTER 25

Tex Scully had his job to do riding the stage, but his brother Mark substituted as an observer to report any movements of the enemy in Copper Fork. He had as an assistant a girl who was a very good friend of his, Mary Landon. Their watchful eyes noted that six riders on very weary horses reached town six or seven hours after the fugitives. Three of the party were Curt Faunce, Jasper Pike, and Yeager.

They dismounted in front of the Crystal Palace and disappeared inside of it. A few minutes later Mark Scully pushed through the batwing doors and stopped at the bar for a beer. Four of the men were lined up there washing their dry throats with drinks. Faunce and Pike were seated at a corner table in the rear with Heilman, their heads close together in low-voiced talk.

The Circle C F men at the bar, Mark gathered from what they said to one another, had been in the saddle all night and as yet had not breakfasted. They were surly and annoyed because Curt had let them know that probably they would take the road again in an hour or two.

Mark drifted out to the street and presently saw all of them except Faunce go into the Miners' Chop House for food. The Circle C F owner had crossed the street and gone into the Landon rooming house.

Faunce had noticed when they stopped there on the way to the ranch how friendly the two girls had become and it had occurred to him that if Fallon's party had come to Copper Fork they would have put up at the Landon place.

From Mary he got no help. She had seen nothing of either Fallon or Nancy. It was not likely they could have been in town and not stayed with her, she told him. He could search the house if it was in his mind that she might be hiding them. The rancher did not trouble to do that. His opinion was that

Fallon had bypassed Copper Fork. Heilman had been positive that the escapees could not have been here without being seen.

Yet there was a lurking doubt in his mind. This girl had been a witness for Fallon at the miner's trial and she had shown kindness to Nancy. His questioning of her was rough and curt.

"If you are lying to me it will go hard with you," he threatened.

She flung out with unexpected spirit, "I suppose you will beat me as you did Nancy after you kidnapped her."

His heavy jaw set. "Keep a civil tongue in your head," he snarled.

Later she was surprised at her own courage. "I'm not your daughter. You daren't touch me. I'd tell everybody in town if you did."

He knew she was right. He could not afford to mistreat her. Her reputation was of the best. All the residents of Copper Fork respected her as a good girl and admired her for the competence with which she was earning a living for herself and Billy. The rough chivalry of the mining camp would tolerate no harm to her.

Angrily he turned away. She followed him to the door. "I hope you don't find them," she cried after him.

He swung around on the pavement, his face stamped with appalling malignity. "I am going to find and kill Fallon for certain."

Mark Scully slipped into the rooming house a few minutes after Faunce had left. "What did he want?" Mark asked. He could see that Mary was frightened.

"To find out if they had been here. He says he is going to find Tom and kill him. He is a dreadful man, Mark."

"Don't worry. I'd bet my boots Tom outlives him. I'll be going up to the camp of the boys after dark. Tex has an idea that it would be best for Miss Faunce and the others to go out with the stage tomorrow and take the train to Tucson. I'm going along. Nobody is going to attack five armed men."

"But Faunce will be waiting at Tucson."

Mark grinned cheerfully. "That's a bridge we'll cross when we come to it."

A man sitting on a rickety bench in front of a dilapidated

log cabin came to attention when he heard the sounds of a horse's hoofs striking the stony rubble. Before he could challenge the rider a voice called information to him.

"Mark Scully," it announced.

The two men by the campfire rose to meet him. While Mark unpacked tobacco and food from his saddlebags he gave them his news. "The whole caboodle of them left this afternoon. Some of them were growling like billy-be-damn because they hadn't had any sleep but Curt put the kibosh on that. He got fresh mounts and kicked them into the saddles, as you might say."

"Then he didn't find out we had been in Copper Fork," Tom said.

"No, but he did a lot of questioning before he left. The old skunk dropped in on Mary but she told him off proper. Last thing he told her was that he aimed to kill you sure."

"He certainly has a single mind about that," Tom commented. "He keeps on trying."

Mark explained to them his brother's suggestion that they leave with the stage, Miss Faunce inside and the others on horseback flanking it. This would of course be relayed to Curt but the news would not reach him before they had taken the train to Tucson. A wire to Sheriff Marshall would insure his meeting them at the station.

Tom accepted this plan but with an amendment. "I'd like to take another passenger with us as far as Tomahawk."

Husky slanted a grin at him. He knew the passenger Tom had in mind. They had broken the lock of the tin box and examined its contents and found evidence of more than one of Curt's crooked deals but the paper interesting them most was the letter from Heilman.

"Mr. Lawman aims to combine business with pleasure," Husky explained to the others.

"With the help of Tex," the deputy added. "Todd did some talking while we were alone. This letter from Heilman to Curt will help hang Harry. I'm going to take him to Sheriff Dunham if I can."

"You or Harry, one will go out in smoke," Mark predicted. "He is a guy tall in the saddle."

"Unless we can trap him. If we are lucky we can." Tom outlined the scheme. They would delay their departure for a day. The morning after the return of Tex on the stage from

156

Tomahawk Tex would send a boy to Heilman with the message that he had a letter from Faunce he had been asked to deliver personally. Last night he had got in too late and now he had not time to go to the Crystal Palace but Harry could get it if he came down to the stage office. Taken by surprise, with luck Heilman could be arrested before he had a chance to draw a gun.

"Maybe he won't come down to the office," Mark suggested.

"If he doesn't I'll have to come back here later and get him," Tom said. "But I think he'll bite. He'll be anxious to hear whether Faunce captured us and he knows a letter may come from his sidekick any time."

"I can't get used to the idea that Harry Heilman is a crook," Slim Hardy put in. "I've always liked him. He treated me fine."

"He has always treated me well too," Tom replied grimly. "Except the time when he ambushed me at night and just missed killing me. But I get your point, Slim. He is a big handsome man, hearty and popular, game as they come. If he hadn't a twisted mind he might be a big man in this territory instead of being a miscreant who has to be rubbed out to protect society. At some turn of the road he went bad."

"You let Rufe Todd go," Hardy protested. "Can't you forget Heilman?"

"I let Todd go because his presence interfered with a more urgent matter, the rescue of Miss Faunce. Anyhow, Todd was only a weak tool of stronger men. He was no good. But he wasn't important. Heilman is a much greater danger. Maybe he can get off with a life sentence. I have a sneaking hope he does. There is something about him you can't help liking. But that does not mean I can shut my eyes to what he has done. He knew what he was getting into and he has to pay for it."

Hardy nodded assent. "You're right. I see that. It's just that he is so much a man I hate to think he's rotten."

They discussed the details of their plan. It was important that the timing be perfect.

CHAPTER 26

After an early breakfast Nancy Faunce walked down the ledge trail with Tex Scully in front of her and Mark behind. The town was coming to life for the day. On Cochise Street stores were opening and miners carrying dinner pails were going to work. In the corral back of the stage office the hostler was busy harnessing the horses.

Bert MacIntosh, the driver, came in to pick up any valuables that were to be put in the strong box. At sight of Nancy he showed surprise. He had heard rumors about her being a captive at her father's ranch. But since this was none of his business he ignored it.

"I'll promise you a safer trip than that lickety-split one we took last month," he said to her.

There were more surprises for him. Three horsemen tied their mounts at the rack in front of the saloon next door and came into the office. One of them was the deputy Tom Fallon who had been making such a sensational reputation in the district. It struck Bert that something unusual and mysterious was taking place.

Tom asked Tex Scully, "Have you sent the kid with the message yet?"

The shotgun guard nodded. "Our friend ought to be here soon—if he is coming."

Husky and Tom stepped into the baggage room at the rear and left the door half closed. Nancy had already disappeared into it.

The clerk behind the counter questioned Tex. "What about the three seats you reserved? Are the passengers here?"

"Two of them," Tex answered. "The third is on his way, I hope."

Heilman walked into the room and waved a cheerful hand in greeting to include all present. "I'll take my letter, Tex," he said. "Much obliged to you for bringing it."

The look in Scully's eyes told him that something was

wrong. He was sure of it when Tom and Husky stepped into the room. They stood silently one on each side of him. "So it's a frame-up," he said, his eyes narrowing.

"You're under arrest, Heilman," Tom told him.

Their gazes locked, hard and unflinching. Neither of the men made any motion toward the weapons at their sides, but Fallon knew the gambler was weighing his chances.

"Under arrest for what?" Heilman asked quietly.

"For robbery and murder." The answer was low-toned and even as the question. No hint of urgency was in the voice of either.

Heilman laughed scornfully. "My friend, you are getting too big for your boots. Be careful somebody doesn't cut you down to size."

"I'm doing a job that has to be done. I don't like it."

"You've set out to be a hero. Nothing will stop you. So you listen to a lot of loose talk by that fool Rufe Todd and go crazy."

The gambler was talking for time. It was not likely that he would reach for his gun. Tom knew that, yet when the man made his move he was not prepared for it. One moment Heilman was leaning against the counter, an elbow resting on it; the next his other arm was lashing out at the deputy's face, the drive of his lithe strong body back of it. Tom could not escape the blow entirely but by a shift of the head he caught it on his cheek. He was flung back against Husky and hung in his friend's arms inert from the shock. While a heart could beat twice.

Heilman made for the door, thrusting aside Slim Hardy, but he stumbled over Mark Scully's outstretched foot and fell headlong. While he was rising Tom's shoulder, plowing into his chest, crowded him to the counter. One of Tom's encircling arms, pressed hard against Heilman's holstered pistol, prevented a draw of the weapon but left his face unprotected. The gambler sent savage jolts at the head trying to find cover against his body. Tom was at a disadvantage in that he could neither attack nor defend himself. If he freed the man's waist Heilman would drag out the revolver and fling a bullet into his stomach.

Tex Scully moved in and slipped the revolver from under Tom's arm, then flung it back of the counter. Fallon stepped

159

back, his face battered and one eye partially closed. He lifted an uppercut that hurt Heilman but did not stop him from pressing the attack.

Husky lunged at the gambler and tried to pin down his flailing arms. A stabbing right landed on his chin and flung him back. Tex had a lock on Heilman's neck and put his strength into it to pull the man down, but in the mêlée the hold was broken.

The outlaw almost tore free but Husky tackled him around the hips as he stumbled toward the door. He was amazingly strong. The huddled fighters swayed across the floor and crashed into a pot-bellied stove so hard that several lengths of pipe tumbled down. By the sheer weight of his assailants Heilman was forced from his feet. Even then it was several minutes before they could rope his wrists securely.

It had been the plan to take him in the coach to Tomahawk but they saw now it would not do to let him ride with Miss Faunce. He was helpless while bound, but unconquered. He was in a fury of frustrated rage. Tom decided to have him put on Husky's horse and let the cowboy ride in the coach.

Heilman swore he would not ride a foot of the way.

"That's up to you," the deputy said. "You'll ride or be dragged at the end of a rope."

A rope was fastened around his waist and the other end tied to the horn of Tom's saddle, after which he was hoisted into the hull. He made no attempt to fling himself out of it. He recognized that at present there was no escape for him.

When Nancy came out of the back room she stared at Tom's fast-closing eye in a face of purple wheals and bruised cuts.

It hurt him to smile but he managed a gargoyle grin. "I must have run into a door," he told her.

While the coach was coming to the front he bathed his face with a wet towel and made what repairs he could. A few astonished miners on their way to work watched the stage and its guarding cavalcade start down the gulch. Within an hour all the residents of Copper Fork knew that Harry Heilman had been arrested, charged with being one of the bandit gang who had raided the town.

Husky noticed that Nancy looked worried, the lovely

160

color washed out of her cheeks. He reminded her that all is well that ends well.

"I'm afraid we haven't reached the end yet. My father will never quit."

"Curt won't make it. He used to be the big mogul of the San Simon. All he had to do was snap his fingers and a dozen gunmen would come running. Where are they now? Bob Wheldon and Jeb Purdy are dead, Dutch Frater shot up and probably in jail, Heilman on his way to prison, and Rufe Todd skedaddlin' for the border. The rest of Curt's gang are drawing away from him like rats out of a sinking ship. They are for him strong while he is ridin' high but they don't aim to back a losing horse."

"I know," Nancy agreed. "I can't thank all of you boys enough. A girl never had better friends."

"We would of been a pretty scurvy bunch if we hadn't come through when you needed us." Husky chuckled. "That Tom Fallon! I never saw his beat. First off I figured him just a nice friendly guy to have fun with, then before you've got time to say Jack Robinson backward he has cleaned up this Copper Fork raid and put the bandits out of business. On top of that he butts in and upsets Curt's apple cart sure enough."

"With a lot of help from Husky Sowers," Nancy mentioned.

"Me, I just went along for the kick," her companion said.

Nancy was feeling much better. The cheerfulness of Husky was contagious. She glanced at his bruised jaw and the cut below his right eye. "You seem to have got several. And poor Tom. He looks as though he had been fighting a wildcat."

"I'll give it to Heilman," conceded Husky. "He came near licking the whole lot of us." The range rider slanted a smile at her. "I came out best. Here I am taking it easy with the prettiest girl in Arizona while Tom has to ride herd all day on his prisoner. Serves him right for being a lawman."

"You really like him awf'ly well, don't you?" Nancy asked.

"That's right," he nodded and inquired impishly, "don't you?"

There was color enough in Nancy's face now. She said primly, "Of course I'm grateful to him."

Apparently apropos of nothing connected with their talk, Husky gave expression innocently to his thought. "I always did want to bust into society and be one of these best men at a wedding."

Nancy retorted promptly. "Can't you do better than that and be the groom? Think what a catch you would be for some poor lonesome girl."

His reply was immediate and fervent. "No, ma'am. Much obliged. I ain't broke to double harness. I'm a lone wolf."

Nancy sighed and told him that he dashed her hopes cruelly.

CHAPTER 27

After dark the stage drew into Tomahawk but passed the company office and went direct to the home of Sheriff Dunham. His wife insisted that Miss Faunce stay with them overnight. There would be no danger. Curt Faunce, Jasper Pike, and Yeager had been in town the previous day but had left before sunup that morning. Evidently the rest of the pursuing party had been sent back to the San Simon country. It would not do for Faunce to arrive at Tucson accompanied by so many gunmen.

It might be true that Faunce had gone to Tucson but Tom was taking no chances. He stayed at the house when the stage, its guards, the sheriff, and his prisoner left for the jail.

Mrs. Dunham was a plump smiling woman of about forty as friendly as a wriggly-tailed pup. Though she and her husband had eaten, she made supper for the two hungry travelers. While they were enjoying the hot biscuits and strawberry jam she hovered over them to make sure they had plenty of food.

From their hostess Tom learned an important piece of news. The sheriff had brought Dutch Frater to Tomahawk and his trial was set for the next week. The man was recovering so rapidly from his wounds that Dunham had felt it safer to hold him here in jail. Owing to the illness of the district attorney James Saunders of Tucson had been appointed special prosecutor. Tom was glad to hear this. Saunders was both a good lawyer and a responsible citizen.

When Mrs. Dunham was out of the room both of the young people spoke only stiff commonplaces to cover embarrassed silences. Since that impassioned kiss of goodbye at Tex Scully's house they had not seen each other alone. Tom did not know whether it was better to ignore his indiscretion or to apologize for it. She had been emotionally upset, he thought, and might welcome a chance to put him in his place. She had been tired and forlorn, and it had been his good fortune to bring her through what must have seemed to her a desperate venture. He had taken advantage of her dependence on him to act like a brash cowboy at a barn dance. Nancy was not like the girls he had romped with after riding forty miles to an all-night hoedown. She was a special job, like a piece of fine china. No wonder she was standoffish now and resented his action.

"About that kiss, Miss Nancy," he began abruptly, blundering into an explanation. "I didn't mean a thing. I guess I was just loco. I—I—"

He stuck in the middle of this apology. Her slender body had stiffened and her eyes sparked.

"What kiss?" she demanded.

Nothing could have deflated him more. She was challenging the fact that there had been one. He had been a fool. They had been friends until he had spoiled everything.

"I thought—"

She cut his sentence off sharply. "If you have been kissing girls don't come boasting to me about it," she said icily.

Mrs. Dunham walked into the room with a wedge of apple pie for each of them. Nancy rose. She was very tired and would like to go to her room if Mrs. Dunham would excuse her, she requested.

Her hostess went with her. A few minutes later Mrs. Dunham returned. She looked at Tom with humorous understanding eyes. He was confining his attention unhappily to the pie in front of him.

"Don't act so whipped out," she advised. "I heard it all. You were sure dumb but that is not fatal. Maybe you'll learn about girls someday." She put her hand to her lips to suppress a giggle. "My goodness! After you have kissed a girl

163

you don't go around explaining to her it didn't mean a thing. You are expected to feel pleased and happy about it."

Since she already knew of what he had done Tom took her into his confidence. "We were good friends and today she acted as if I was a stranger. I reckon I didn't make things any better by bringing it up. All I wanted to say was that I was sorry if I had made her mad at me."

"Just forget it and stay away from her for a while," Mrs. Dunham advised. "When she is good and ready she will forgive you. Don't be so scared of her. Funny about you. My husband says he never met anybody with more cold nerve than you. Yet you wilt before a little girl who is crazy about you."

He shook his head. "No, ma'am, you've got that wrong. There is another man, an officer in the army."

"When a girl is as pretty as Nancy there is always another man. Go in and win."

Husky and Slim escorted Nancy to the train next day, Tom following behind as a lone rear guard. She was very lively and gay but none of her charm was for Tom.

Husky sat beside her in the car. "Looks like poor Tom is in the doghouse," he presently mentioned.

Nancy did no pursue that opening.

"He must have lost his grandmother. Or maybe his best girl." Husky slanted a grin at her.

Miss Faunce looked out of the window. "How different the bleak plains look now from the way they do when the desert flowers are blooming in April," she said.

"Yes," he agreed. "He probably put his big foot in it somehow. When a fellow worships a girl he isn't at his best with her, especially one like Tom who hasn't had much experience."

"He worships some girl, does he?" Nancy's voice was very casual.

"That's right. His sun rises and sets in her. He thinks there never was anybody like her."

"Really." She was still apparently contemplating the scenery and her question showed indifference. "Is she a nice girl?"

Husky gave that consideration. "Well, she is pretty as a new painted wagon. Some spoiled, but after she has washed the duds of the kids for a few years she will get over that.

164

There aren't many girls good enough for Tom but I think this one may work out all right."

"He is so wonderful that I suppose she will jump at the chance to get at that washtub," Nancy said tartly. "You picture a lovely future for her."

"I'll backtrack some on that washtub," he conceded. "Tom is going places. There's something about him—darned if I know what it is—that tells me he'll be a big man one of these days if he lives."

Nancy felt that Husky's prediction might be right but his rider to it set a fear whispering in her mind, *If he lives, if he doesn't get killed.*

James Saunders and Jeannie Harshaw met them at the Tucson station. Sheriff Marshall was also there. Tom's glance swept the platform swiftly. The sheriff interpreted that searching look.

"Faunce is in town, boiling mad, but he isn't at the depot. Fact is, he has run into something that worries him. I'll tell you about it as we walk to the house." Marshall dropped to the rear of the party with Tom. "This town and Tomahawk have both got set on one thing, to try these outlaws and see they are hanged. It gripes Faunce to find out that what he wants doesn't matter at all."

The whole party stopped at Mrs. Harshaw's house to eat a dinner already prepared for the guests. When the time came to carry out the dishes before the desert Nancy rose and glanced at Fallon.

"Maybe Tom will help me carry them out," she suggested.

Tom followed her with two plates into the kitchen. He murmured "Thank you," scarce daring to look at her.

CHAPTER 28

Curt Faunce dropped into the sheriff's office to quiz and placate him. He knew that his daughter had reached town and was at her aunt's but he made no effort to see her. That could wait. His attention was concentrating on the impending trial at Tomahawk. He did not like the shape of events.

Word had reached him of the arrest of Heilman. His trial would follow immediately after that of Dutch Frater. The jail was being guarded very closely.

Both of the prisoners would expect him to save them by one means or another. He could not do it. His strength had fallen away from him. When he walked down Congress Street he realized that the eyes of men who formerly had been very polite to him now held condemnation. To make any move that allied him with Frater and Heilman would be disastrous. This whole southeast corner of Arizona was clamoring for the extermination of the bandits. Yet if he stood aloof Frater would surely drag him into the net.

Sheriff Marshall was writing a letter when Faunce came into the room. He put down the pen and gave his attention to his visitor but he did not rise to shake hands.

Faunce flung himself into a chair. "What's the matter with this town?" he demanded. "It's gone hog wild for what it calls law and order. Tomahawk too. They are making a tin god out of that killer and desperado Fallon. On top of his other murders he shot my foreman less than a week ago and left him lying between life and death. Any crime he commits is all right but those poor devils lying in the Tomahawk jail are going to be railroaded to the scaffold."

"They will have a fair trial," the sheriff disagreed. "The evidence against them is strong, especially in the case of Frater. It is quite true that young Fallon is very popular just now. He has done a fine job cleaning up this Copper Fork robbery. I'm going to say something personal, Curt. I am sure you won't take it wrong. You don't like Fallon. I hope your feeling will not get out of hand. It would be very dangerous for anybody to injure him."

"That's a threat," stormed the ranchman.

"Call it a warning. The public feeling is running high."

"After killing one of my riders and almost killing another he goes down to my ranch, knocks out two of my men, attempts to kill another, steals one of my horses and private papers, and drags my daughter away with him. And you tell me to lay off him." In Curt's eyes was a raging but frustrated fury.

The sheriff's cold gaze measured the man. "I'll tell you something else. You got away with a jail break on me but you can't pull that trick twice. I'm giving it to you straight.

If you lift a hand to help those two bandits in jail you'll land in a cell beside them. Most of the people in Tucson believe you left Purdy here to kill Tom Fallon and slipped up. Already I am being blamed for not putting handcuffs on you. You're skating on damned thin ice, Faunce."

"You never saw the day you could put cuffs on me," exploded Faunce. "I don't take talk like that from any man. You are practically claiming I was in on that Copper Fork raid. Say it point blank and, damn it, we'll settle this right here. Only one of us will go out of this room alive."

Marshall answered, his voice low and even, his eyes steady. "I'm making no such charge. I'm telling you for your own sake just where you stand. Get it into your head that law has come to this country. Time was when you could bull anything through. Those days are gone forever. Face the facts, Curt."

"What facts? That your pet Fallon can pull off any crime he pleases against us San Simon settlers and your kind of law backs him to the limit? You bet we'll face that—with our guns blazing if it has to be that way."

Faunce stormed out of the office. His arrogant temper had got the better of him. His purpose in calling on the sheriff had been to ease the situation by posing as a law-abiding citizen who had been put in the wrong. Instead of that he had foolishly let his anger carry him to a defiance of the authorities he had no power to enforce. There was some devil in him that could not take opposition.

For it stood out like a sore bandaged thumb that he had to cut himself loose from Heilman and Frater and if they tried to implicate him play the part of an honest indignant citizen. This was bitter as wormwood to him. He had ridden down competitors savagely for years and it rankled that he must give way now to forces he could not control. His hatred centered on Tom Fallon. The intention to kill him remained fixed but he must be careful how he did it.

He was puzzled at this heat of resentment beating on him. For years this troubled district had been infested by rustlers and outlaws. Citizens grumbled but accepted the condition as a matter of course. Now they were resolved to put an end to it. He ought never to have allowed the raid on Copper Fork. If he had foreseen what was to occur he would not have let that upstart Fallon get away from the town alive. This young deputy had managed somehow to wreck his grip on the district. Unless he showed strength enough to save Heilman and Frater none of his followers would accept him as a leader. Yet there was nothing he could do for them except hire a defense lawyer.

On Congress Street he met Husky Sowers. The cowboy was going to pass him with a nod but he barred the way.

"You came to my ranch, accepted its hospitality, and abused it," he charged.

"Looking at it that way you are right, Mr. Faunce," the young man acknowledged mildly.

"And stole the best horse on the ranch," Faunce added.

"I'd rather put it that I borrowed it. I was in some hurry and hadn't time to ask your leave. At Tomahawk I hired a fellow to take it back to you. Things being the way they are, I don't reckon it would help any to say I'm much obliged for the loan."

"I'm going to have you arrested, you young scoundrel."

"There is a point you have overlooked, Mr. Faunce," Husky said in amiable irony. "The horse was saddled to go find Tom Fallon. That's what I used it for."

"Don't mock me, you fool." With a sweep of his heavy arm Faunce flung Husky aside and went stamping down the street.

Jasper Pike was sitting on the porch of the Russ House and Faunce took a chair beside him.

"Have any luck with Marshall?" Pike asked.

"No. They have the cards stacked against us."

"Against you," Pike corrected. "My only interest in this is your daughter. The way you're acting looks like I'm drawing to a busted flush and not filling."

"Don't try to ride me, Jasper," growled Faunce. "I'm in no mood to take it. I promised you that when we go back my daughter will travel with us. Leave it lay at that."

"Fine. If you go through."

"Let's get this straight." The cold shallow eyes of Faunce stabbed at those of the other man. "Don't think for a minute you can use me for a cat's-paw. I don't give without taking. These stranglers are using their law to put ropes around our necks. Your neck as well as mine, Mr. Pike. I don't aim to let you forget how you used to raid the Mexican ranches with old man Clanton and how you ambushed and shot the hell

168

out of a bunch of greasers smuggling dobe dollars across the line. Except for a bull or two you bought for breeding there isn't a head of stock on your ranch that didn't come from stolen stuff."

"We'd better let sleeping dogs lie, Curt," protested Pike. "We were wild young fellows in those days. I don't think this situation is half as bad as you figure it is. Dutch Frater will go to the gallows. They have got the dead wood on him. I'm not so sure they will get Heilman. Let's assume Dutch will rat on you. Doesn't mean a thing. He's talking to try to save his neck. Hold your head up and ride it through. The thing for you to do is keep away from both of them. Let them play their own hands."

Pike's argument was along the same line as that of Sheriff Marshall, although the motivation of the advice was different. Curt's own judgment told him this was the right course to follow but he was not going to let Pike think he had influenced him.

"There is no way they can touch me," Faunce said with sharp decision, and wished he knew his words were true. "Just keep in mind you're in this fight as deep as I am."

Faunce took a cigar from a pocket which held several more. He did not offer his companion one, but lit his and walked into the house. The sulky eyes of Pike followed him. If he had yielded to his immediate urge he would have saddled and ridden back to his ranch. But the thought of Nancy restrained him. His greed to get her for his own was inordinate. To leave Faunce now would be to lose her. He had to play the string out, though he felt the sense of danger crowding him.

CHAPTER 29

Tomahawk was bursting at the seams. Cattlemen had left their ranches and cowboys the range to be in at the trial. The exodus from Copper Fork was so great that the mines closed for lack of workers.

The courtroom could not hold one tenth of those who

wanted to be present at the trial of the notorious Dutch Frater. In part Sheriff Dunham solved the pressure by issuing tickets, each good for one session only, nobody to get more than one.

On the faces of the miners was a noticeable grimness that boded ill for Frater. They had come to make sure he got the extreme penalty. Openly they talked of lynching if the jury failed to convict. A restless unease was in the air. Cowboys and miners drifted in and out of saloons, stopped in small groups on the street to talk, but always returned to the square brick courthouse which sat alone in a block ornamented only by rank grass and a few gnarled cottonwoods.

Among the fiddlefooted visitors were a dozen from the San Simon district, several of whom had been associated with Frater in one or another bit of night-riding knavery, but even if they had liked him there would have been no thought in their minds of attempting a rescue. In the courtroom were six armed guards and as many more on the grounds outside.

The trial went badly for the defendant. His lawyer could put up no other defense than one of mistaken identity and that was easily swept aside. Though Tom Fallon was the principal witness against him, damaging testimony was given by a dozen others. Sam Rosenstein identified him as the big bandit who had come into the store with Bob Wheldon. Two miners gave evidence that they had seen him on Cochise Street half an hour before the robbery. A ranchman had caught sight of the three riders heading into the hills after they had found fresh horses and he swore that Frater was leading them on a big white-stockinged bay belonging to Clint Gregory. The owner of the horse followed him on the stand to say that the bay had been stolen from his corral during the night. It was shown that prior to the robbery Frater was broke and that shortly afterward he lost more than a thousand dollars gambling at the Legal Tender in Tucson. His attempt to assassinate Tom Fallon at the corral counted heavily against him.

Throughout the trial the prisoner's worried eyes searched the courtroom again and again for Faunce. Curt never appeared. He remained at Tucson and did not lift a hand to help the man who had been his tool. No word of any kind from him reached either Frater or his lawyer.

170

After the instructions of the judge the jury filed out of the room to reach a decision. Inside of half an hour they returned with a verdict of guilty. Frater behaved like a wild man. He cursed the judge, the jury, and the witnesses who had appeared against him but most of his rage centered on Faunce. He accused the San Simon ranchman of having instigated the raid on Copper Fork and being at the bottom of all the lawlessness in the region for the past fifteen years. Shackled though he was, he tried to break away from his guards and was subdued only after a hard struggle. As they dragged him from the room he was still denouncing Faunce.

Heilman occupied the cell next to Frater and listened to his furious disjointed account of the trial. The gambler's anger at Faunce was deep and bitter. Curt was flinging them to the wolves. Heilman was a man of enduring hatreds and the cold hard resolution was in his mind that as soon as he got out of this trouble—and he felt sure he would escape somehow—he would pay in full the old fox who thought he had side-stepped danger by leaving them to shift for themselves.

The confidence of Heilman had some justification. After supper on the day the Frater trial closed half a dozen men met at the home of Sheriff Dunham to discuss the case of the gambler set to begin at once. James Saunders had called the group together to tell them his opinion of the situation.

His opening surprised them. He said he had no doubt of Heilman's guilt but there was not at present enough evidence to justify a conviction though he intended to go through with the trial. Item by item he went over the evidence. Tex Scully thought he had seen Heilman strangle the bandit Wheldon but since he was not sure no judge would allow that to be brought into the case. Members of the posse felt that the gambler had led the pursuit on a false trail. But that was merely a matter of opinion and not admissible as evidence, since they could not read the man's mind and prove it. The man's letter to Faunce was highly suspicious but made no explicit reference to the raid.

"We can break Frater down and get him to implicate Heilman," Dunham cut in.

Saunders shook his head. "How much weight would that have with a jury that would know he was dragging Heilman in hoping to save his own neck?"

"Harry shot at Tom twice the other night at Copper Fork," Marshall said.

"Will Tom swear he recognized the man shooting at him?" the lawyer asked.

Tom admitted he could not.

"You feel sure it was Heilman and it probably was," Saunders agreed. "But we can't put you on the stand to swear to a guess."

"But I can swear I saw him coming out of a restaurant here with the bandits a day or two before the raid," Tom said.

"Contributary evidence but proves only that he knew them and had been with them recently."

"It sums up to this, that I ought not to have arrested him," Tom said ruefully.

"No," Saunders denied. "You did right. His guilt has been brought out into the open. We'll try him, and if he gets off suspicion will hang so heavily on him that he will have to leave this part of the country or run the danger of being shot down any time."

There was nothing of the hangdog look about Heilman as he walked down a lane between massed men on both sides and into the courthouse. He carried his powerful body with easy grace and his handsome face showed no fear of the issue. To those he knew the prisoner raised his manacled hands in greeting or called them cheerfully by name. The feeling of the crowd was divided. The gambler was popular and many could not believe that there was a tie-up between him and the bandits.

His lawyer Castleman was one of the leading attorneys in the territory. When the time came for choosing the jury he announced that if the judge would pick any twelve men in the room it would be agreeable to the defense. Saunders rose at once and said that would suit him. Both of them knew the judge could not accept the offer, but Castleman's air of bland confidence had its effect.

Tom was the first witness for the prosecution. The defense objected and was sustained when he spoke of Heilman leading the posse astray. In cross-examination Castleman spent an hour trying to discredit Tom as a witness. He brought out adroitly all the circumstances that had pointed to him as an accomplice of the robbers. At the miners' trial had he not been let off because the evidence of his guilt was not quite conclusive? Since that time had he not killed one man in a street affray and at another time left a second foe for dead? Was it true that less than a week ago he had abducted a young lady from her father's ranch and while doing so severely wounded the foreman of the ranch who was trying to defend the girl?

Saunders put Tex Scully on the stand. The stage guard testified that when the battle on Cochise Street ended he was standing just behind Heilman and was convinced the defendant had throttled the wounded outlaw Wheldon to keep him from telling who his accomplices were. Before he had finished the sentence Castleman was on his feet protesting indignantly at this. The judge sustained the objection, ordered the words stricken out, and reprimanded Saunders for leading up to such a statement.

The prosecuting lawyer put another question. "Did you later notice any bruises on the throat of the dead outlaw?"

Tex said he did.

"What did they look like?"

In spite of an objection the judge allowed him to answer. "They looked like the marks of finger pressure," Tex said.

The letter found in the tin box of Faunce was introduced and shown by the testimony of Slim Hardy to have been sent by Heilman. Other bits of incriminating evidence fitted into the case against the gambler. But though there was a strong feeling that he was probably guilty the proof of this was not conclusive. The jury was out an hour and a half before returning with a verdict of not guilty.

Watching Heilman, knowing him for a hardened villain, Tom could not help admiring the cool poise that had not deserted him for a moment during the strain of the ordeal. If there had been any quick pounding of the heart or tightness in the chest as he saw in men's eyes the growing sense of his guilt, no sign of this disturbed his calm assurance.

After the verdict was announced men crowded around him to shake hands in congratulation and others moved away to have no part in it. When he reached the courthouse steps a few minutes later he stopped to light a cigar. A hundred men had waited to see him come out and he knew he was the focal point of all their attention. He knew that in the minds of many of them he was forever damned. His cynical reckless eyes drifted from one another. The man's pride showed in his lifted head and squared shoulders.

"He'll always ride tall in the saddle," a cowboy standing near said to a miner beside him.

"Yes, but I'll never forget that he is a cold-blooded killer," the Cornishman answered.

Heilman's keen hearing picked up the words. He was aware they had not been meant to reach him but this was a chance to declare himself. "I'll let that go once, Rhys," he said, his voice a cold challenge flung out as a warning to all. "But don't say it again unless you are ready to back it."

The miner turned and walked away without a word.

Tom Fallon and Tex Scully came out of the courthouse to the steps. Heilman said angrily, "Two of a kind, both ready to swear a man's life away with lies."

Tex answered quietly. "You squeaked out of it, but my opinion hasn't changed. Better sing soft. The boys won't take much from you now."

A voice shouted, "You can bet yore boots on that, Heilman."

Castleman appeared in the doorway. "Gentlemen—gentlemen!" he protested in his most courtly manner. "My client has been declared innocent by a jury of his peers. We must accept that judgment in the spirit of good Americans who respect the law."

He tucked an arm around the elbow of his client and walked with him to a saloon across the street. A drink seemed called for to celebrate the triumphant acquittal.

Heilman looked grimly at the glass in his hand. "There is a lot of feeling against me," he said grimly. "I'll have to sell out and leave."

"Might be a good idea," the lawyer agreed.

"No word from Faunce yet?" Heilman's low voice held a menacing bitterness.

Castleman smiled sardonically. "You'll hear from him now you are out of the woods. It will turn out that he is your warmest friend but he was afraid it would hurt your cause for him to come into the open."

The gambler spoke as if to himself in a low voice, the words almost dripping from his lips. "I'm going to see Mr. Faunce and thank him before I go."

It occurred to Castleman that he would not like to be in Curt Faunce's place at that meeting nor in fact in Heilman's either. With the gambler in his present mood anything was likely to happen.

To satisfy his curiosity the lawyer ventured an observation. "You don't seem to feel so bitter at Fallon who really dragged you into this trouble."

"Why should I? He is an officer. He played his hand the way it was laid out for him. In his place I would have done the same."

Castleman thought that characteristic of his client.

CHAPTER 30

Sheriff Dunham looked up from the newspaper he was reading when Tom Fallon and Husky Sowers walked into the office. He put a finger on the paragraph he had reached.

"The way this paper looks at it I had better move over and make way for a hell-raisin', crime-bustin' deputy of mine." Dunham was smiling. He liked Tom very much and was not at all jealous of the popularity acclaiming him one of Arizona's great law officers. "Fact is, I've been wanting to quit anyhow. Say the word and I'll turn the headache over to you. My ranch needs attention. I'll be real glad to get back to it."

"You can't do that to me," Tom told him. "I'm beating you to it. Starting from right now I am no longer your deputy but a private citizen. I got into this thing to clear my name. Now that is taken care of I'm through. But I have brought along a better man to take my place—if you figure you need one."

The sheriff looked at Husky and approved of what he saw, a smiling lad, tall and broad-shouldered, with clear direct eyes in a good-looking face. He carried himself jauntily, hat slightly tiptilted, but Dunham liked him none the less for that. Unshaved and unwashed deputies were no recommendation to the service.

175

"Thought you didn't like lawmen," Dunham said.

Husky grinned. "This here son-of-a-gun Tom has done converted me. I'd kinda like to take a whack at it myself."

"I don't want another deputy like Tom," the sheriff explained. "He is a magnet for attracting bullets. It's a miracle we have not had to bury him. I want a nice quiet man who has a gift of keeping out of trouble. Think you can do that?"

"Unless it's laid right in my lap," Husky qualified. "I'm a sure enough peaceable fellow. Why, I even get along with Tom."

Dunham laughed.

"If you hire me," Husky continued, "I'd want a day or maybe two off to go to Tom's wedding. I've picked myself for best man."

Tom made a pass at him that Husky ducked. "Don't pay any attention to him," the ex-deputy warned. "I am not going to be married."

"I'd give him two to one on that if I had a buck in my jeans," Husky retorted. "The lady thinks different from Tom about that."

The sheriff reverted to business. "I might give you a tryout, Husky. But I won't have you bustin' out of the corral every now and then like Tom did. I give the orders here."

Husky said, a gleam of mischief in his eyes, that he was no ball of fire like Tom but a steady dependable citizen who would stay hitched.

The sheriff mentioned some news he had heard. Harry Heilman had sold his dance hall and had given it out that he was leaving for Trinidad, Colorado. All of them hoped it was true.

Tom left for Tucson and on his way to the Orndorff from the train met Nancy and Lieutenant Ramsey riding. They drew up when they saw him. Nancy smiled at him, her eyes star-bright.

His spirits plunged. *She is with the man she loves*, he thought. *That is why she is so happy.*

"My aunt wants to hear all about the trial," she said. "We are glad you are back. Of course you will come to supper tonight and tell us everything."

He said he would, but with a mental reservation. What he wanted to tell her most he could not say, even if Ramsey had not been in the way. He was out of a job, penniless, a cowpuncher on the chuck line, unless part of the reward money should be given him.

As the riders moved down the road, the officer asked a question. "Does that invitation to supper include me?"

"Some other night," she said pleasantly.

Ramsey looked a little sulky. He had proposed to her and been rejected, but he hoped she might change her mind. "Are you in love with this fellow?" he plumped at her.

She raised her eyebrows and her body stiffened in the saddle. "What fellow?" she inquired coldly.

"This Tom Fallon?"

Nancy said, icily gentle, "I do not think it is within your right to ask me that question in regard to Mr. Fallon or anybody else."

"I am in love with you."

"That gives you the right to ask what my feeling is about one person." Her anger at him had gone. She spoke with a friendly kindness in her voice. "You paid me a great compliment, Archie. I have never met a nicer man than you. I like you so much, but—I just don't love you."

He could not understand it. Most of the girls he met would have been glad to marry him. He was young, goodlooking, gay, an officer from West Point. Lovely and charming though Nancy was, her life had been lived on the frontier, far from the social refinements he had known. At first he had meant only to flirt with her and have a good time but there had grown in him a flame that had swept his caution aside. Damn it, she ought to be proud to win him.

Their ride was not a success. The talk they made was forced. In the earlier days of their friendship they had both been full of laughter and chatter with many points of contact. Now the fire had gone out.

CHAPTER 31

Tom was not the only guest for supper at the Harshaw home. James Saunders was there. This was not a surprise to Tom, for Nancy had told him of the lawyer's engagement to her aunt. But he was at once aware of a change in Jennie Harshaw. He had never seen her without reacting to her charm and friendly personality. It seemed to him now that life had quickened in her. She looked years younger. Love had warmed and irradiated her.

Then Nancy came into the room from the kitchen and his thoughts were of her only. She lowered her hand from touching back a truant lock of her dark hair to give it to him with her quick lovely smile. An odd breathless heat of excitement brushed through him as her small soft palm fitted into his.

It was a gay little supper with interludes of seriousness. During one of these Saunders asked Tom about his plans for employment. Tom was not sure. He thought he might look for a homestead claim on which to locate. The lawyer had a suggestion. He was part owner of an outfit freighting to and from the mines south of Tucson. His partner and he needed a manager. There was a future in it, Saunders thought, and Tom could take over if he wished. They felt they would be lucky to get him.

Tom was pleased. This was a piece of good fortune. He would not have to go back to chasing cattle out of the brush, and he could spend a good deal of his time in Tucson.

The maid was clearing the dishes for dessert when a man walked into the house without knocking. Jennie rose from her seat swiftly, her eyes angry and disturbed.

"How dare you come into this house, Curt Faunce?" she demanded.

The dull eyes in the man's heavy face shuttled from one to another of them sourly and came to rest on Tom. "I have come to find my daughter who was kidnaped from her home by that killer sitting beside you." A biting venom rode in his voice.

"Kidnaping is a strange word for you to use," his sister-in-law told him scornfully. "And killer is another. You forget easily."

"That gunman there won't think that I forget quickly," he retorted fiercely. "The fellow is close to the end of his last crooked mile."

Tom said quietly, "Is this the place to discuss that, Mr. Faunce?"

178

"You can talk big when you are sitting behind the skirts of two women." The passionate hatred of the rancher leaped into words. "Come into the street and we'll settle this now."

"I don't fight duels," Tom told him.

"You use a gun only when you feel sure it is safe," Faunce spat at him contemptuously. He turned on Jennie Harshaw. "I came to tell you that I am leaving here with my daughter the day after tomorrow."

"No," Nancy broke in. "I won't go."

Faunce swung round on the lawyer. "It's my legal right to take her. You can't tell them anything different, Saunders."

"Your legal but not your moral right," the attorney answered. "You have forfeited the claim on Nancy you once had."

"Damn your quibbles. I'm her father. She goes with me."

He reached the door before Jennie's challenge stopped him. "I'm going to have you arrested at once for murder."

"Try to bring up that lying charge and see how far you get." In his rage he brushed a lovely vase from the top of a cabinet to the floor and stormed out of the house.

The vase lay on the floor broken into a hundred pieces. Nancy shuddered. She was thinking that this brutal man, whose shallow eyes had glared at them with such burning hatred, was her father.

Jennie was the first to speak. "What do you think, James? Can I have him arrested for killing Tom's father?"

Saunders shook his head. "He would be released on bail. The evidence is not enough to hold him."

After some discussion it was decided that perhaps the best plan would be to send Nancy secretly to Phoenix or Prescott for a time. Tom offered to see that she reached her destination safely.

Presently the lawyer said, "We must not let this spoil our evening. We are not going to let him take Nancy. Won't you play for us, Jennie?"

As Mrs. Harshaw moved to the piano her niece whispered to Tom. "I think they would like to be alone for a little while."

The two younger people stepped into the patio. It was a warm velvet night with just a sliver of crescent moon in the sky.

"Do you remember the night when we rode into Copper Fork?" he asked her. "That was a lovely night too, but you were so dreadfully tired."

"I remember," she replied in a low voice.

At dinner she had been gay and full of laughter. Now she seemed to him shy and fragile as a rose, once more dependent on him. The arm resting under his trembled a little.

"Don't be afraid of Curt Faunce," he told her. "I'll not let him get you."

"I'm not afraid now, but he'll follow and find me wherever I go."

That was true, Tom knew. She needed the protection of a man. It had become urgently necessary that he know whether Lieutenant Ramsey was that man. He asked her bluntly.

"Are you still trying to marry me to Archie?" she smiled. "I must disappoint you again. Today was our last ride together."

"You have quarreled perhaps."

"No." Her monosyllable did not invite further questioning.

In the darkness her face was a soft and shining oval. A deeper color painted her clear lovely skin. His eyes searched hers while the blood pounded in his veins.

She had to break the deep silence. "Why are you looking at me like that?" she asked in a small voice.

"I am thinking that you are the loveliest girl alive."

Nancy had taken her arm from his and was facing him. "Something more for me to remember," she said, then leaned forward and brushed his cheek lightly with her lips.

He caught her hands in his. "Does that mean anything?"

Nancy tried to escape from her boldness. "As much as the one you gave me once," she told him.

"Mine meant that I love you terribly," he cried.

A heat ran through her slender body. She laughed, breathlessly. "It has taken you a long time to tell me, sir."

Her lips turned to his and his arms went around her.

"This is how it should be," Tom said, after they found time for words.

"Oh my dear, I want to begin everything with you—a new life—to share everything with you. Always." She caught herself wondering at this passionate emotion, this assurance that she was in a newborn world because a man loved her.

"Tomorrow," Tom answered. "If you are my wife Curt Faunce will have no legal claim on you. Or tonight. Why not tonight?"

"Give me a little time," she demurred. "I want to dream about it. Let's say next week."

"If we wait you'll be back at the ranch next week," he reminded her.

"And if we don't wait—" She stopped, appalled at the picture in her mind. "Nothing could prevent him from killing you. He would be insane with anger. We can't go on with it—not now."

"You heard his threat," Tom said. "Whether I do or don't marry you makes no difference to my safety. But it makes all the difference in the world to you. That man Jasper Pike is in town with him. You know why. To back Curt Faunce's claim to take you back to the ranch and then to drive you into a marriage with him. For us to run away is no solution. Faunce would find you. But if we are married he is barred. He can't touch you."

"But he can kill you," Nancy protested unhappily.

"No. His power is gone. The whole district would be for us and against him. He has no gunpackers left who would dare touch me. Not with Frater sitting in jail waiting to be hanged."

"I saw his eyes when he looked at you. There was a devil of hate in them."

"Admitting that he does not like me, he will play it safe just the same." He took her in his arms again. "Don't worry, dearest. It's going to be all right."

They walked into the house and announced their news. Jennie jumped up and kissed first Nancy and then Tom.

"I hoped it would turn out like this," she said.

"Good," Tom replied. "We'll be married tomorrow morning and take the night train for Phoenix."

Both Mrs. Harshaw and Saunders agreed it would be well for them to leave and stay away for a week or two. Neither of them mentioned Faunce but he was in their mind.

Tom walked back to the Orndorff, a song in his heart. Yet he took no unnecessary risks but followed back streets and alleys. The assurance to Nancy of his safety was not convincing to him.

CHAPTER 32

The news of the marriage swept through the town like tumbleweeds in a heavy wind. Jennie's next-door neighbor, Matilda Bartells, saw to that. Her little eager eyes had noticed the unusual bustle at the Harshaw house. She had not missed noting the new suit Tom was wearing nor the arrival of the minister. At the earliest opportunity she buttonholed the young Papago maid and corkscrewed the facts from her. Inside of ten minutes she was on her way to tell a few intimate friends under a pledge of secrecy that the young cowpuncher Fallon had just been married to Nancy Faunce. She did not forget to add that though the girl's father was in town he had not been present.

Jasper Pike picked up the story at a pool hall and carried it to Faunce. The occasion was not a pleasant one for either of the men. Pike's disappointment made him sore as a wounded bear with cubs but his resentment was nothing like the furious rage that swept over his companion. With difficulty he restrained Faunce from setting out to shoot down Tom Fallon on sight. If Curt felt he had to kill the fellow he had better wait until darkness covered the deed. After Faunce's first burst of uncontrollable anger he recognized the wisdom of this. Fallon would die after dark, shot by an unknown assassin.

Pike made some discreet inquiries for him and learned that Fallon was still at the Orndorff or at least had not yet moved his belongings. The young people expected to leave on the night train for Phoenix. Casually Pike mentioned another bit of information. Harry Heilman had reached town on the morning train. This gave Curt some uneasiness. No word had come to him after Heilman's acquittal but he had no doubt the gambler was a good deal annoyed at him. He would have to explain to the man why it seemed better to stay in the background during the trial. Heilman was a hard stubborn man. It would not be easy to placate him.

182

But a possible way occurred to him. He had seen Heilman's eyes rest on Nancy and guessed what was in the man's mind. Why not flaunt the girl before him with the promise of her for his wife? The gambler was a handsome bold dashing man. It might be a good deal easier to drive Nancy into a marriage with him than with a heavy clod like Pike.

"I'd better have a talk with Harry, Jasper," he said. "If you know where he is staying send him round. We ought to have him on our side."

"He is at the Orndorff. I wonder what he is doing here."

"We'll find out." A possible reason came to his mind. "He must hate Fallon for what he has done to him. Maybe he has come to get another crack at him."

Pike found Heilman in the Legal Tender and delivered his message. The gambler listened to him with an impassive face that told nothing.

"I'll see him," he said.

As they walked down to the Russ House the San Simon rancher let his jealous anger at Fallon spill out in words. Faunce had promised the girl to him and this tramp Fallon had stepped in and married her. The fellow had stirred up a hornets' nest that had made trouble for all of the honest settlers in this part of the territory. Somebody ought to stop his clock.

"Why not you?" Heilman asked with obvious sarcasm. Pike was known to be gun-shy.

"I'm too old to go on the warpath," Pike admitted.

"You're not much over fifty," Heilman jeered. "Just the right age for a beautiful girl of seventeen."

Pike answered doggedly, "Her father promised her to me."

They found Faunce in the lobby of the hotel. He rose with a welcome smile and held out his hand. "I'm sure glad that jury had the good sense to free you, Harry."

Heilman did not take the offered hand. He said, "I understand you want to see me."

"That's right. Come to my room. You'll excuse us, Pike."

Curt closed the door of the bedroom. "Sit down, Harry. We'll have a drink to celebrate this occasion."

"No drink," Heilman told him. "Nothing to celebrate. You slid out like the rat you are and left us to hang."

Faunce was determinedly friendly. "Those are hard words,
183

Harry, but under the circumstances I'll take them from you until we have cleared away this misunderstanding."

The gambler listened to the explanation. Faunce did not wait for an answer but pushed on to the proposal he had thought up. He had long had the purpose of arranging a marriage between his daughter and Harry. Now this saddle-bum Fallon had upset any hope of it unless somebody rubbed him out, in which case Nancy would still be available.

Heilman's gorge rose at the man. Faunce was rotten to the core, false to every shred of decency. He had offered to sell his daughter to Pike and now at the cost of another murder was proposing to sell her to him. The gambler had gone bad but there were limits to his villainy. To save himself and his partners in crime he had squeezed the last moments of life out of a man already practically dead. He had tried to shoot Fallon without warning. Up to this time he had not been quite sure how far his anger against Faunce would take him. But he knew now. The fellow was talking himself to death and did not know it.

"Is it your idea that I should go get this interfering fool?" he asked.

"You and I could lay for him tonight. He is expecting to take the midnight train for Phoenix with his bride. I could check out of this hotel, leave town, and then slip back after dark. With Fallon out of the way a big fine-looking fellow like you ought to have no trouble winning the girl."

Heilman thought that might be true. He was a man that women fell in love with. The old devil was certainly baiting the hook with a tempting fly. He yielded reluctantly to the urging of Faunce and at last he agreed to go along with him. Fallon had been asking for this a long time.

There would not be many chances to catch him alone but since Heilman was staying at the hotel he could watch his goings and comings carefully. Word could be got to him that Faunce had left town. With his enemy gone he would be off guard. Against two good shots pumping lead at him he would have no chance.

Heilman had not come to Tuscon looking for Fallon. Another man had been in his mind. But it seemed as if a break was coming his way. He could clean the slate by settling two debts of vengeance at the same time.

It would have to be a smooth job with no witnesses present. Faunce would destroy his enemy without warning and then the old devil would get his. Nobody could doubt that the two had met and killed each other.

CHAPTER 33

Heilman and Fallon came face to face in the lobby of the Orndorff. Two cattlemen were talking with the hotel owner and a drummer for dress goods was writing a letter at a table. The conversation died away. The eyes of those engaged in it fastened on the two who had met unexpectedly. There might be trouble.

"So you are a happy bridegroom, Mr. Deputy Sheriff," Heilman said. "Congratulations."

Tom was too full of good will to the world to resent the sarcastic tone. "Ex-deputy," he corrected. "I have resigned. And let me congratulate you too, Mr. Heilman."

"What for?" the gambler wanted to know.

"For the favorable verdict of the jury."

"You were plugging for me all the time, I suppose."

"Not exactly." Tom spoke amiably. "But believe it or not I was rather glad the trial turned out as it did. You acted friendly toward me when I was in a jam that first night we met."

"Everybody makes some mistakes as I did then," Heilman replied coldly. He shrugged his shoulders. "But that is all water over the dam. You go your way. I go mine. After today we'll probably never meet again. That will suit me fine."

He stepped past Tom and went down the corridor to his room. Lying on the bed, he went over in his mind what he meant to do that night. Part of it gave him no satisfaction. But he was an obstinate man. What he had set himself to do he would do. Because of Fallon he had been forced to sell his business for less than half of what it was worth. The deputy had driven him out of Arizona. Why should he interfere to save him? It would be Faunce's gun and not his that flung the bullets into him.

Tom had an appointment to meet the partner of Saunders in the freighting business. On the way he met Johnny Adler, the owner of the Longhorn Corral. After thumping the bridegroom on the back and telling him how glad he was to hear of his marriage to Nancy, he mentioned a piece of news that greatly relieved Tom's mind. Curt Faunce had paid his bill for horse feed at the corral and set off for the ranch.

"Did you see him go?" Tom asked.

"Sure I did. He went all right. Tim Beecher came in an hour later and said he met him five miles out."

Saunders also was glad to know that Faunce had left Tucson. "I have been a little worried," he said. "The man is a thoroughly bad character, violent and vindictive. I judge he knows he can't outrage public opinion any more and has thrown in his hand."

The lawyer's partner, Madison Purcell, was very pleased to get Tom as manager of the freighting outfit and a contract was signed with a liberal salary for Tom who was to begin work when the honeymoon was over. Saunders guessed that Tom must be pressed for money and paid him one hundred dollars in advance to seal the agreement.

Tom had so much to do before taking the train that he had kissed his bride goodbye half an hour after the ceremony with a promise to be back as soon as he could. He reached Mrs. Harshaw's house just before supper time.

Nancy flew into his arms. "A fine husband you are," she said, her eyes dancing with the joy of meeting him. "To run away from your bride on your wedding day on account of business."

"I have been with you every minute in spirit," he said in justification.

"And I have worried every minute for fear something had happened."

"Three things have happened, none of them bad. I met Harry Heilman. He congratulated me and hoped he would never see me again. I signed a contract to manage for a year the Tucson Freighting Company. And I learned from Johnny Adler that Curt Faunce has left town and was seen several miles out heading for his ranch. So you need not worry any more. Fair weather ahead for Nancy and Tom Fallon." He sealed that promise with a long and ardent kiss.

After supper Jerry Harshaw walked to the Orndorff to

186

help Tom carry back his telescope valise and war sack.*
Jerry was highly elated at having Tom for a cousin-in-law. It
was his opinion that Nancy had done far better in marriage
than she had any right to expect. His mother was much
amused at this. Though she agreed with him in approving
Nancy's choice, from a wordly viewpoint a penniless cowboy could not be considered exactly a bargain for a girl like
her niece.

"We are going to leave most of this stuff at your mother's
until we come back," Tom explained.

He let the boy take his rifle but wore the belt with the holstered revolver. Tom noticed while he was settling his bill
that Heilman was lounging in one of the lobby chairs reading a newspaper. The gambler gave no sign of knowing that
they were in the room.

The distance from the hotel to Jennie Harshaw's house
was not more than three hundred yards but in this residence
section of the town there were no lights except the lamps in
the houses which were built well back from the road.

Jerry said cheerfully, "Gee, I'm glad that old Curt Faunce
has pulled his freight from here."

"Count me in on that," Tom agreed. "He has had me buf-
faloed since the first day I met him."

An adobe wall surrounding a small pasture ran parallel to
the street. As they approached it a sharp voice cut into the
stillness of the night.

"Look out, kid," it warned.

A pistol shot rang out. Tom threw Jerry to the ground
and crouched over him. The second bullet flung up a spatter
of dirt beside them. Fallon fired at the flash. Jerry tried to
scramble out from under Tom to run.

Another weapon sounded, a dozen yards farther down the
road than the first. *Two of them,* Tom thought, *they'll get us
sure.* But they were safer here, if there was safety anywhere,
in the shadow of a large cottonwood tree close to the road.

"Crawl back of the tree, Jerry," he ordered, and waited
until the boy had found cover before he drew trigger at the
gunman opposite.

The crash of guns came again, almost simultaneously. Tom
slid back of the tree in front of Jerry. He did not understand

* A cowboy's blankets and impedimenta.

what was going on. He was no longer the target of the hammering weapons.

A voice cried, "You've killed me, you damned doublecrosser."

The figure across the street, vaguely defined in the darkness, slumped to the ground and huddled into itself. Tom held his fire. An unrecognized friend had come to their rescue.

A pistol roared once more.

Out of the gloom words came. "That will be all. Curt is deader than a stuck shote. Put up your gun."

Tom holstered his revolver. The man who moved slowly forward and looked down at the man he had killed was no friend of Fallon. The sight of him startled Tom. He was Harry Heilman. A thin film of smoke rose from his .45.

The gambler said coldly, "He has been due for this a long time."

His eyes met those of Tom. They could hear the whimpering of the boy behind the tree.

Tom spoke first. "You saved our lives."

Heilman would have none of his gratitude. "I came here to watch him kill you and then send him to hell. The kid balled that up. I knew Curt would have to shoot him down too."

That there was no longer any danger from this man Tom knew. "If you want me dead you can finish the job and light out."

"With the kid a witness against me? Thank him, not me."

Some sure instinct told Tom that even if Jerry had not been present Heilman would have interfered to save him. But he knew the gambler would never admit it.

The door of a house opened and a man shouted, "What are all the fireworks about?"

Tom said quickly to Heilman, "You're in the clear. I'll see to that." He answered the question. "A man has been killed—Curt Faunce. He tried to ambush us and Mr. Heilman had to kill him to save us."

Jerry came into the open and clung to Tom. "I was scared to death," he said, a catch still in his voice.

Four or five men had come out of the near houses.

"Thank Mr. Heilman for saving us. He shouted a warning and when that didn't stop Faunce he had to kill him."

188

Heilman let it go at that. "If the sheriff wants me I'll be at the Orndorff," he said coolly, then walked away.

James Saunders was one of the men who had arrived. "They must have heard the shooting at Jennie's house. You and Jerry had better go there and let them know you are safe. I'll attend to the body."

There was a chance that one of the bullets in the body of Faunce came from Tom's gun, but that was something he never intended to mention. After all the man was Nancy's father.

They met Jennie and Nancy running to meet them. From Tom they learned what had occurred. He held Nancy's slender body close. It was shaken by sobs. The racketing guns had alarmed the girl greatly and she clung to her husband almost hysterically.

"I thought—I was afraid—Oh, thank God—thank God," she cried.

Tom comforted her gently. The last danger to him had been removed. Stretching ahead were long years of happiness. There was no longer anything to fear.

Jerry was in his mother's arms. Her soft hand stroked his hair and patted his shoulder softly. Presently she looked up at the lovers, a glad light in her eyes. The words of a great poet came to her mind. "Port after stormie seas."